Grace Livingston Hill is one of the most popular authors of all time because of her unique style of combining elements of the Christian faith with tasteful and exciting romance.

Find out why generations of readers of all ages have been entertained and inspired by the fiction of Grace Livingston Hill.

Grace Livingston Hill ... fiction that fills the heart as well as the spirit!

GRACE LIVINGSTON HILL

A Daily Rate
A Chautauqua Idyl
The Parkerstown Delegate

Three complete and unabridged novels in one volume

Barbour Books
164 Mill Street
Westwood, New Jersey 07675

Typesetting by:
Typetronix, Inc., Cape Coral, FL

ISBN 1-55748-121-0

A
DAILY RATE

1

The world would not have looked quite so dreary to her perhaps, if it had not been her birthday. Somehow one persists in expecting something unusual to happen on a birthday, no matter how many times one has had nothing but disappointment.

Not that Celia Murray was really expecting anything, even a letter, on this birthday, though she did stand shivering in the half light of the dim, forlorn front room that served as a parlor for Mrs. Morris' boarding-house, watching for the postman to reach their door. She did it merely because she wished to be near, to get the letter at once, — provided there was a letter, — and not that she really hoped for one.

It was Saturday evening, and the close of a half holiday in the store in which she usually stood all day long as saleswoman. The unusual half day off was on account of some parade in the city. Celia had not spent her afternoon at the parade. Instead, she had been in her small, cold, back bedroom on the third story, attending to various worn garments which needed mending. They had been spread out on the bed in a row, and she had gone steadily down the line putting a few stitches here, a button there, and setting in a patch in another, counting every minute of daylight hoping to finish her work before it faded, for the gas in her room was dim, the burner being old and worn out. She tried to be cheerful over the work. She called it her "dress parade." She knew it was the best way in which to accomplish as much as she wished to do.

And now it was six o'clock, and she had turned down the wretched, flickering light in her room and descended to the parlor to watch for the postman.

He was late to-night, probably on account of the parade. She leaned her forehead against the cold glass and looked out into the misty darkness. Everything was murky and smoky. The passers-by seemed tired and in a hurry. Some had their collars turned up. She wondered where they were all going, and whether there were pleasant homes awaiting them. She let her imagination picture the homes of some. There was a young working man hurrying along with breezy step and swinging dinner pail. He had not been to the parade. His parade was at home awaiting his coming, — a laughing baby, a tidy wife, and the house redolent of fried onions and sausage. She had passed houses often at night where these odors were streaming forth from quickly opened and closed doors. The young man would like it; it would be pleasant to him. And the thought brought no less cheer to the watching girl because to her this supper would not be in the least appetizing.

1

There passed by a strong old German, a day laborer perhaps. She pictured the table full of noisy children of various ages, and the abundance of sauerkraut and cheese and coffee and other viands set out. Then came a stream of girls, some clerks like herself, and some mill girls. On other evenings they would present a different appearance, but many of them to-night were in holiday attire on account of the half holiday which had been generally given throughout the city. These girls, some of them, had homes of more or less attractiveness, and others, like herself, were domiciled in boarding-houses. She sat down on one of the hard haircloth chairs and looked around the parlor. In the dimness of the turned down gas, it appeared more forlorn than usual. The ingrain carpet had long ago lost any claims to respectability. It had a dragged out, sodden appearance, and in places there were unmistakable holes. These, it is true, had been twisted and turned about so as to come mostly under the tables and sofa, but they were generally visible to the casual observer. The parlor suite of haircloth, by reason of being much sat upon, had lost the spring of youth, and several of the chairs and one end of the sofa looked like fallen cake. There was an asthmatic cabinet organ at the end of the room which had been left by some departing boarder, (under compulsion) in lieu of his board. There were a few worn pieces of music scattered upon it. Celia knew that the piece now open on the top was that choice selection "The Cat Came Back," which was a great favorite with a young railroad brakeman who had a metallic tenor voice and good lungs. He was one of the boarders and considered quite a singer in the house. There was a feeble attempt at the aesthetic in the form of a red, bedraggled chenille portière at the doorway, bordered with large pink cabbage roses. The mantel had a worn plush scarf embroidered in a style quite out of date and ugly in the extreme. On it stood a large glass case of wax flowers, several cheap vases, and a match safe. Over it hung a crayon portrait of the landlady's departed husband, and another of herself adorned the opposite wall, both done in staring crayon work from tin types of ancient date, heavily and cheaply framed. These with a marriage certificate of the clasped-hand-and-orange-wreath order, framed in gilt, made up the adornments of the room.

Celia sighed as she looked about and took it all in once more. It was a dreary place. She had been in it but a week. Would she ever get used to it? She did not curl her lip in scorn as many other girls would have done over that room and its furnishings. Neither did she feel that utter distaste that is akin to hatred. Instead was a kind of pity in her heart for it all, and for the poor lonely creatures who had no other place to call home. Where there is such pity, there is sometimes love not far away. She even rose, went to the doorway and looped the loose, discouraged folds of the chenille curtain in more graceful fashion. Somehow her fingers could not help doing so much toward making that room different.

Then she sighed and went to the window again. She could see the belated postman now across the street. She watched him as he flitted back and forth, ringing this bell and that, and searching in the great leather bag for papers or packages. His breath showed white against the dark greyish-blue of the misty evening air. His grey uniform seemed to be a part of the mist. The yellow glare of the street-lamp touched the gilt buttons and made a bright spot of the letters on his cap as he paused a moment to study an address before coming to their door.

Celia opened the door before he had time to ring and took the letters from his hand. There were not many. The boarders in that house had not many correspondents. She stepped into the parlor once more, and turned up the gas now for a moment to see if there were any for herself. Strange to say, there were two, rather thin and unpromising it is true, but they gave a little touch of the unusual to the dull day. She noticed that one bore a familiar postmark and was in her aunt's handwriting. The other held the city mark and seemed to be from some firm of lawyers. She did not feel much curiosity concerning it. It was probably some circular. It did not look in the least interesting. She pushed them both quickly into her pocket as the front door opened letting in several noisy boarders. She did not wish to read her letters in public. They would keep till after supper. The bell was already ringing. It would not be worth while to go upstairs before she went to the dining-room. Experience taught her that the supper was at its very worst the minute after the bell rang. If one waited one must take the consequences, and "the consequences" were not desirable. The meals in that house were not too tempting at any time. Not that she cared much for her supper, she was too weary, but one must eat to live, and so she went to the dining-room.

Out there the gas was turned to its highest. The coarse tablecloth was none of the cleanest. In fact, it reminded one of former breakfasts and dinners. The thick white dishes bore marks of hard usage. They were nicked and cracked. There were plates of heavy, sour-looking bread at either end of the table. The butter looked mussy and uninviting. The inevitable, scanty supply of prunes stood before the plate of the young German clerk, who was already in his chair helping himself to a liberal dish. The clerk was fond of prunes, and always got to the table before any one else. Some of the others good-naturedly called him selfish, and frequently passed meaningful remarks veiled in thin jokes concerning this habit of his; but if he understood he kept the matter to himself, and was apparently not thin-skinned.

There was a stew for dinner that night. Celia dreaded stews since the night of her arrival when she had found a long curly hair on her plate in the gravy. There were such possibilities of utility in a stew. It was brought on in little thick white dishes, doled out in exact portions. There were great green fat pickles, suggesting copper in their pickling, and there was a plate of cheese and another of crackers. A girl brought each one a small spoonful of canned corn, but it was cold and scarcely cooked at all, and the kernels were large and whole. Celia having tasted it, pushed her dish back and did not touch it again. On the side table was a row of plates each containing a slim, thin piece of pale-crusted pie, its interior being dark and of an undefined character. Celia tried to eat. The dishes were not all clean. Her spoon had a sticky handle and so had her fork. The silver was all worn off the blade of her knife, and she could not help thinking that perhaps it was done by being constantly used to convey food to the mouth of the brakeman with the tenor voice.

One by one the boarders drifted in. It was surprising how quickly they gathered after that bell rang. They knew what they had to depend upon in the way of bread and butter, and it was first come first served. Little Miss Burns sat across the table from Celia. She was thin and nervous and laughed a good deal in an excited way, as if everything were unusually funny, and she was in a constant state of embarrassing apology. There were tired little lines around her eyes, and her mouth still wore a baby droop, though she was well along in years. Celia noticed that she drank only a cup of tea and nibbled a cracker. She did not look well. It was plain the dinner was no more appetizing to her than to the young girl who had so recently come there to board. She ought to have some delicate thin slices of nicely browned toast and a cup of tea with real cream in it, and a fresh egg poached just right, or a tiny cup of good strong beef bouillon, Celia said to herself. She amused herself by thinking how she would like to slip out in the kitchen and get them for her, only — and she almost smiled at the thought — she would hardly find the necessary articles with which to make all that out in the Morris kitchen.

Next to Miss Burns sat two young girls, clerks in a three-cent store. They carried a good deal of would-be style, and wore many bright rings on their grimy fingers, whose nails were never cleaned nor cut apparently — except by their teeth. These girls were rather pretty in a coarse way, and laughed and talked a good deal in loud tones with the tenor brakeman, whose name was Bob Yates, and with the other young men boarders. These young men were respectively a clerk in a department store, a student in the University, and a young teacher in the public schools. Celia noticed that neither the student nor the school-teacher ate heartily, and that the young dry goods salesman had a hollow cough. How nice it would be if they all could have a good dinner just for once, soup and roast beef, and good bread and vegetables, with a delicious old-fashioned apple dumpling smoking hot, such as her aunt Hannah could make. How she would enjoy giving it to them all. How she would like to eat some of it herself! She sighed as she pushed back her plate with a good half of the stew yet untouched, and felt that it was impossible to eat another mouthful of that. Then she felt ashamed to think she cared so much for mere eating, and tried to talk pleasantly to the little old lady beside her, who occupied a small dismal room on the third floor and seemed to stay in it most of the time. Celia had not yet found out her occupation or her standing in society, but she noticed that she trembled when she tried to cut her meat, and she was shabbily clothed in rusty black that looked as if it had served its time out several times over.

Mrs. Morris came into the dining-room when the pie was being served.

She was large and worried-looking, and wore a soiled calico wrapper without a collar. Her hair had not been combed since morning and some locks had escaped on her neck and on her forehead and added to her generally dejected appearance. She sat down heavily and wearily at the head of the table, and added her spiritless voice to the conversation. She asked them all how they enjoyed the parade and declared it would have been enough parade for her if she could have "set down for a couple of hours." Then she sighed and drank a cup of tea from her saucer, holding the saucer on the palm of her hand.

It all looked hopelessly dreary to Celia. And here she expected to spend the home part of her life for several years at least, or if not here, yet in some place equally destitute of anything which constitutes a home.

Except for her brief conversation with the old lady on her right, and a few words to Miss Burns, she had spoken to no one during the meal, and as soon as she had excused herself from the pie and folded her napkin, she slipped upstairs to her room, for the thought of the two letters in her pocket seemed more inviting than the pie. She turned the gas to its highest, though it did screech, that she might see to read her letters, and then she drew them forth. Her aunt Hannah's came first. She tore the envelope. Only one sheet and not much written thereon. Aunt Hannah was well, but very busy, for Nettie's children were all down with whooping cough and the baby had been quite sick, poor little thing, and she had no time to write. Hiram, Nettie's husband, too, had been ill and laid up for a week, so aunt Hannah had been nursing night and day. She enclosed a little bookmark to remember Celia's birthday. She wished she could send her something nice, but times were hard and Celia knew she had no money, so she must take it out in love.

Hiram's sickness and the doctor's bills made things close for Nettie or she would have remembered the birthday, too, perhaps. Aunt Hannah felt that it was hard to have to be a burden on Nettie, now when the children were young and she and Hiram needed every cent he could earn, but what else could she do? She sent her love to her dear girl, however, and wanted her to read the verse on the little ribbon enclosed and perhaps it would do her good. She hoped Celia had a nice comfortable "homey" place to board and would write soon.

That was all. The white ribbon bookmark was of satin and bore these words:

"His allowance was a continual allowance ... a daily rate. 2 Kings 25:30," and beneath in small letters:

> "Charge not thyself with the weight of a year,
> Child of the Master, faithful and dear,
> Choose not the cross for the coming week,
> For that is more than he bids thee seek.
> Bend not thine arms for to-morrow's load,
> Thou mayest leave that to thy gracious God,
> Daily, only he says to thee,
> 'Take up thy cross and follow me.' "

2

Celia read the words over mechanically. She was not thinking so much of what they said, as she was of what her aunt had written, or rather of what she had not written, and what could be read between the lines, by means of her knowledge of that aunt and her surroundings. In other words Celia Murray was doing exactly what the words on the white ribbon told her not to do. She was charging herself "with the weight of a year." She had picked up the cross of the coming months and was bending under it already.

Her trouble was aunt Hannah. Oh, if she could but do something for her. She knew very well that that little sentence about being a burden on Nettie meant more than aunt Hannah would have her know. She knew that aunt Hannah would never feel herself a burden on her niece Nettie, — for whom she had slaved half her life, and was still slaving, unless something had been said or done to make her feel so; and Celia, who never had liked her cousin-in-law, Hiram, at any time, for more reasons than mere prejudice, knew pretty well who it was that had made good, faithful, untiring aunt Hannah feel that she was a burden.

Celia's eyes flashed, and she caught her hands in each other in a quick convulsive grasp. "Oh, if I could but do something to get aunt Hannah out of that and have her with me!" she exclaimed aloud. "But here am I with six dollars and a half a week; paying out four and a quarter for this miserable hole they call a home; my clothes wearing out just as fast as they can, and a possibility hanging over me that I may not suit and may be discharged at any time. How can I ever get ahead enough to do anything!"

She sat there thinking over her life and aunt Hannah's. Her own mother and Nettie's mother had died within a year of each other. They were both aunt Hannah's sisters. Mr. Murray did not long survive his wife, and Celia had gone to live with her cousins who were being mothered by aunt Hannah, then a young, strong, sweet woman. Her uncle, Mr. Harmon, had been a hard working, silent man, who had supplied the wants of his family as well as he could, but that had not always been luxuriously, for he had never been a successful man. The children had grown fast and required many things. There were five of his own and Celia, who had shared with the rest, — though never really getting her share, because of her readiness to give up and the others' readiness to take what she gave up. Somehow the Harmon children had a streak of selfishness in them, and they always seemed willing that aunt Hannah and Celia should take a back seat whenever any one had to do so, which

6

was nearly all the time. Celia never resented this for herself, even in her heart; but for aunt Hannah she often did so. That faithful woman spent the best years of her life, doing for her sisters' children as if they had been her own, and yet without the honor of being their mother, and feeling that the home was her own. She had never married, she was simply aunt Hannah, an excellent housekeeper, and the best substitute for a mother one could imagine. As the children grew up they brought all their burdens to aunt Hannah to bear, and when there were more than she could conveniently carry, they would broadly hint that it was Celia's place to help her, for Celia was the outsider, the dependent, the moneyless one. It had fallen to her lot to tend the babies till they grew from being tended into boys, and then to follow after and pick up the things they left in disorder in their wake. It was she who altered the girls' dresses to suit the style, and fashioned dainty hats from odds and ends, turning and pressing them over to make them as good as new for some special occasion. And then when it came her turn, it was she who had to stay at home, because she had nothing to wear, and no time to make it over, and nothing left to make over, because she had given it all to the others.

Then had come the day, — not so many weeks ago: Celia remembered it as vividly as though it had happened but yesterday; she had gone over the details so many times they were burned upon her brain. And yet, how long the time really had been and how many changes had come! The boy came up from the office with a scared face to say that something had happened to Mr. Harmon, and then they had brought him home and the family all too soon learned that there was no use in trying to resuscitate him, — all hope had been over before he was taken from the office. Heart failure, they said! And instantly following upon this had come that other phrase, "financial failure," and soon the orphans found they were penniless. This was not so bad for the orphans, for they were fully grown and the girls were both married. The three boys all had good positions and could support themselves. But what of aunt Hannah and Celia? Nettie and Hiram had taken aunt Hannah into their family, ill-disguising the fact that she was asked because of the help she could give in bringing up and caring for the children, but Celia had understood from the first that there was no place for her.

She had been given a good education with the others; that is, a common school course followed by a couple of years in the high school. She had her two hands and her bright wits and nothing else. A neighbor had offered to use her influence with a friend of a friend of a partner in a city store, and the result was her position. She had learned since she came that it was a good one as such things went. She had regular hours for meals and occasional holidays, and her work was not heavy. She felt that she ought to be thankful. She had accepted it, of course, for there was nothing else to be done, but she had looked at aunt Hannah with a heavy heart and she knew aunt Hannah felt it as keenly. They had been very close to each other, these two, who had been separated from the others, in a sense, and had burdens to bear. Perhaps their sense of loneliness in the world had made them cling the more to each other. Celia would have liked to be able to say "Aunt Hannah, come with me. I can take care of you now. You have cared for me all my life, now I will give you a home and rest." Ah! if that could have been! Celia drew her breath quickly, and the tears came between the closed lids. She knew if she once allowed the tears full sway, they would not stop till they had swept all before them, and left her in no fit state to appear before those dreadful, inquisitive boarders, or perhaps even to sell ribbons in Dobson and Co.'s on Monday. No, she must not give way. She would read that other letter and take her mind from these things, for certain it was that she could do nothing more now than she had done, except to write aunt Hannah a cheering letter, which she could not do unless she grew cheerful herself.

So she opened the other letter.

It was from Rawley and Brown, a firm of lawyers on Fifth Street, desiring to know if she was Celia Murray, daughter of Henry Dean Murray of so forth and so on, and if she was, would she please either write or call upon them at her earliest possible convenience, producing such evidence of her identity as she possessed.

The girl laughed as she read it over again. "The idea!" she said, talking aloud to herself again as she had grown into the habit of doing since she was alone, just to feel as if she were talking to some one. "If they want to identify me, let them do so. I'm not asking anything of them. If I'm I, prove it! How very funny! What for, I wonder? There can't be a fortune, I know, for father didn't have a cent. I'm sure I've had that drummed into my head enough by Nettie, and even uncle Joseph took pains to tell me that occassionally. Well, it is mysterious."

She got up and began to walk about the room singing to herself the old nursery rhyme:

> " 'If it be me, as I suppose it be,
> I've a little dog at home and he'll know me;
> If it be *I*, he'll wag his little tail,
> And if it be *not* I, he'll bark, and he'll wail.' "

"Dear me!" said Celia, "I'm worse off than the poor old woman who fell asleep on the king's highway. I haven't even a little dog at home who'll know me." She sighed and sat down, picking up the white ribbon that had fallen to the floor. Then she read it over again carefully.

"How like aunt Hannah that sounds!" she said to herself, as she read the poem slowly over, " 'Child of the Master, faithful and dear,' I can hear aunt Hannah saying that to me. She was always one to hunt out beautiful things and say them to me as if they had been written all for my poor self. If aunt Hannah had ever had time, I believe she would have been a poet. She has it in her. How entirely I have been doing just exactly what this poem says I must not do: choosing my cross for the coming week. Yes, and bending my arm for to-morrow's load. I have been thinking what a dreary Sunday I should have, and wondering how I could endure it all day long in this ugly, cold room. And I won't stay down in that mean parlor and listen to their horrible singing. It wouldn't be right anyway, for they have not the slightest idea of Sabbath keeping. Last Sunday was one hurrah all day long. I wonder what that verse at the top is — 'His allowance was a continual allowance.' I declare I don't remember to have ever read it before. But trust aunt Hannah to ferret out the unusual verses. I must look it up. Second Kings: who was it about, anyway? The twenty-fifth chapter. Oh! here it is!'' She read:

" 'And it came to pass in the seven and thirtieth year of the captivity of Jehoiachin king of Judah, in the twelfth month, on the seven and twentieth day of the month, that Evil-Merodach king of Babylon in the year that he began to reign did lift up the head of Jehoiachin king of Judah out of prison;

And he spake kindly to him, and set his throne above the throne of the kings that were with him in Babylon;

And changed his prison garments: and he did eat bread continually before him all the days of his life.

And his allowance was a continual allowance given him of the king, a daily rate for every day, all the days of his life.' "

Celia paused and read the verses over again.

She began to see why her aunt had sent it to her, and more than that why her heavenly Father had sent it to her. It was the same thought that was in the bit of a poem. God was taking care of her. He was a king and he was able to lift her head up out of prison, if this was a prison, and set her even on a throne, and change her prison garments, and more than that give her an allowance of grace to meet all the daily needs of her life. A continual allowance: she need never worry lest it should give out. It was "all the days of her life." And aunt Hannah was his also. He would care for her in the same way. There was nothing to be done but to trust and do what he gave her to do. Perhaps it was unusually hard for her to do that. She had always been so accustomed to looking ahead and bearing burdens for others and planning for them. She recognized her fault and resolved to think more about it. Meantime, obviously the next duty for her to perform, and one by no means a cross, was for her to write a long cheery letter to aunt Hannah, who she could easily see was homesick for her already, though it was but a week since they had been separated. She gathered together her writing materials, drew her chair a little nearer the poor light, put on her heavy outdoor coat, for the room was chilly, though it was only the latter part of October, and began to write; thinking meanwhile that she could perhaps make a pleasant Sabbath afternoon for herself out of the study of Jehoiachin, who was so much a stranger to her that she had hardly remembered there was such a person spoken of in the Bible.

The letter she wrote was long and cheerful. It abounded in pen pictures of the places and things she had seen, and it contained descriptions in detail of the different boarders. She tried not to tell the disagreeable things, for she knew aunt Hannah would be quick to understand how hard it all was for her to bear, and she would not lay a feather's burden upon those dear hard-worked shoulders. So she detailed merry conversations, and made light of the poor fare, saying she had a very good and a very cheap place they all told her and she guessed they were right.

She also drew upon her imagination and described the dear little home she was going to make for aunt Hannah to come and rest in and spend her later years, and she told her she was going to begin right away to save up for it. She made it all so real that the tears came to her eyes for very longing for it, and one dropped down on the paper and blotted a word. She hastily wiped it out, and then took a fresh page, for aunt Hannah's eyes were keen. She would be quick to know what made that blot. She paused a minute with her pen in the air ere she closed the letter. Should she, or should she not tell aunt Hannah of that letter from the lawyers? No, she would not until she saw whether it came to anything, and if so, what. It might only worry her aunt. There were worries enough at Hiram's without her putting any more in the way. So she finished her letter, sealed and addressed it, and then ran down to put it in the box.

As she returned from her errand into the misty outdoor world, and closed the door behind her shivering, glad she did not have to go out any more, she met the tall, lanky cook in untidy work dress and unkept hair. Celia noticed instantly that it was curly hair and black, like the one she found in the stew the night she came. She was passing on upstairs but the cook put out her hand and stopped her.

"Say," she said in a familiar tone. "I wish you'd jes' step into Mis' Morris' room and stay a spell. She's took dreadful sick this evenin', and I've ben with her off an' on most all the time, an' I've got pies yet to bake fer to-morrow, an' I can't spend no more time up there now. She ought to have some one, an' the rest seems all to be gone out 'cept that ol' lady up there, an' she's gone to bed by this time, I reckon."

Celia could do nothing but consent to go, of course, though the task looked anything but a pleasant one. Mrs. Morris had never struck her pleasantly. She enquired as to the sickness. The woman didn't exactly know what was the matter. No, there had not been any physician sent for. "There wan't no one to go in the first place, and, secondly, doctors is expensive things, take 'em anyway you will, medicine and all. Mrs. Morris can't afford no doctors. She's most killed with debt now."

Celia turned on the stairs, and followed the woman's direction to find Mrs. Morris' room.

Over in her mind came those words she had read a little while ago.

> "Daily, only, he says to thee,
> 'Take up thy cross and follow me.' "

She smiled, and thought how soon the cross had come to her after she had laid down the wrong one of a week ahead, and tapped softly on Mrs. Morris' door, lifting up her heart in a prayer that she might be shown how to do or say the right thing if action were required of her. Then she heard a strained voice, as of one in pain, call "Come in," and she opened the door.

3

Mrs. Morris lay on her unmade bed, still in the soiled wrapper. Her expansive face was drawn in agony and she looked white and sick. She seemed surprised to see Celia, and supposed she had come to prefer a request for another towel, perhaps, or to make some complaint.

"You'll have to ask Maggie," she said without waiting to hear what the girl had to say. "I can't talk now, I'm suffering so. It's just terrible. I never was so sick in my life."

"But I've come to see if I can't help you," explained Celia. "Maggie told me you were sick. Tell me what is the matter. Perhaps I can do something for you. I know about sickness and nursing."

"Oh, such awful pain!" said the woman, writhing in agony, "I suppose it's something I've et. Though I never et a thing, all day long, but a little piece of pie at dinner to-night and me tea. Me nerves is all used up with worrying anyway, and me stomach won't stand anything any more."

Celia asked a few practical questions, and then told her she would return in a minute. She found her way in haste to the kitchen, though she had never before penetrated to that realm of darkness — and dirt. She ordered Maggie peremptorily to bring her a large quantity of very hot water as soon as she could, and send somebody for a doctor. Then she went up to her own room and hastily gathered a bottle or two from her small store of medicines and a piece of an old blanket she had brought from home. She hesitated a moment. She ought to have another flannel. The woman was too sick to find anything, and she had said she did not know where there were any old flannels. It was necessary. She must take up this cross to save that poor woman from her suffering and perhaps save her life, for she was evidently very sick indeed. She waited no longer, but quickly took out her own clean flannel petticoat. It was nothing very fine, and was somewhat old, but it was a sacrifice to think of using any of her personal clothing down there in that dirty room, and for that woman who did not seem to be scrupulously clean herself. However, there was no help for it, and she hurried back as fast as she could. She gave the poor woman a little medicine which she thought might help her, and she knew could do no harm till the doctor could get there, and then plunging the cherished blanket into the hot water, she wrung it as dry as she could and quickly applied it to the seat of pain, covering it with the flannel skirt. She knew there was nothing like hot applications to relieve severe pain. She saw by the look of relief that passed over the sick woman's face that the pain had relaxed to some

12

extent. After a moment, Mrs. Morris said:

"I don't know as you'd a needed to send for a doctor, this might have helped me without him. I can't bear to think of his bill. Bills'll be the death of me yet, I'm afraid."

But a spasm of pain stopped her speech, and Celia hastened to repeat the applications.

It was some time before the doctor arrived. The girl had to work fast and hard. It was evident when he came that he thought the patient a very sick woman. Mrs. Morris realized this, too. After the doctor was gone and Celia was left alone with her, she asked her if she supposed the doctor thought she was going to die.

"Though I ain't got much to live for, the land knows — nor to die for either for the matter of that."

"Oh, you forget!" said Celia, reverently, aghast that one should speak in that tone of dying. "There is Jesus! Don't you know him?"

The woman looked at her as if she had spoken the name of some heathen deity, and then turned her head wearily.

"No," she said, "I don't suppose I am a Christian. I never had any time. When I was a girl there was always plenty of fun, and I never thought about it, and after I got married there wasn't time. I did tell the minister I would think about joining church the time of my daughter's funeral, but I never did. I kind of wish I had now. One never is ready to die, I s'pose. But then living isn't easy either, the land knows."

A grey ashen look overspread her face. Celia wondered if perhaps she might be dying even now. She shuddered. It seemed so terrible for any one to die in that way. She had never been with a very sick person near to death, and she did not know the signs well enough to judge how much danger there might be of it. She felt, however, that she must say something. The woman must have some thread of hope, if she should be really dying. She came close to her and took her hand tenderly.

"Dear Mrs. Morris! Don't talk that way. Dying isn't hard, I'm sure, if you have Jesus, and he's always near and ready, if you will only take him now. I know he helps one to die, for I can remember my own dear mother, though I was but a little girl. She had a beautiful look on her face, when she bade me goodbye, and told me she was going to be with Jesus, and that I must always be a good girl and get ready to come to her. She looked very happy about it."

Mrs. Morris opened her eyes and gave her a searching look. Then she said in a voice halfway between a groan and a frightened shout:

"Why do you talk like that? You don't think I am dying, do you? Tell me, quick! Did the doctor say I was going to die? Why did he go away if that was so? Send for him quick!"

Then the inexperienced young girl realized that she had made a mistake and been too much in earnest. There was danger that the woman might make herself much worse by such excitement. She must calm her. To talk to her thus would do no good. She must wait until a suitable season.

"No, Mrs. Morris," she said, rising and speaking calmly, "He did not say so, and I do not believe you are going to die. You must not get so excited, or you will make yourself worse. Here, take your medicine now, for it is time. I did not mean you to think I thought you were dying, and I'm sorry I spoke about my mother's death, it was very foolish of me. Please forget it now. I only wanted to tell you how Jesus was standing near, ready to be a comfort to you always, whether you lived or died. But now you ought to go to sleep. Would you like me to sing to you? Is the pain a little easier? The doctor said you must lie very quiet. Can I get you anything?"

By degrees she calmed the woman again, and then sat down to watch and give her the medicine. There seemed to be no one whose business it was to relieve Celia. Maggie put her head in the door about midnight to say she was going to bed now and had left a fire, if any more hot water was needed. Celia sat there gradually taking in the fact that she was left to sit up all night with this sick woman, an utter stranger to her. It was scarcely what she would choose as a pleasant task. But she recognized it as the cross the Master had laid upon her with his own hand, and there was a sense of sweetness in performing this duty which she would not have had otherwise. It occurred to her that it was well this was Saturday night instead of some other, for she could ill afford to sit up and lose all her sleep when she had to stand at the counter all the next day. She smiled to herself in the dim light and thought this must be part of the Master's plan to fix it so that she could do this duty and her others also. This was all he asked her to do, just what she had strength for. He gave her the daily allowance of that. But what if she should have to sit up to-morrow night? "Daily, only, he says to thee," and "Thou mayest leave that to thy gracious Lord," came the answering words, for now she knew the little poem by heart. She went upstairs, hastily changed her dress for a loose wrapper, and secured her Bible and one or two articles which she thought might be useful in caring for the sick woman. When she came down again Mrs. Morris seemed to be asleep, and Celia settled herself by the dim light with her Bible. She felt that she needed some help and strength. She had not read long when Mrs. Morris said in a low voice, "Is that the Bible you've got? Read a little piece to me."

Celia hardly knew where to turn for the right words just now, but her Bible opened easily of itself to the twenty-third psalm and she read the words in a low, musical voice, praying the while that they might be sent of the Spirit to reach the sick woman's heart. When she stopped reading, Mrs. Morris seemed to be asleep again, and Celia settled herself in the least uncomfortable chair in the room, and began to think.

But she had not long for this occupation, for this was to be a night of action. The terrible pain which for a time had been held by some powerful opiate the doctor had given when he first came in, returned in full force, and the patient soon was writhing in mortal agony once more. Celia was roused from her thoughts. She called Maggie and sent for hot water and the doctor again, and it was not until morning was beginning to stain the sky with crimson that she sat down to breathe and realize that Mrs. Morris was still alive. It seemed almost a miracle that she was, for the doctor had said when he arrived that there was doubt whether he could save her.

Early in the morning Miss Burns came in to relieve her watch, and Celia snatched a little sleep, but she found on awaking that she was needed again. Mrs. Morris had asked for her. She went down to the breakfast table and found, what she had not supposed possible, that the breakfast was so much worse than former breakfasts, since the mistress was sick, that it was hardly possible to eat at all. It seemed that Mrs. Morris had made some difference in things, though Celia had thought the night before that they could not very well be much worse. She had yet to find that there were many grades below even this in boarding-houses.

The Sabbath was not spent in studying Jehoiachin. It was full, but not with attending church services. She did not stay in her cold little room. She would have been glad to have been allowed to flee to that refuge. Instead, she made her headquarters in Mrs. Morris' room and from there she began by degrees to order things about her, for Mrs. Morris seemed to have placed all her dependence upon her. It was she who answered the questions of Maggie about this thing and that, and who kept the entire list of boarders from coming in to talk to Mrs. Morris and commiserate with her. She also cleared up the room and gave a touch of something like decent care to the sick woman and her surroundings. Once or twice the patient opened her eyes, looked around, seemed to see the subtle difference, and then closed them again. Celia could not tell whether it pleased her or whether she was indifferent. But it was not in Celia's nature to stay in a room and not make those little changes of picking up a shoe and straightening a quilt and hanging clothing out of sight. She did it as a matter of course.

Occasionally, when she had time to do so, she wondered what aunt Hannah would think if she could see her now, and she smiled to think that this was just what she seemed to have had to do all her life, — give up to help other people. Then she thought perhaps it was the most blessed thing that could happen to her.

Occasionally there would come to her a remembrance of that letter from the lawyers, and she would wonder what it meant, and how she could possibly go to work to find out.

Sunday evening she sat with her landlady for a couple of hours. The pain seemed to be a little easier, though she had spent an intensely trying day. She seemed worried and inclined to talk. Celia tried to soothe her and persuade her to get calm for sleeping, but it was no use.

"How can I sleep," answered the woman impatiently, "with so many things to fret about? Here am I on me back for the land knows how long, and the doctor wanting me to go to the hospital. How can I go to the hospital?

What will become of me house, and me business if I up and off that way? And then when I get well, if I ever do, what's to become of me? Me house would be empty, or me goods sold for grocery debts and other things, and I should starve. I might as well take the chances of dying outright now as that. I know I'd die in the hospital anyway, fretting about things. That Maggie never could carry on things, even if I was only to be gone two days. She never remembers to salt anything. Those two girls from that three-cent store have been complaining about the soup today already. They say it was just like dish water. And that German fellow came and told me tonight, with me lying sick here, that he'd have to leave if things didn't improve. He said I ought to get better help! Think of it! How am I going about to get help and me on me back not able to stir? I don't much care if he does leave, he always ate more than all the rest of them put together. But land, if I should get well right away and keep on, I don't see where I'm coming to. There's bills everywhere, milk and meat and groceries and dry goods. I don't know how I'm ever to pay 'em. It'll be just go on and pay a little, and get deeper into debt, and pay a little of that and make more debt, till I come to the end sometime, and I s'pose it might as well be now as any time."

Poor Celia! She had no words ready for such trouble as this. Debt had always been to her an awful thing, a great sin, never to be committed. She never realized that there were people to whom to be in debt seemed the normal way of living from day to day. She tried to think of something comforting to say, for how could a woman get well with such a weight as this on her mind? It would do no good to quote verses of Scripture about taking no thought for the morrow, nor to quote that sweet poem of hers about not bearing next week's crosses. The poor woman would not understand. She had not so lived in the past as to know how to claim the promise of being cared for. She would scarcely understand if Celia tried to tell her that if she would but cast her care now on Jesus he would help her in some way at once. This was what she longed to say, but her experience of the night before led her to fear saying anything which might excite the poor nervous woman.

"How much money do you need to pay all your debts and set you straight again?" she asked, thinking a little opportunity to go over her troubles might quiet her.

"Oh, I don't know," wailed the poor woman. "If I just had a thousand dollars, I'd sell out me business and go somewhere and get out of it. Things seem to be getting worse and worse." She began to cry feebly, and Celia was at her wits' end. Everything she said seemed to make matters worse. Suddenly she began to sing in a low soft voice,

> "Jesus, Saviour, pilot me,
> Over life's tempestuous sea."

Her voice was sweet and pure, and the woman paused to listen while Celia sang on until she fell asleep.

4

Celia discovered that the firm of lawyers who had written her, had their office in a building not many blocks from Dobson and Co.'s store. She felt anxious to find out what they wanted of her, and so the next morning she obtained permission for a few minutes' extra time at the lunch hour and hastened there.

She reached the number at last, and searched the dirty sign board for the names "Rawley and Brown." There it was, almost the last one on the list, "Fourth floor, back." She climbed up the four flights of stairs, for the elevator was out of order, and arrived panting before the dingy office. When she entered the room, two elderly men sat at desks on which were piled many papers, and each was talking with a client who sat near his desk. They did not cease their talking with these men until Celia had stood for some moments by the door. Then the elder of the two looked over his glasses at her, and she ventured to say she was Miss Murray come in response to their letter. She was given a chair and asked to wait until Mr. Rawley was at leisure, and in the course of a few minutes both the clients had withdrawn, and she was left alone with the two lawyers. Over in the corner behind a screen she could hear the click of a typewriter and see the top of a frizzy head which she knew must belong to the operator, probably the one who had written the letter to her.

Mr. Rawley at last turned to her and began a list of questions. Celia answered everything she could, wondering when this mystery would be explained. As soon as she had finished telling Mr. Rawley the names of her different living relatives, he cleared his throat and looked at her sharply and yet thoughtfully:

"Miss Murray," said he, as if about to ask something very important, "did you ever hear your father speak of having a great uncle?"

Celia paused to think a moment. She had been but ten years old when her father died. She could remember some conversation between her father and mother about relatives whom she had never seen. She searched her mind.

"I'm not sure about the 'great' part of it. He might have been a great uncle, but I know there was one father called uncle Abner. He must have died long ago. He was a very old man then. I can remember father saying laughingly to mother one day that he would never see anybody prettier than she was, not if he lived to be as old as uncle Abner."

"A-ahem!" said Mr. Rawley, uncrossing his feet and recrossing them again and putting his two thumbs together as he looked at them seriously under his bushy eyebrows. "Yes. Ah! Well, and did that uncle have any — ah — heirs?"

Celia wanted to laugh. She had already begun to plan how she could make aunt Hannah laugh by a letter she would write describing this interview with the lawyers, but she kept her face straight and answered steadily.

"I do not know."

"Well, I must say, my dear young lady," remarked Mr. Rawley, after a somewhat prolonged pause, "that your evidence is somewhat — that is to say, — inadequate. You could hardly expect us, with so little to go upon — that is to say, without more investigation, you could hardly expect us —"

"You forget, sir," said Celia, really laughing now, "that I have not the slightest idea what all this is about. I expect nothing. I came here to be informed."

The old lawyer gave her another searching look and then seemed to conclude that she was honest.

"Well, young lady, I think I may safely tell you this much. There was property of Mr. Abner Murray's, which naturally descended to his only son. That son had been in India for years. He did not return at his father's death, and in fact his whereabouts was not definitely known, until a very short time ago, when positive information of his death without heirs was received. The property would then revert to Mr. Abner Murray's next of kin, and his heirs. Mr. Abner Murray had a brother, who is supposedly your father's father. If this should prove to be the case, through his death and your father's, his only heir, you being the only living child of your father, the property would naturally fall to you. Do you follow me closely?"

Celia looked at Mr. Rawley respectfully now and very gravely. The matter had taken on a different aspect. It was a complete surprise. She had not even in her wildest dreams allowed herself to hope for any such thing. Fortunes only fell to girls in books, not to flesh-and-blood, hard working, everyday girls.

She looked at the lawyer in silence a minute and then she smiled gravely and said:

"That would be very nice if it's true. I wish it might be. And now I suppose you are done with me for the present, until you have investigated the truth of my statements."

Mr. Rawley seemed surprised that she took it so coolly and asked no more questions. She rose as if to go. The truth was she had caught a glimpse of the clock and she saw that she had barely time to reach her counter before the limit of her nooning would be over, and she had had no lunch. Her position might be forfeited if she exceeded her time. This was worth to her at present all the mythical fortunes that the future might hold for her. So, without more ado, she hurried away, and not even stopping for a single bite to eat, laid aside her wraps and was in her place behind the counter when the minute hand pointed just one minute after the time allotted her.

It was a very busy afternoon. She had not much time to think. Everybody seemed to want ribbons. "Perhaps I shall be in a position to buy some of these yards myself, instead of measuring them off for other people, some time, if that old Mr. Rawley ever finds out whether *I* am *I*," she thought to herself as she skillfully clipped off two yards of blue satin and three yards of pink taffeta.

"Property!" he had said. What did property mean? Had great uncle Abner left an old house standing somewhere, which would be of no earthly use to anybody unless sold, and bring nothing then? Or perhaps it was some musty old library. She had no faith that there was much money. Such things did not run in their family. It would turn out to be very little. But oh, what if it should be something worth while? What, for instance, if it should be a thousand dollars! What might she not do? Why, a thousand dollars would enable her to do some of the nice things she longed so to do. She could bring aunt Hannah here to the city, and set up a tiny house with her in it somewhere. With that much money to start on, they could surely make their living, she in the store and aunt Hannah at home sewing. It flashed across her mind that that was just the sum Mrs. Morris had wished for. She had said if she only had a thousand dollars she could pay her debts and have enough left to start on and get out of her uncomfortable life.

How nice it would be if she, Celia, could have money enough to say, "I have the thousand dollars, Mrs. Morris, and I will give it to you. You may pay those people and go away to some more quiet, restful life." Then how delightful it would be to take that poor miserable boarding-house and make it over. Make the boarders' lives cheerful and pleasant, give them healthful food and clean, inviting rooms to live in! What a work that would be for a lifetime! If she ever did get rich, she believed she would do just that thing. Hunt up the most wretched boarding-house she could find and take it, boarders and all, and make it over. She believed she could do it with aunt Hannah's help. Aunt Hannah could cook and plan, and she could execute and beautify. The thought pleased her so well that she carried it out into details, during the long walk back to her boarding-house that night. She even went so far as to think out what she would give them for dinner the first night, and how the dining-room should appear — and how their faces would look when they saw it all. What fun it would be! Miss Burns should have something every night that would tempt her appetite, and the poor old lady in the third story should be given the very tenderest cut in the whole steak, so she need not tremble so when she cut it. And there was that poor young school-teacher, he needed rich creamy milk. She had heard him decline the muddy coffee several times and once he asked if he might have a glass of milk, and Maggie had told him they were all out of milk.

She debated whether she would retain her position in the store and decided that she would for a time, because that would give her a chance to carry out some plans without letting the boarders know who was at the bottom of it all. Things should not be changed much at first, except that everything should be made entirely clean and wholesome. Then gradually they would begin to beautify. Perhaps the others would help in it. Perhaps she could lure the young man from the dry goods store into spending an evening at home and helping her. She had a suspicion that he spent his evenings out, and remained late in places which did him no good, to say the least. It would do no harm for her to try to get acquainted with him and help him, even if she never got a fortune to enable her to raise her neighbors into better things. She would begin the reformation of young Mr. Knowles that very evening, if there came an opportunity. With these thoughts and plans in mind she completed her long walk in much shorter time than usual and with a lighter heart. It did her good to have an interest in life beyond the mere duties of the hour.

She found Mrs. Morris in much the same state of depression as on the day before. The doctor had urged again that she go to the hospital for a regular course of treatment. She was as determined as ever that she would not, or rather *could* not do it. She wanted Celia to come and sit with her. She had taken a liking to her new boarder, and she did not hesitate to say so, and to declare that the others were an unfeeling set who bothered her and didn't care if she was sick. Celia tried to cheer her up. She gave her a flower which one of the other workers in the store had given her, and told her she would come up after dinner was over. Then she went down to the table, and found Mr. Knowles seated before his plate looking cold and coughing. She wondered if her opportunity would come. His seat was at her left hand. They exchanged some remarks about the weather, and Celia told him he seemed to have a bad cold. He told her that was a chronic state with him, and then coughed again as he tried to laugh. She entered into his mock gaiety, and told him that if his mother were there she would tell him not to go out that evening, in such damp weather and with that cough.

His face grew sober instantly, and he said very earnestly: "I suppose she would."

"Well, then, I suppose you'll stay in, won't you?" said the girl. "It isn't right not to take care of yourself. The wind is very raw tonight. Your cough will be much worse tomorrow if you go out in it. You ought to stay in for your mother's sake, you know."

It was a bow drawn at a venture. Celia stole a glance at him. He looked up at her quickly, his handsome, gay face sober and almost startled.

"But mother isn't here," he said, his voice husky. "She died a year ago."

"But don't you think mothers care for their sons even after they have gone to heaven? I believe they do. I believe in some way God lets them know when they are doing right. You ought to take care of yourself just the same, even if she is not here, for you know she would tell you to do it, now wouldn't she?"

"Yes, I know she would," he answered, and then, after a minute's pause, he added, "but it is so hard to stay in here. There is no place to sit and nothing to do all the evening. Mother used to have things different."

"It *is* hard," said Celia, sympathizingly, "and this is a dreary place. I've thought so myself ever since I came. I wonder if you and I couldn't make things a little pleasanter for us all, if we tried."

"How? I'm sure I never thought I could do anything in that line. How would you go about it?"

"Well, I'm not just sure," said Celia, thinking rapidly and bringing forth some of her half made plans to select one for this emergency. "But I think we ought to have a good light first. The gas is miserable."

"You're right; it is that," responded Mr. Knowles.

"Didn't I see a big lamp on the parlor table?"

"Yes, I think there is a lamp there, but it smokes like an engine, and it gives a wicked flare of a light that stares at you enough to put your eyes out."

"Well, I wonder if we couldn't do something to cure that lamp of smoking. I'm somewhat a doctor of lamps myself, having served a long apprenticeship at them, and I think if you'll help me I'll try. I have some lovely pink crepe paper upstairs that I got to make a shade for my room, but I'll sacrifice that to the house if you can get me a new wick. What do you say? Shall we try it? I'm sure Mrs. Morris won't object, for it will save gas, besides making things pleasanter for the boarders. I have a book I think you will enjoy, after the lamp is fixed for reading. If you are going to be a good boy and stay at home tonight I'll bring it down."

The young man entered into the scheme enthusiastically. He was a very young man, not more than nineteen, or Celia would not have cared or dared to speak to him in this half-commanding way. But she had been used to boys, and to winning them to do what she wished, and she won her way this time surely. The young man was only too glad to have something to keep him in, and his heart was still very tender toward his lost mother. Celia saw that he would not be hard to influence. She wished she were wise and able to help him. Her soul felt with oppression the need of all these other souls in this house with her, and she wished to be great and mighty to lift them up and help them. How strange it was that the way kept opening up before her for daily helping of others. She seemed to be the only Christian in this house full of people. What a weight of responsibility rested upon her if that was so. How she ought to pray to be guided that she might be wise as a serpent and harmless as a dove; that she might, if possible, bring each one of them to a knowledge of Jesus Christ. And what was *she* to do all this? A mere weak girl, who was discouraged and homesick, and could not get enough money together to keep herself from need, perhaps, nor grace enough to keep her own heart from failing or her feet from falling. What was *she* to think of guiding others? How could she do all this work? She must shrink back from the thought. She could not do it. It was too much. Ah! She might leave all that to her gracious Lord. She had forgotten that. All he wanted her to do was to take the duty of the hour or the minute and do it for him. What matter whether there were results that showed or not so long as he was obeyed? When she slipped up to her room for that pink crepe paper she knelt down and asked that it and the book and the lamp and her little effort for the evening might be blessed. Then she went down to conquer that lamp.

"For the land sake! Yes," said Mrs. Morris, turning wearily on her pillow, "do what you please with it. I wish it was a good one. I'd like to afford a real good one with a silk shade with lace on it, but I can't. There's lots ought to be done here, but there's no use talking about it. I'm clean discouraged anyway. I wish I could sell out, bag and baggage, and go to the poorhouse."

"Oh, Mrs. Morris, don't talk that way!" said Celia, brightly. "You'll get well pretty soon. Don't think about that now. We'll try to keep things in order till you are able to see to them yourself. And meantime, I believe I can make that lamp work beautifully. I'll come back by and by and report progress. Now eat that porridge. I know it can't hurt you. The doctor told me it would be good for you. I made it myself, and it's just such as aunt Hannah used to make for sick people. There's nothing like twice boiled flour porridge. Is it seasoned right? There's the salt."

Then she flitted downstairs to the lamp.

Young Mr. Knowles was already on hand with the new wick he had purchased at the corner grocery, having carefully taken the measure of the burner.

Celia, with experienced hand, soon had the lamp burning brightly. Frank Hartley, the university student, had been attracted by the unusual light and declared he would bring his books down to the parlor for a while. It was cold as a barn in his room anyway. He and Harry Knowles stood by watching with admiring eyes, as Celia's fingers, now washed from the oil of the lamp, manipulated the pretty rose-colored paper into a shade, and when it was done, with a gathering string, a smoothing out on the edges and a pucker and twist here and there, and then a band and bow of the crepe paper; it all had looked so simple that they marveled at the beauty of the graceful fall of ruffles, like the petals of some lovely flower.

She put the promised book in Harry Knowles' hand, a paper-covered copy of "In His Steps," and saying she would come down later to see what he thought of the story, she slipped away to Mrs. Morris' room. She must get time to write to aunt Hannah some time to-night about her visit to the lawyers, for aunt Hannah might have some evidence which would serve her in good stead, but this duty to the sick woman came first. She turned her head as she left the room and saw the two young men settling themselves in evident comfort around the bright lamp. The school-teacher, George

Osborn, came in the front door just then, and catching the rosy light from the room stepped in, looked around surprised, then hung up his hat and went in to stand a minute before the register to warm his hands. It was a touch of cheer he had not expected. Presently he went upstairs and brought down a pile of reports he must make out, and seated himself with the other two around that light.

Celia upstairs was telling Mrs. Morris about the lamp, how well it burned, and giving a glowing account of the three young men seated around it. Mrs. Morris listened astonished.

"Well, I've told them boys time an' again that they ought to stay at home, but they never would before. It must be some sort of a spell you've worked on them. Of course, that teacher he stays up in his room a lot. But he's trying to support his mother and put his brother through college, and you can't expect much of him. He'll just give himself up entirely to them and that'll be the end of his life. There's always some folks in this world have to be sacrificed to a few others. It's the way things are. I'm one of those meself, though the land knows who's the better for me being sacrificed. It does seem as if I had had to give up every blessed thing I ever tried for in me life. Just set down a while. I feel a little easier this evening and I've been a-doing a powerful lot of worrying all day. I haven't a soul to advise me that knows anything. You seem to be made out of good stuff, and you've been real good to me, and I just wish you'd tell me what you think I ought to do."

Celia sat down. She wondered what could be coming next. It was strange to have her advice asked this way. Coming out into the world alone to earn one's living placed a great many responsibilities upon one sometimes. She felt very incapable of advising. She felt she had not wisdom to settle her own life, let alone another's, and one so much older than herself, that it would seem as if experience ought to have taught her much. But she tried to be sympathetic, and told Mrs. Morris to tell her all about it, and she would do the best she could. In her heart she prayed the Father that she might have the wisdom to answer wisely.

"Well, you see it's this way. I'm just deep down in debt. I told you that before. It's been going on worse and worse every year, and every year I'd hope by the next to make the two ends meet somehow. But they never did. I've cut down and cut down. And then I got left two or three times by boarders going off without paying what they owed after I had trusted them a long time. There was that Mr. Perry now, he left that old rickety organ. It was well enough to have an organ for the boarders, but you see I can't afford to have one. If I could have, I'd have bought a new one, you know. Well, things like that have happened time and again. Once a woman who recited pieces for a living came into the house. She had a lot of dirty satin clothes, and afterward she left quite suddenly and I never knew she was gone till a man came for her trunk. Of course I got the trunk for her board. She had been here two months and only paid one week's board, kept putting me off and off. When I had that trunk sold at auction it brought me in just one dollar and sixty-two cents. What do you think of that? And she had the second story front alone too; and *airs,* why she'd have her breakfast sent up every morning about ten o'clock. She made me think she was a great woman. Well, I learned better. But it does seem as though I've had more trouble with folks. There was the time the woman was here with her little girl, and the child took scarlet fever and the Board of Health came in and sent everybody off, and scared them so 'twas a long time before I could get them back. Well, there's been a plenty of other things just like that. You don't wonder, do you, that I'm in debt? The worst of it is it's been getting worse and worse. That Maggie just wastes everything she lays her hands on, and I don't know's I'd better myself any if I tried to get somebody else. There's always changes and new things to buy. Now what would you do? You see it's this way. I've got a sister out west that lives by herself in a little village. She's a widow and she's got enough to live on, and she's written to me to come out and live with her, and she thinks I could get a little sewing now and then, and I could help her in her house. I can't ask her for money, for I haven't got the face to, having asked her once before. Besides, she's not one to give out and out that way, even if she could afford to, which I guess she can't, though she'd be willing and glad to give me a home with her. I'm too proud to borrow what I know I never could pay, and I won't skip out here as some would and leave me debts behind me. I'm honest, whatever else I ain't. Now what would you do? No, I don't own this house; if I did I'd been bankrupt long ago with the repairs it needs, that I couldn't get out of the landlord. But I took it for the rest of the year, and the lease won't run out till April, so you see I'm in for that. It's just the same old story. 'A little more money to buy more land, to plant more corn, to feed more hogs, to get more money, to buy more land, to feed more hogs.' Only, I always had a little less of everything each time. Now Miss Murray, what would you do if it was you?''

"Haven't you anything at all to pay with? No,'' — she hesitated for a word and the one she had heard that day came to her — "Haven't you any property of any sort? Nothing you could sell?''

Celia was always practical. She wanted to know where she stood before she gave any advice. Mrs. Morris looked at her a moment in a dazed way, trying to think if there was anything at all.

"No, not a thing except my husband's watch and this old furniture. I suppose I might sell out me business, but nobody would buy it and I'd pity 'em, poor things, if they did.''

She talked a long time with the woman, trying to find out about boarding-houses and how they were run. Before she was through she began to have some inkling of the reason why Mrs. Morris had failed in business and was so deeply in debt. She was only a girl, young and without experience, but she felt sure she could have avoided some of the mistakes which had been the cause of Mrs. Morris' trouble. Finally, she said in answer to the twentieth "What would you do if you was me?''

"Mrs. Morris, I don't quite know till I have thought about it. I will think and tell you to-morrow, perhaps, or the next day. It seems to me though, that I would stop right now and not run on and get more deeply in debt. That cannot better matters. I think somebody might buy your things, and — some way might be found for you to pay your debts, — but, in the first place, you must get well, and we'll do the very best we can to get on here till you are well enough to know what you will do. Now may I read to you just a few words? And then you ought to go to sleep. Just you rest your mind about all those things, and I promise you I will try to think of something that will help you."

She turned to the little Bible she had brought in with her and read a few verses in the fourteenth chapter of John "Let not your heart be troubled; ye believe in God, believe also in me."

She was very tired when she reached her room that night. The letter she intended to write to aunt Hannah was still unwritten. The book she had taken from the public library to read was lying on her bureau untouched. She had been bearing the burdens of other people, and the day had been full of excitement and hard work. She threw herself on her bed, so nervously tired that she felt convulsive sobs rising in her throat. What had she done? She had promised to think up some way to help Mrs. Morris. Mrs. Morris was nothing to her, why should she take this upon herself? And yet she knew, as she asked herself these questions, that she had felt all along that God had as truly called her to help that poor woman as ever he had called her to sell ribbons for Dobson and Co., or to help aunt Hannah with the mending. She had not wanted to do it, either. It was very unpleasant work indeed, in many ways, and had required sacrifices of which she had not dreamed when she began. There was the pretty lampshade she was planning to have. She had given that up for the general good of the house. Now, when she got the lamp she intended to buy at a cheap sale somewhere, she would have to wait till she could afford more paper and a frame for her shade. Well, never mind! She surely was repaid for that act, for those young men had enjoyed it. How much pleasure a little thing can give! How many things there were about that house which might be easily done to make things brighter and pleasanter, and how much she would enjoy doing them, — if aunt Hannah were only here! How nice it would be if she had some money and could buy Mrs. Morris out and help the poor thing to get off to her relatives, and then get to work and make that house cheerful and beautiful and a true home for its present inmates. How aunt Hannah would enjoy that work too! It was just such work as would fulfill that good woman's highest dreams of a beautiful vocation in life.

Suddenly Celia sat bolt upright on the hard little bed, and stared at the opposite wall with a thoughtful, and yet energetic expression on her face.

"What if it should!" she said aloud. "What if there should be some money, say as much as a thousand dollars, and maybe a little over, for an allowance lest we might run behind. Wouldn't that be grand! Oh, you dear old uncle Abner, if it proves true, and if you up in heaven can see, I hope you know how happy you'll make several people. I'll do it. I surely will! And aunt Hannah shall come and run the house and be the housekeeper, and maybe we can get old Molly, for I'm certain we never could do a thing with that Maggie, she's so terribly dirty, and Molly would leave anywhere to be with aunt Hannah! There now, I'm talking just as if I was a 'millionairess' and could spend my millions. I ought not to have thought of this, for it will turn my head. I shall be so disappointed when Mr. Rawley tells me, to-morrow or next day, that I'm not myself, or that the property is some old hen house and a family cat, that I'm afraid I shall not be properly thankful for the cat. I wonder if it isn't just as bad to take up the happy crosses for the coming year as the uncomfortable ones. I wonder how that is. I must think about it. Meanwhile, aunt Hannah must be written to, for Mr. Rawley wanted some marriage certificates she has, and somehow I feel quite happy." She sprang from the bed and jumped around her room in such a lively fashion that Miss Burns who roomed below wondered what was the matter.

Writing to her aunt sobered her down somewhat. She began to think of herself a little.

"Celia Murray, do you know what you are doing?" This was what she heard whispered to her from behind. "You have come to the city to earn your living, and you have come here to board, not to nurse sick landladies, nor to become a guardian angel for stray young men, nor to exercise the virtue of benevolence. You must think of yourself, somewhat. How in the world will you ever be fit for your work if you spend so much time and energy on working for other people and staying up nights? Had you better seek out another boarding-house? There must be plenty in this city, and probably if you looked about a little you might find one where you would have more conveniences and a better room and board. Leave Mrs. Morris to get along the best way she can. You are not responsible for her. She is a grown woman and ought to know enough to take care of herself. Anyway, she is only suffering the consequences of her foolishness. Better try to-morrow to find another boarding-house."

Yet, even as Celia heard these words spoken in a tempting voice, she knew she would not go. She was not made of that kind of stuff. Besides she was interested. Whatever her cross for the coming week was to be, it would not be one to her to remain here now and help work out God's plans, if she might be permitted so to do.

"And if it might only please my King to lift my head up out of prison and set me up where I might help others in this boarding-house, I would try to make as good a use of my liberty and my allowance as Jehoiachin did. I wonder what he did do with his allowance anyway. And it must have been such a pleasant thing to him to know, to fully understand that his allowance would not fail all the days of his life. I wonder if he got downhearted sometimes, and feared lest

Evil-Merodach might die and leave him in the lurch, or whether he might turn against him some day. Now with me it is so different. My King is all-powerful. What he has promised, *I know* he will perform. I need never dread his dying, for he is everlasting. I can trust him perfectly to give me an allowance all the days of my life of whatever I need. And yet, daily and hourly I distrust, and fear and tremble, and dread lest I may be left hungry some day. What a strange contradiction, what an ungrateful, untrustful, unworthy child of the King I am.''

Then she turned out her light and knelt to pray.

6

It is said that Satan trembles when he sees the weakest saint upon his knees. It is probably true that he also hurried him away to take counsel with his evil angels to see if they cannot by some means overtake that saint in his resolves and endeavors, and make him tremble, and perhaps fall. It certainly seemed to Celia the next morning as if everything had conspired to make her life hard.

In the first place it was raining. A cold, steady drizzle, that bade fair to continue all day and for several days, if it did not turn into snow. The furnace, none too good at any time, was ill-managed. Mrs. Morris usually regulated it herself, but Maggie made a poor hand at it. She chose this morning to forget to see to it at all until the fire had gone out. There was no time to build it up then, for she had breakfast to get for the boarders who must be off to their work at their appointed hours. Celia dressed quickly, for her room was so cold she was in a shiver. With her blue fingers she tried to turn the pages of her Bible to read a few words while she combed her hair, but finally gave it up she was so cold. She was sleepy, too, for she had lost much sleep of late, and it was hard to get up before it was fairly light and hurry around in the cold. Life looked very hard and dreary to her. She thought of aunt Hannah getting breakfast for Nettie's family, and buttoning the children's clothes between times. Somehow the thought of aunt Hannah weighed heavily upon her this morning. She could not get away from it. It brought a sob in her throat and a pain at the heart. Why did they have to separate? It was cruel that life was so. The tears came to her eyes. She jerked a snarl out and broke two teeth of her comb at the same time. This did not serve to help her temper. She did hate to use a comb with the teeth out and once out there was no putting them back. Neither could she afford a new comb for some time to come. She glanced at her plain little silver watch and saw it was later than she usually rose, and she hurried through her toilet as much as possible, and ran downstairs to the dining-room. The clerk stood at the dining-room door, an expression of belligerence on his face and his attitude one of displeasure. He filled up the door so completely that Celia was obliged to ask him to let her pass before he moved. She was indignant at him for this. She found herself likening him to one of the animals condemned in the Bible. It was unchristian of course, but Celia did not feel in a very sweet spirit this morning. She recalled what Mrs. Morris had said and wished he would leave the house. He looked like a man whom it was impossible to please anyway. But she found the cause of his displeasure was that there was no breakfast forthcoming as yet. Mr. Knowles came down, greeted her pleasantly, looked at the empty table, and the clock, filled his pocket with some crackers on a plate there, and remarked that he guessed he would skip, that it was as much as his place was worth if he did not get to the store on time, and he would have to run all the way to the car to make it now, it was so late. Celia felt indignant that this young man was obliged to go to a hard day's work unfed. But there was nothing to be done now, he must go. It was the hard fate of the wage-earner. He must be on time, if the house fell. She went to the kitchen door and peered in. Maggie was slamming about in a grand rage. The biscuits she was baking were not even beginning to brown yet, as Celia saw by a glimpse into the oven door when Maggie opened it and slammed it shut. There was some greasy-looking hash cooking slowly. It did not look as if it ever would be done at the present rate it was cooking. The stove looked sulky and the ashes were not yet taken up.

"Maggie," she said, "can I help you get something on the table? These people all have to go to work and so do I. If we can't eat in five minutes we'll have to do without."

"Well, then, go without!" said Maggie, rising in a towering passion. "I'm sure it won't hurt you fine folks once in a while. I never hired out to do everything and I ain't responsible. I'll get the breakfast as soon as I can and not a bit sooner, and you can get out of my kitchen. I don't want you bothering 'round. I get all flustered with so many folks coming after me. Go on out now, and wait till yer breakfast's ready. And tell the rest I won't cook any dinner fer 'em, if a soul comes in this kitchen again."

Celia retreated, indignant and outraged. To be spoken to in such a manner when she was but offering help was an insult. It was a peculiarity of hers that when she felt angry the tears would come to her eyes. They came now. It was exasperating. She went quickly to the window to hide them, and looked out in the dim little brick alley that ran between the houses and watched the rain drop all over the bricks. There was a blank brick wall of the next house opposite her, and a little further toward the front she could see a window and some one standing at it. She turned quickly away again. There was no refuge there. Taking in at a glance the table with its unbrushed crumbs, and the dishes of uncooked hash and underdone biscuits that Maggie was just bringing in, she resolved to follow the example of Mr. Knowles and take some crackers. Then seizing her hat and coat from the hall rack where she had put them, on coming downstairs, she started for the store. It was a long, cold walk and she got very wet, but she did not feel justified in spending the five cents which would have carried her there. In her present mood she had no faith in uncle Abner's fortune. It would probably turn out to be some poor land somewhere which would never be worth a cent. That was the kind of inheritance which usually came to any one in their family, like the lot in a new town out west that was left to aunt Hannah by her eldest brother, where the city authorities compelled property holders to pave the streets and pay large taxes and where there were no purchasers. Such inheritances one was better off without. She felt very bitter in her heart. As she walked along in the rain, she remembered that she had forgotten to kneel by her bedside in prayer before she left her room that morning, it was so cold and late. She knew that must be the reason why she felt so cross and unreasonable, and she tried to pray as she walked along in the rain, but there were many things to distract her thoughts, and she had to watch carefully that she did not run into some one with her umbrella turned down in front of her to keep off the driving rain. She thought of aunt Hannah again, now probably washing the breakfast dishes, or doing some sewing or ironing, and she sighed and felt that earth was wet and cold and dreary. Half-way to the store, she encountered a little newsboy who followed by her side, and begged her to buy a paper. He looked hungry. His feet were out at the toes from his shoes, much too large. Celia had no money to buy a paper and she answered the boy in a decided negative and made him turn hopelessly away. It made her cross to see his need, when she had no power to help him. She realized how cross her voice had been and that vexed her. Then she blindly stepped into a mud puddle and splashed the water over the tops of her shoes. She shivered as she felt the dampness through the thin leather of her boot, and wondered what she would do when the inevitable sore throat, which always with her resulted from getting her feet wet, arrived. And so she hurried on, tugging after her the heavy cross which she had carefully made that morning for herself to carry, out of bits of her own and other people's troubles, and letting it spoil the sweet peace God had sent her, and soil the clean heart he had washed from sin for her. It was too bad. Her guardian angel pitied her that she could so soon forget her high resolves, and her heavenly Father.

Matters were no better when she reached the store. One of the girls who belonged at the ribbon counter with her was sick. Celia had to do her duty and the girl's also. This might not have been so bad if she had been left to herself, but the head of that department, a young woman with a sour expression and disappointed eyes, was also out of temper, and did her ordering in an exceedingly disagreeable manner. She found a great deal of fault and kept demanding of Celia more than she could well accomplish in a given time. Celia had hoped it would not be a busy day on account of the rain, but on the contrary every woman in town seemed to be in need of ribbon and to have hit upon that particular rainy morning in which to shop, thinking doubtless that the others would stay at home and leave the store to her. When the noon hour came Celia was cut down to half time on account of the rush, and obliged to take a few precious minutes of that in putting up some ribbons left carelessly on the counter by another saleswoman who had gone to her luncheon leaving them there. To the young girl new to her work, and fresh from a home where every *necessary* comfort at least had been hers, it was a long, hard day, and she looked forward with no hope of a let-up to the evening that was to follow. She grew crosser as the day began to wane, and she grew hungry, and then faint, and then lost both those feelings and settled down to a violent headache. It was then that a new cause for trouble loomed up before her imagination. What if she should get sick? Who would take care of her and how should she live? Aunt Hannah would have to come, and what an expense that would be! — No, aunt Hannah could not come. There was no money anywhere to pay her fare, or her board when she got there, and she was bound to stay with Nettie and Hiram as long as they were supporting her. She would have to get along without telling aunt Hannah. What would become of her? Oh, why of course, she would have to go to the hospital among strangers and be nursed, and perhaps die, and aunt Hannah never hear and then worry and worry and no one would tell her.

It was just in the midst of these thoughts that there came the clear voice of the floor walker:

"Miss Murray, will you step to the office a moment. There is a message there for you, a special delivery letter I believe."

With her heart throbbing violently at thought of the possibilities contained in a special delivery letter, she walked the length of the long store. Aunt Hannah must be sick and they had sent for her. Surely they would do that if aunt Hannah should be so ill she needed care, for Nettie would never care for her, she was no nurse and hated sick rooms. Besides, to be perfectly honest, Nettie would have enough to do in caring for her home and children. There was no hospital in the little town where Hiram lived, so he would, of course, rather pay her fare and keep her while she did the nursing than to hire some one to care for aunt Hannah. All this reasoning went clearly through her brain, as she walked swiftly in the direction of the office. It seemed as if the writing of her name on the receipt book was one of the longest actions she ever performed, and her hand trembled so when she retired to the little cloak room to read her letter that she could scarcely open the envelope, nor take in at first that the letter bore Rawley and Brown's printed heading. And then she read just a few lines from them asking her to call once more upon them and as soon as possible. She went back to her place among the ribbons feeling almost angry with Rawley and Brown that they had frightened her so, and yet relieved that there was nothing the matter with aunt Hannah.

It was nearly five o'clock, and the crowd of women who were doing rainy day shopping had gone home. The rain was pouring down harder than ever. The store was comparatively empty. Perhaps she might get away for a few moments now; she would ask. Permission was granted her, as she had had only half her noon hour, and she hurried up to the dark little office again.

She found that she was not too late, for Mr. Rawley had not yet gone home, though he had his overcoat on as if about to depart. It appeared that he wished to ask a few more questions to establish certain facts. Celia answered them as best she could, and then as he seemed to be through with her, she asked timidly:

"Would you be so kind as to tell me what this is all about, anyway? You said there was property. If it should turn out to be mine, what would it be? I suppose you do not mind giving me a general idea of that, do you?"

He looked at her almost kindly under his shaggy brows. "Why no, child!" he said. "That's perfectly proper, of course. Why, I haven't the exact figures in my head, but it's several thousands, well invested, and an old farm up in New York state that's well rented. There would be enough to give a pretty good income every year, you know, and if you left the investments as they are, it would be a continuous one, for they are not likely to fail or fall through. Then, too, there is a considerable accumulation owing to the doubt about the heir. I hope you'll turn out to be that heir and I have no doubt you will. Good-afternoon." Celia tripped down the dark old staircase as if it were covered with the softest carpet ever made. Several thousands! What wealth! What luxury! She had wished for one single thousand, and her Father had sent her not one, but many. For she began to believe now that the money was hers. All the evidence seemed to point that way. The lawyer seemed to be convinced, and it needed only the coming of a few documents in possession of her uncle Joseph's old lawyer to corroborate what she had told him. She felt pretty sure that it was all true. And here she had been cross and growling all day, and worse than that, she had been carrying crosses not meant for her shoulders, and probably leaving undone the things God had laid out for her to do. What wickedness had been hers. Only last night she had knelt in earnest consecration, and now to-day she had fallen so low as almost to forget that she had a Father whose dear child she was, and who was caring for her. Could she not retrieve some of the lost day? She had but one hour left in the store. She would try what she could do. She smiled on the beggar child who stood looking wistfully in at the pretty things in the store window as she passed in to her work. When she reached the ribbon counter again, she found the head of the department looking very tired, and complaining of a headache. There were other burdens besides her own she could bear. She might offer to do her work for her and let her rest, and she could bring her a glass of water. It was not her business to put up certain ribbons not in her own case, but she could do it for the other girl who was absent and save the head girl. As she made her fingers fly among the bright silks and satins, she wondered if there were more burdens for her to bear for others when she reached the boarding-house, and whether Mrs. Morris would be better to-night and able to sit up and direct things a little, and then there came to her mind the joyous thought that perhaps she was to have the means soon to make that house permanently better in some ways and help its inmates. How light her heart and her shoulders felt now that she had laid down that heavy self-imposed cross! It was wonderful! Oh, why could she not learn to trust her Master? The verse of a loved hymn came and hummed itself over in her mind.

"Fearest sometimes that thy Father
          Hath forgot?
When the clouds around thee gather,
          Doubt him not!
Always hath the daylight broken —
Always hath he comfort spoken —
          Better hath he been for years,
          Than thy fears."

7

Miss Hannah Grant sat in her room under the eaves darning little Johnnie's stocking. Her hair was grey and rippled smoothly over her finely shaped head. Her sweet face wore a sad, far-away expression. It had grown habitual with her ever since she had come to live with her niece Nettie. Perhaps a close observer would see that the sadness was a shade deeper this afternoon. Her eyes were deep grey and seemed to go well with her hair. She gave one the impression of being able to see further with them than most people, and there was a luminousness about them that lit up her otherwise plain face, and made it truly beautiful. Her gown was plain and old and grey. She always wore grey dresses. They had been becoming long ago in the days when it mattered whether she wore becoming things, and now that she cared no more about the becomingness, she wore them for sweet association's sake, and for the sake of one long gone who used to admire them when she wore them. She did not seem to know that they still suited her better than any other color, or absence of color, could have done.

The hole was large and ill-shaped, for Johnnie was hard on his stockings, but she darned it patiently back and forth, and seemed to be thinking of something else. Once she laid it down and went to the closet for her little grey worsted shawl to throw around her shoulders, for the room was heated only by a drum from the stove downstairs and she felt chilly. She usually sat in the sitting-room in the afternoon to sew or mend, but there had been a reason for her coming up here today. She had settled herself as usual by the west window downstairs to get a good light on her work. She had a large peach basket full of stockings by her side, and her workbasket on the window. The baby, creeping about the floor, had upset the peach basket and scattered its contents around, and Nettie, coming down just then in a new red cashmere shirt waist she had finished the day before, had jerked him unceremoniously away from among the stockings and hastily bundled them all into the basket, shoving it behind aunt Hannah's chair and out of her reach. As she did so, she remarked in a disagreeable tone that she wished aunt Hannah wouldn't bring that old thing into the sitting-room. Couldn't she bring a pair of stockings at a time, and not litter up the whole room? She was expecting Mrs. Morgan and her sister in with their embroidery and crocheting, and she did like to have things look a little nice. Aunt Hannah had meekly disposed of the stocking basket behind her ample apron, and there had been silence in the room for a few minutes. Then young Mrs. Bartlett remarked:

34

"Aunt Hannah, I think you had better go and change your dress, if you are going to sit there. That old grey thing doesn't look very well. I wish to goodness you had a black silk, or something, like other folks. You always waste your money on grey things when you have to buy anything. It's a dreadfully gloomy color. It makes you look sallow, too, now you're getting older."

Nettie had gone out in the kitchen then for a minute and returned just as aunt Hannah was starting upstairs with the darning basket.

"Aunt Hannah!" she called, "take your shawl and bonnet up with you, won't you? I s'pose you'd just as soon keep them up there, wouldn't you? Hiram says he hates to see the hall rack cluttered up so."

Aunt Hannah put down the basket on the stairs, descended swiftly, gathered her shawl and bonnet and one or two other belongings of hers which were downstairs, in inconspicuous places, and carried them all upstairs. She was not in the habit of leaving her bonnet and shawl on the rack, and had only done so last night when she came in from prayer-meeting, because she had buckwheat cakes to set before going to bed, and when that was done and she started to take them away, Nettie had asked her to carry a lamp and two comfortables up for her, and in doing so the shawl and bonnet had escaped her notice. It was a little thing, and she realized that the hall rack looked better without her shawl and bonnet, but somehow it was one of the many things that gave her the feeling that she had no home. She had put them all meekly away and sat down in her little cold room near the drum to darn. She had done what she was asked to do with one exception. She did not change her dress and go down again. She saw that Nettie would like to have her out of the way for the afternoon, and she did not wish to remain where she was not wanted. She did not sigh as some women would have done. Instead, her eyes took on that far-away look. She was beginning to long so sorely for the open gates of her home above where she need never more feel that desolation of not belonging, and where she would meet loved ones, and above all her Father, face to face. Yet she knew her heavenly Father was with her, even in this home where she was treated as a burden, and she could be content to stay and do his bidding, only sometimes that great longing for the face to face view grew upon her till her heart ached with the desire to go.

In her bureau drawer, safe hid in tissue paper in a white box smelling of rose leaves there were some letters, and an old daguerreotype. The picture was in an old-fashioned leather frame that closed with a little brass hook, and was lined with stamped purple velvet. The face inside was of a young man with sweet, serious eyes, a grave, handsome face, smoothly shaven, heavy, dark hair tossed back from a high white forehead, and the dress of the olden time — a high rolling collar and stock. The letters were from this man to Hannah Grant, written when he was in the theological seminary, and they contained bright glad plans for the future, Hannah's and his. They might not have seemed bright to some women, for they were planning, as soon as he had finished his ministerial training, to go to the Foreign Mission field and work together for the Master they both loved better than anything else. And next to him they had loved each other. How bright her life had seemed to her then as she did her daily duties; sang about them; thought of the future and wrote her happy letters; and thanked the Lord daily that she was to be permitted to do his work in this honorable way. The time had gone by rapidly then, and the years of study had been completed. Hannah's wedding day was set, her simple lovely wedding gown was finished, and it was grey. He loved grey. It had little touches of soft white about the throat and wrists, just enough to bring out the coloring of Hannah's delicately cut face. And then, — suddenly there happened one of those mysteries of the kingdom which we shall understand by and by, and to which now we can only say, "It is the Lord, let him do what seemeth him best," and trust. The earnest young missionary was taken up higher, there to receive his reward. His bride, when she could rally from the shock of the sudden ending of her life joy, bowed to the will of him to whose keeping she had long ago given her will and her life, and was enabled to say with tears of triumph that like that man of God of old her beloved had "walked with God and was not, for God took him."

She had thought even then to go alone, and take the message of Jesus to those who knew him not, and bear her sorrow more easily by thinking she could do some of the work which they would have done together. But God opened another door for her and showed her plainly that he had called her to a duty at home, and so she took her saddened heart, her sweet face and her tender ways to her sisters' motherless little children and had lived there ever since. Sometimes now, when she thought how she was not wanted in this home, and yet could not go anywhere else by force of circumstances, she would take out that pictured face and wonder if James could know how she was being treated, what he would think and feel about it, and think how he would guard her from the world and shield her if he were only here. And then she would be glad that he could not know, or that if he could, he was where he knew it would not any of it be for long, and that she would soon come home to be with Jesus and with him forevermore, and that time to him was only a brief space. It was at such times that her eyes would take on their far-away look.

So she sat and worked and thought that afternoon. In due course of time the expected visitors arrived. The woman upstairs heard their voices, and presently they drew nearer to the stove in the sitting-room. Their talk could be quite distinctly heard now, but Hannah was absorbed in her own thoughts, and she paid no attention as they gossiped on about this one and that, with "You don't say sos," and "Well, I always thought as muchs," and "Did-she-say thats," until she heard Nettie say, "Yes, she will stay with us this winter anyway. No, it isn't quite as pleasant as to be alone you know, but then what could we do? She had no home to go to. My husband wanted my cousin to come, too, though it was more than we really could afford to do to feed and clothe two more, but she was very ungrateful, and wanted to have her own way and see the world a little. I expect she'll come back humbly enough when she's been away a couple of weeks longer, and if she does I'm sure I don't know what in the world we shall do with her. Oh yes, aunt Hannah helps me a little here and there, but you can't ask much of people that are getting on in years. (Aunt Hannah was forty-nine.) My father always kept her in luxury as she was my mother's only sister. Yes, people do get spoiled sometimes that way. But, dear me, all she can do wouldn't make up for the outgo. Yes, she was a sort of acting housekeeper in our home after mother died, but you know no one can ever take a mother's place. (Johnnie, shut that door and go away and stop your coaxing, or I'll take you upstairs and give you a good spanking. No, you *can't* go down by the pond to play to-day.) No, I never had so much to do with her as the younger children. I was the elder daughter, you know."

Aunt Hannah quickly and noiselessly moved away from her position by the drum to the other side of the room. And this from the little girl she had so carefully mothered, and tended, and tried to train! And had loved, too, for Hannah Grant loved all that God loved and placed in her way. Ah, this was hard! And must she go on living here and knowing that she was not wanted, that she was a burden, and that lies — yes, actually lies, for there was no use trying to call them by a softer name — were being told to the people in the village about her? How could she? She could see just how it would go on from year to year. Hiram would come in cross at night and either ignore her altogether, or else contradict every word she spoke, and find fault with anything he knew she had done, in a surly, impersonal way, which he knew and she knew he meant for her. The children would grow up to disrespect her, as they were beginning to do already. And her dear Celia! She was toiling bravely far away from her! There was no prospect of anything better for years to come, perhaps never so long as she lived. She knelt down by her bed, and prayed for a long time. Then she arose quietly and went back to her window, a chastened look upon her face. This was not more than he had helped her to bear before. Indeed, it was not nearly so much. It was what Jesus had himself borne, being despised and rejected of men. She darned on till the room grew dark, and then she sat in the twilight and thought. She could not bring herself to go downstairs yet, not till she must get supper. She thanked the Lord she had a room to herself where she might take refuge alone and think of him. It was seldom that aunt Hannah had had even this privilege in the daytime since she had come to live with Nettie, there was always so much to be done, and Nettie seemed to expect it to be done quickly.

The company below had departed, but Miss Grant took no heed. She sat and watched the grey sky grow into night. There was no sunset. It had been a grey day. There was not even a point of light to make the sky lovely. It sank into darkness, quietly, soberly, unnoticed and unlovely. She thought it was like herself. But then there had been some reason why God had not made a bright sunset to-night, and there surely was some reason why he had wanted her life grey instead of rose-colored. She sighed just a little, and now that the darkness had stolen softly upon her, she let a tear have its way down her cheek.

Downstairs Nettie was growing restless. Hiram came in a little earlier than usual with a sour look and asked how long it would be before supper. Nettie said it would not be long, and wondered why aunt Hannah did not come downstairs. Hiram remarked that if the old woman was getting lazy and taking on fine-lady airs they had better give her a warning, for he couldn't support her for nothing. He threw a letter for her upon the table while Nettie was lighting the lamp. Nettie took it up, glanced at the writing, then sent Johnnie up with it and told him to tell aunt Hannah his father had come and wanted his supper right away.

"It's from Celia again," she said, in a contemptuous tone. "She wastes more money on postage. I don't think it's right to do that in her position. If she has any extra money she better save it up and help with supporting aunt Hannah. A great fat letter, too. I don't see what she finds to write about. This is the third one this week. It's perfectly absurd!"

But aunt Hannah did not hear what they said; she was not sitting near the drum, and would not again, even if she was cold.

Johnnie came down and reported that aunt Hannah had a light in her room and Nettie rattled the stove with all her might, and slammed the dishes around more than was necessary, but still aunt Hannah did not come, and finally Nettie began to get supper herself. She sent Johnnie up again pretty soon to tell aunt Hannah she wished she would come downstairs, that she needed her, and Johnnie came back and said aunt Hannah told him to tell mamma she would be down pretty soon, she could not come just now.

"Well, really!" said Hiram, looking up from his paper, "seems to me she is putting on airs at a great rate. If I were you, Nettie, I would just sit down and wait till she comes. I wouldn't get supper at all. If you haven't the grit to tell her to come down now when you send for her, I'll do it for you."

But Nettie rattled the stove and the dishes and managed to get supper ready pretty soon. She did not quite understand her aunt. This was a new development. Never in all the years she had known her and been cared for by her had aunt Hannah ever refused a request for help. It must be something serious. Was she sick? Nettie had some little heart left in her, and it irritated her to have her husband speak so of her relatives, so she bristled up at him, while she made the coffee.

"You'll not do any such thing, Hiram Bartlett. I guess she has a right to stay in her room once in a while. I'm sure I never knew her to do the like before in the whole of her life. If she was your aunt, you wouldn't speak of her in that way. I think you ought to be a little grateful for the way she took care of you last week when you were so sick, and me with the baby sick, too. If she hadn't been here I should have had my hands more than full. I don't know what I should have done. Johnnie, make that baby stop crying! Lillie, pick that doll up off the floor! I keep walking over something of yours all the time. I s'pose Celia's got into some trouble and aunt Hannah's worried about her. I expected as much. That girl hadn't experience enough of the world to go off to the city alone. Somebody ought to have taken her home to live. If one of the boys had been married she could have gone with them, but the boys are so selfish they never think of other people. If you had any sense of the fitness of things you'd have done it yourself."

They talked on in a wrangling way until supper was ready, but it was not until they had nearly finished the evening meal that the hall door opened and aunt Hannah walked in.

8

Aunt Hannah had lighted her lamp a few minutes after the light of the day went out, to get a little comfort from her Bible before going downstairs to face her trials, for it must be confessed that aunt Hannah had not had a cross so heavy to bear in many a year, as it was for her to go downstairs that night and face Hiram and Nettie calmly after the words she had heard her niece speak. She had tried to think of all the comfort in the Bible as she sat in the twilight. She had a great store of the precious words to draw from, for her Bible had ever been her chief delight. She knew just where to turn in her memory for the right help and it came trooping forth.

"Fear thou not; for I am with thee: be not dismayed; for I am thy God: I will strengthen thee; yea, I will help thee; yea, I will uphold thee with the right hand of my righteousness ... When thou passest through the fire, thou shalt not be burned ... God is faithful, who will not suffer you to be tempted above that ye are able; but will with the temptation also make a way to escape, that ye may be able to bear it ... Blessed is the man that endureth temptation: for when he is tried, he shall receive the crown of life, which the Lord hath promised to them that love him ... For I reckon that the sufferings of this present time are not worthy to be compared with the glory which shall be revealed in us ... All things work together for good to them that love God ... To be conformed to the image of his Son ... If God be for us, who can be against us? ... Nay in all these things we are more than conquerors through him that loved us."

Then she lighted the lamp to search out another promise, for it seemed to her as if just to look upon the words would somehow help her. It was at that moment Johnnie brought up Celia's letter. She opened it quickly, the anticipation of another trouble arising in her mind, for what might not have happened to Celia so far away in that great city alone, since the last letter she wrote?

It was a thick letter and she read it slowly through, taking no thought of time because the matter it contained absorbed her mind completely, and when Johnnie came up the second time, she had something new to think about which demanded immediate attention and had claims prior to any downstairs. The letter read thus:

"DEAR AUNT HANNAH:
"Do you remember the words on the little bookmark you sent me for my birthday? I know you do, for you have a way of hiding all such

40

words away in that wonderful memory of yours. You know the heading was about an allowance, from the king, a continual allowance. When I read it I knew just what you meant by sending it to me. You wanted to remind me that my King had plenty of extra strength to give me, and that he had promised to furnish me with enough for every day of my life to bear that day's trials. It did help me, for I knew I was trying to bear some of them all by myself, and that I often and often forget that I do not have to take up next year's crosses and worry about them. But I remember, when I first read the words, I couldn't help longing deep down in my heart, that I could have a real earthly allowance of money, just solid hard dirty monty, coming in every week, and every month, and every year, and enough to supply all the actual needs that I might live with you and work for you and have you all to myself. Then I felt indeed that my head would be lifted up out of prison forever — for I read the chapter about Jehoiachin as you meant I should, you dear good auntie — and it helped me too. You see, I had been taking up a big heavy cross for the year to come for you. I didn't feel happy about you there at Hiram's, for in spite of me I cannot like Hiram's ways and I don't believe you do. I know for one thing, and a very small thing, that you hate tobacco smoke and have never been used to it, and yet Hiram smokes all over the house whenever he pleases, without even so much as caring whether it is repulsive to you or not. In fact, I am wicked enough to suspect that he might do it the more, just because you don't like it, to show you he is master of his own house. I am so sorry I have to feel that way about my cousin-in-law, but I can't help it. There is this comfort about it, I don't believe Nettie minds, and as she is the one that has to be his wife and go through life with him, it is a relief to think she doesn't. But there! This is all out of the way, and unchristian, and I have been too much blessed to allow myself to say anything unchristian about any one. Only I did want you to understand that I appreciated how hard it was for you to cheerfully accept Nettie's proposal and go to live with her for a few years. I did not say so then because I thought any words would only make it harder to bear, and I know my own dear auntie's old way of always finding a thing easier to bear if she succeeds in making other people think she is perfectly happy. That is just one way, and the only way in which you ever are the least little bit dishonest.

"But I must hurry on with my main theme which has not even been hinted at yet. And I have a great deal to write, and must get it in to-night, for I cannot bear to have you wait a minute longer than is necessary to hear the good news.

"In the first place, you are not to stay at Nettie's another day — that is not unless you prefer to, of course — but you are to pack up every scrap that belongs to you and take the first train to Philadelphia, sending me a telegram (at my expense) to say what train you start on. You must come to the Broad Street station — have your trunks checked there too, and don't leave any of your things behind, for there is plenty of room to put all your things here, and you are not to go back to Nettie's unless you go on a visit of pleasure."

Aunt Hannah glanced up to see if the little room with its old ingrain carpet and cheap furniture was still about her. She was almost breathless with the proposal of the letter. Things seemed to whirl around her. She wanted to get something to steady her before she read on. She saw the black side of the sheet-iron drum and remembered this afternoon, and a glance toward her open Bible showed her the lines "God is faithful ... will with the temptation also make a way to escape, that ye may be able to bear it." She drew a long breath and closed her eyes for a minute's lifting of her heart to God. He was going to make the way to escape. She did not yet understand how it was to be done, but her faith caught at the fact that it was to be done. Then she went back to the letter.

"You are to give your checks to the porter on the car — and you are to take a sleeper if you come at night, or a parlor car if you choose to come in the daytime. I enclose your ticket."

Aunt Hannah noticed then that a small pink and white paper had fallen from the letter when she opened it, and slipped to the floor. She stooped and picked it up in a dazed way. Good for one trip to Philadelphia it certainly was. This was something tangible and brought her back to everyday life. She really was to go, for here was the ticket. She went on with the letter eagerly now.

"You are to have the porter carry your satchel into the station for you, and I will meet you at the gate and take you home. Yes, HOME, aunt Hannah, yours and mine, do you hear that? It isn't very pretty, nor inviting yet, but it is ours for a while, for as long as we want it, and we shall fix it into a charming home. And now you want to know how it all happened and what it means.

"Well, this morning I was sent for again to come to Rawley and Brown's office on very important business, and as they told me it might keep me some time I asked for the day off at the store. I couldn't have had that, if I had not done double duty for the last week in place of a girl who was sick. Mr. Dobson was very nice and said certainly in such a case he would give me permission. Of course, I suppose I'll lose my pay for that day, but it had to be done, and it doesn't matter now anyway. Well, Mr. Rawley hemmed and hawed a good deal, and finally told me that everything was satisfactorily settled at last and that I had been duly declared by the court to be uncle Abner's heir, without any question or doubt anywhere, and that he wished to go over the papers with me and place the property in my hands. There was some red tape to be gone through which I needn't stop now to tell you about. It was all very interesting to me, the number of times I had to sign my name, and all the witnesses, and I felt just like a girl in a book, but I haven't time for that. There is better to come. It seems uncle Abner had a farm where he lived after he got old, and his wife died and his son went to India, and there was a young farmer and his family who lived there and took care of him, and they have rented the house ever since. They still live there. The farm is pretty good, way up in New York somewhere I think, I didn't pay much attention to it. Then he owned an interest in a coal mine near Scranton and a few government bonds, not many of those, but the whole is well invested and brings in a nice little income every year, sure, and I couldn't help thinking of Jehoiachin when Mr. Rawley was telling me about it. He said it was so well invested that it was, as near as anything earthly could be, sure, a continual 'income as long as I lived' if I kept things in their present shape, for uncle Abner had been a very careful man and always invested in pretty safe things with what little he had. I didn't tell him I considered it much instead of little, though. It seemed a fortune to me. I suppose I shall learn better hereafter, but I am going to try to be very wise with it anyway, with God's help.

"Now you want to know how much it is, I know. Well, it amounts to about nine hundred dollars a year at the lowest calculation, besides several years of accumulated interest not invested yet. Isn't that riches? Why, you've often told me that not many ministers and few missionaries get more than that. Now then, why shouldn't you and I be missionaries? I know it has been your dear desire all your life, and I don't know of anything that would be grander work. And as we can't go as foreign missionaries just now, what if we should be home missionaries? Of course, two lone women couldn't take mortar and bricks and build a church and preach, at least I shouldn't like to try it, though I'm not at all sure but I could do it. You know we always thought, if we had the time and the material and the pattern, you and I could do almost anything anybody else could if we tried. Well, I began to think about a mission for us, and before I had gotten half-way home to write to you it came to me just what I would like to do. Why shouldn't you and I make a real home mission for ourselves right here in the city of Philadelphia, by making a good home for a few people who have none of their own? It seems to me there is as much gospel sometimes in a good sweet loaf of bread such as you can make, as there is in — well — *some* sermons. Don't you think so? Then we could get a hold on the people who ate it, and get them to go to the churches, and try to help them in their everyday lives. Why, some of the young men here would stay at home evenings occasionally, perhaps regularly, if they had a pleasant, warm, light place to stay in. Instead of that they go out to the saloons, perhaps. Anyway, auntie dear, they don't look rested in the morning when they come down to breakfast. And oh, what a breakfast we did have this morning! It seems as though I never can like hash again, though I always used to enjoy ours so much at home when you made it. But hash in Mrs. Morris' boarding-house is a very different dish indeed. When I got home I went straight up to Mrs. Morris' room. She has not gotten entirely well from her severe sickness of a few weeks ago yet, though she goes around and directs things, but she seems to be so worried all the time. You know I told you how many bills she has unpaid and how hard times have been for her. You wouldn't wonder a bit if you could be here and watch the way things go a little while. She was lying on her bed when I went in and looking as if she would like to cry, if she only were young enough and had the energy. She told me right away that she was in trouble again. She was a month behind in her rent, and the agent had been around and said it must be paid in advance after this and he couldn't wait longer than till five o'clock. She only pays twenty-five dollars a month, and with all her boarders you might think she could pay it, but she doesn't, that's all. While she was talking I began to revolve my plans very rapidly. I didn't want to act too rashly, for you know you always tell me that is one of my great faults, but I knew if I did anything it ought to be done very soon. Probably it would have been wiser to have asked Mr. Rawley's advice, and perhaps some of my relatives, but I had an innate suspicion that I would not be allowed to do it at all, if I asked. And why shouldn't I? The money is mine, and I am of age if I am not very experienced. I knew you would like it, at least I felt very sure you would, and if you and God like a thing I don't care what all the rest of the world think. So I asked Mrs. Morris a lot of questions, some I had not asked her before. You see I had a whole two hundred dollars in my pocketbook, Mr. Rawley had given me. He said it was mine, and I might as well take it to begin on. So I took it. I knew I would want to do a lot of things right away, and that the first one would be to get you here at once, and to buy your ticket. I was just aching to spend some money, for it was the first time in my life I ever had much to spend. I asked Mrs. Morris about her butcher's bill, and her grocery bill, and things and I found they were not so very big as she had made me think at first. Then I asked her point blank how she would like to let a woman come in here in her place for three months or so, and take the boarding-house off her hands, paying the bills for the present, and letting her pay them by and by, if she chose, or if not, holding the furniture as collateral. She didn't know what I meant by collateral, but she soon understood, and said she would be only too glad, only she never could find any woman who would be so foolish. She said, too, that she was afraid if she once got away she would never be willing to come back, but just stay and leave the old furniture to make it right with her debts, and she sighed and returned to her trouble and began to cry. Then I couldn't stand it any longer. I told her I thought I knew the right one for her, and I would write to her at once and attend to it all if she was sure she agreed to it. It did not take her long to decide what she would do after she was fully convinced that I meant what I said. She began to pack up her clothes right away and to talk about what she would take with her. She hasn't much worth while, I guess. She will want those horrid crayon portraits of her family and herself, I hope, and a few other ornaments. But when we had gotten to this point, we found it was five o'clock, and the door bell made Mrs. Morris remember the rent agent. Sure enough, he had come, and Maggie came up to call Mrs. Morris. She looked at me blankly as much to say: 'What shall I do?' She had forgotten all about him. I thought just a minute and then I told her I had some money, enough I thought to pay the agent and satisfy him, and I would go down and see if I could make him behave till we got things settled. Then I went downstairs and put on my most dignified air. He bristled at me and demanded Mrs. Morris.

" 'Mrs. Morris is not well and is lying down,' said I, 'and I have come down in her place. Is there anything I can do for you?'

" 'Well, I've got to see her if she *is* lying down,' he said in a loud voice, and he took a couple of steps toward the stairs as if he would go up to her at once. 'She's got to pay her rent. She'll be put out if she don't do it at once. This thing has gone —'

" 'Oh,' I said, 'it isn't in the least necessary for you to get excited, if that is all. I can attend to the rent as well as anything else. Are you the agent?'

" 'Yes, I *am*,' he said, 'and I won't have any more talk either. I want my money.'

"I had my pocketbook in my hand, and I tried to freeze him with a look as I opened it. When he saw me bring out a big roll of bills he almost looked faint, he was so astonished.

" 'How much is it that is back?' I asked.

" 'Two months and a half,' he snarled.

"I began to count out the money, and then I remembered my own experience with Rawley and Brown and thought I would give him a little taste of it. I drew back and said, 'You are sure you are the agent and fully entitled to receive this money? Can you give me any credentials?'

"He was very much taken aback, and got red and embarrassed and at last remembered that Mrs. Morris knew him. Then he grew angry again and demanded to see her. I sent a message up to Mrs. Morris that if she was able we would like to have her come down, and she came. When it was finally all settled and the receipt signed, I told the young man that he might tell the owner that the rent hereafter would be paid in advance and on time, and that there were a few repairs which needed immediate attention and we would like to have him call at his earliest convenience. He went away quite crestfallen, and I began to feel quite like a householder. The only thing that troubles me is Mrs. Morris' extreme gratitude, because, dear auntie, I'm afraid I haven't loved her as much as I ought to for Christ's sake, and I therefore can't take to myself the credit she would give me. It is all very selfish in me.

"Now the matter stands this way. If you possibly can come this week, do so. Mrs. Morris will be ready to leave on your arrival. She will go to her sister out West, and I doubt if she ever returns. I have given her some money to go with. It isn't always you can buy a full fledged boarding-house, boarders and all, so cheap. I suppose some one would call it dear, but I am happy in my purchase. I shall keep my place in the store till you come anyway, for I don't care to have the boarders find out my connection with the business, till they see some of the changes I want to have made for the better. The only servant here is worse than none. She is so dirty and saucy you never could stand her. If you possibly can induce Molly to come with you, bring her. I enclose a New York draft which I think will be all the money you will want to bring here, and pay any little bills till you get here. And now, dear auntie, I do hope and pray you will say yes, and come at once, and not find any 'oughts and ought nots' in the way, as you sometimes do. You see I have gone ahead and burned my bridges behind me, because I felt that you 'ought' whether you think so or not, for I mean to take care of you now myself and you are working too hard there. Here we will keep you in pink cotton and only let you direct. I shall keep good servants, and if I don't always make the two ends meet why I shall have 'a continual allowance' given me of my King to draw upon.

　　　　　　　　　　　　　　"Your loving, eager
　　　　　　　　　　　　　　　　"CELIA."

There was a calmness and "upliftedness" about Miss Grant's face as she entered the dining-room that the people about that table did not understand, and it rather angered them than otherwise. She walked quietly to her accustomed chair and sat down. Nobody spoke, but she had so far forgotten her afternoon's troubles as to be oblivious of this. Hiram was trying to think of the most sarcastic thing he could say, and so failed to say anything, while Nettie in her various revulsions of feeling did not know how to begin. Aunt Hannah herself opened the conversation in the calmest, most self-contained tone possible, as if the question she asked was one she asked of her nephew.

"Hiram, can you tell me what time the through Philadelphia trains go?"

Hiram raised his cold, black eyes to her face in astonishment, a moment, and stared at her as much as to say, "What possible concern of yours is that?" and then dropped them to his plate again and went on eating. After a suitable pause he said freezingly, "No." Aunt Hannah tried again.

"Isn't there a time-table in the paper? Could you find out for me?"

"I don't know," said Hiram, this time without looking up. "I suppose if it's there you can find it as well as I can."

"What in the world do you want with the time-table, aunt Hannah?" asked Nettie, peevishly, with an undertone of anxiety in her voice. "There isn't anything the matter with Celia, is there? I presume she has lost her place and is coming back on us. I always supposed that was the way her venture would turn out. She ought to have tried to get a place in the country for housework. It was all she was ever trained to do. Anybody might know she couldn't get on in the city."

"Nothing is the matter with Celia, Nettie," answered her aunt, "except that she has written me to come to Philadelphia. She has found something there for me to do, and I have decided that it will be best for me to go at once. I shall have to start to-morrow, if possible, because I am being waited for."

"You go to Philadelphia!" exclaimed Nettie dropping her fork. "The perfect idea! Has Celia gone crazy? Why aunt Hannah, you couldn't get along in the city. Why, you — you — wouldn't know how to get anywhere. You don't understand. Philadelphia is a large city and you couldn't get across the street alone. And what could you do? You are not going to start in as a clerk in a store at your time of life, I hope. You would break down at once, and then we should have you both to care for, and you know aunt Hannah, willing as we are, we are not able to do that." Nettie paused for breath.

Then Hiram turned his little black eyes on her and asked contemptuously, "And who is going to pay your fare on this pleasure excursion you are going to take? You certainly can't expect me to do it. I think I've done all I'm called upon to do. I understood the bargain was that you were to work for your board here."

Hiram had never been so openly insolent before. If he had, Miss Grant would have left long ago, even though she had been obliged to walk the streets in search of work for her living. She turned her clear eyes upon him full, and said quietly with the strength of the grace the Father gave her from her communings with him:

"Yes, Hiram, that was the bargain, and I certainly have worked. I consider that I have fully earned all that I have eaten, and the amount of shelter that has been given me. As for any further assistance, I think I have never yet asked it, and I hope I may never be obliged to do so. Celia has sent me money and a ticket,—and I shall not be obliged to ask any favors of any one."

"Celia sent you money!" Nettie fairly screamed it. "Where in the world did she get money?"

"Yes, where did Celia get money?" asked Hiram, sharply. "It seems to me there's something pretty shady about this business. Miss Celia 'll get into serious trouble which will bring no credit to her family, if she keeps on."

Aunt Hannah rose from her untasted supper, drew herself up to her full height and looked down upon Hiram Bartlett till he seemed to shrink beneath her glance. There comes a time when a strong sweet nature like Hannah Grant's can be roused to such a pitch of righteous indignation that it will tower above other smaller natures and make them cower and cringe in their smallness and meanness. She had reached one of those places in her life. Nettie, as she watched her, thought to herself that aunt Hannah must have been almost handsome once when she was young.

"Hiram," said aunt Hannah, and her voice was quite controlled and steady, "don't you ever dare to breathe such a thought as that again about that pure-souled girl. You know in your inmost soul that what you have said would be impossible. Some time, when you stand before God, you will be ashamed of a good many of your other words and actions." That was all she said to him. She did not lose her temper, nor say anything which she did not feel she ought to say, or which she would have taken back afterward. Then she turned to Nettie and quietly said:

"Celia has had a little estate left her from her father's great uncle Abner. She is now quite independent as regards money, and she wishes to have me with her as soon as possible, and I intend to go to-morrow evening, if I can get ready."

She turned from the room then and went upstairs, but when she got there, instead of going to work at packing, she turned the key in the lock and knelt down by her bed, to pray first for Hiram, and second that God might overrule anything that she had said amiss.

Meantime below stairs there was astonishment and confusion. Celia as a poor shop girl, and Celia with money were two very different people. Even Hiram felt that. He retired behind his paper till a suitable time had elapsed for his wife to talk out her anger, astonishment, and humiliation, and then he began to reflect that it would be a very convenient thing to have the management of Celia's money, even though it was not much, for he was just beginning business for himself and every little helped in the matter of capital.

"It would just serve you right, Hiram Bartlett, if Celia should turn out to be rich," said his wife, angrily. "The way you have treated her and aunt Hannah ought to make you ashamed, but I don't suppose it will. Now what am I to do I should like to know? Three children, and one a fretful baby, and all my housework to do all alone. If you had treated aunt Hannah nicely, she would have stayed anyway. Maybe Celia would have come here to live and taught the children. She is real good at teaching little children anything, I remember she used to be so patient with the boys at home. It would be awfully convenient to have somebody around with money."

In the course of the evening, while aunt Hannah swiftly gathered her possessions in array preparatory to packing, Nettie knocked at her door. She wanted to ask a great many questions, and she wanted to argue with aunt Hannah and show her the inadvisability and impossibility of her thinking of such a thing as going to Philadelphia to live with Celia, when her plain duty was here with Nettie and her family. When she saw she was making no headway, she tried to work on her aunt's strong sense of duty, and finally cried, and told her she never thought she would be left by aunt Hannah in that way, with all those children and no help, that she always knew aunt Hannah cared more for Celia than for any of them, and that it was not fair when they offered her a home and done everything for her, and she had come there with the understanding that she would stay several years anyway. It wasn't fair to Hiram.

When she had talked this way for some time, her aunt turned to her almost desperately. She did not want to say anything rash. But Nettie must be shown how inconsistent she was.

"Nettie," said she, just as calmly as she had talked to Hiram, "you know that you and Hiram never wanted either me or Celia with you. You know that you consider me in the way, and that I am only good to work. I don't say anything against that, for that may be true, but you know that you grudge me my home here, and that you are giving out to your friends that you are doing a great deal of care for me in my helpless old age, and that I am a burden. You know yourself whether that is quite fair, and whether I have not worked as hard as any woman could for my board and lodging. But that is not to the point. You have a perfect right to think so about me. It may be all true, and I cannot stop you in saying such things to outsiders, but I have a right to say whether I will be taken and disposed of as if I was a piece of goods, and cared for as if I was a baby. I am not quite so infirm yet but that I can earn my living where I shall be more welcome. I thank the Lord that a way has been opened for me to go where I am wanted, but I must honestly tell you, Nettie, that I should have gone just the same if I had known that you felt so, for I feel that my place is with Celia, if I can be with her. She is alone in the world. You have your husband and your children. She has nobody but me. I bear you no grudge, Nettie, and I think you will be happier with me away." Then she went on packing and Nettie retreated to talk with her husband.

The result was a proposition that they should coax Celia to come home and live with them, and Nettie said a few nice things which she hoped would patch up aunt Hannah's feelings, but aunt Hannah was firm, and would not even delay to write to Celia. She went diligently on with her preparations.

Gradually they settled down to the inevitable, and by the next noon had so far calmed down as to be able to ask some questions about the more definite details. Aunt Hannah had started out on an expedition very early in the morning without telling them where she was going, or without seeming to remember that there was breakfast to be gotten and cleared away. She seemed to be living by faith. She certainly ate nothing that morning. She visited a certain little house in a by-street where lived an old servant, Molly by name, who had declined the most earnest solicitation of Nettie to live with her at exceedingly small pay, and preferred to earn her living by doing fine ironing. She also visited the station, the telegraph office, the bank, and the expressman's office, and then went back to her packing again. Later in the afternoon, she went out again and made a few calls, on the minister's wife and the doctor's wife and a few very dear friends, bidding them a quiet good-bye, for she wished to slip away without making any more talk than was necessary. But it was at the dinner-table that Celia's whole plan was ferreted out by Nettie.

"Celia has bought a boarding-house!" exclaimed Nettie. "What an absurd idea! What does she or you either know about keeping boarders? You'll both let them run right over you. You'll get in debt the very first week. Why, aunt Hannah, you have no right to encourage Celia in such a scheme. She's too young, anyway, to be away off there in a city without a guardian. She ought to be here. Hiram could manage her money and make it double itself in time, and if she really has as much as you say, she has plenty to live quite comfortably without doing anything. You ought to tell her so."

But aunt Hannah did not seem to be intimidated by this. Nettie tried again.

"And then think how plebeian it will be! It was bad enough to work in a store, but a boarding-house keeper, and for one who has money of her own. It is simply unheard-of. I shall be ashamed to death to have Mrs. Morgan know about it. I think I have had trouble enough without having to be ashamed of my family. Celia always did do queer things, anyway. Don't you think it is very impractical, Hiram?"

Nettie asked his opinion as if that would settle the matter for everybody concerned, and he answered in the same manner.

"I certainly do think it is the most wild and impossible scheme I ever heard of, and one which ought not to be permitted. It will be the ruin of Celia's property, and when that is all gone, and you and Celia are in trouble, I suppose I shall be called upon to help you out. Of course I shall do the best I can, but you must remember that I have not very much money to throw away on wild childish schemes." He spoke with the air of a martyr, and aunt Hannah answered him cheerily. She had recovered her spirits since she had sent her telegram.

"You needn't worry, Hiram. I don't believe either Celia or I will ever be in need of your help. But if we are, I don't think we shall trouble you. You know they have a good many charitable institutions in the City of Brotherly Love, and we shall surely be well cared for if the improbable happens." Then aunt Hannah placed her nicely prepared little coals of fire in the hands of her two grand nephews and her grand niece, and went smiling upstairs. The coals were tiny paper parcels each containing a bright five dollar gold piece. She had lain awake last night, worried about the sharp words she had felt obliged to speak, and the sentence Nettie had flung out about her leaving her without help, and she wanted to show that she bore no grudge for what they had said. Celia had sent her the money to spend as she thought best, and aunt Hannah knew her girl well enough to feel she would say this was a good way to spend it. Besides, she felt sure she could run a boarding-house successfully in a financial way, as well as some others, if she had the chance, so she might by and by have more five dollar gold pieces to do with as she chose. She was beginning to be very happy, as she packed and strapped the last trunk, and smoothed her hair and tied on her grey bonnet and grey veil. At the last Hiram and Nettie behaved quite well. Those five dollar gold pieces had gone a long way toward making the bereavement of aunt Hannah's departure felt. Hiram took her satchel down, and Nettie walked beside her carrying her umbrella and wheeling the baby, while Johnnie and Lily trotted on ahead. There was an éclat and importance attached to a sudden and first-class departure such as aunt Hannah's was turning out to be, which could not well be carelessly neglected. They made an interesting procession down the street. More than one neighbor looked out of her window, and a few knew that Miss Hannah was going away. But they had said good-bye, and only turned their heads the other way to wipe away a tear of regret, or sigh perhaps that their good friend was not to be near any more with her cheery face and her words of comfort. When it was observed by one or two that Molly Poppleton had also passed down the street accompanied by an old man wheeling her ancient trunk on a wheelbarrow, and carrying a good-sized bundle, several of the good women came to their gates to look down the street, and wait till Nettie returned to ask what it all meant. And Nettie enjoyed a triumphal march back to her home. "Yes, she's gone, we shall miss her very much." Her nose was red with being rubbed and her eyes had a suspicious redness about them. "No, Celia isn't ill, but she couldn't stand it any longer without aunt Hannah. You know Celia has had a fortune left her? Oh yes, she'll have plenty now. Yes, aunt Hannah has to go and be her chaperone. I suppose she'll quite come out in society now she has money enough to do about as she pleases. Oh yes, she's very generous, she always was. She sent the children each handsome presents in gold. Yes, aunt Hannah has taken old Molly for a maid. She'll be obliged to have a maid there, you know. Funny, isn't it, that a woman who knows how to work should need a maid? I shouldn't like it myself, but then one has to do as other people do." Then Nettie went home and got supper and washed up her dishes and put her three babies to bed, and sat down wearily and wished for aunt Hannah.

But aunt Hannah sat serenely in the sleeper, waiting for her berth to be made up, and thinking to herself that she also, like Jehoiachin, had had her head lifted up out of prison.

10

It was perhaps one of the happiest nights that aunt Hannah ever spent. She lay down in her bed in the sleeper and slept like a little child for she was as tired as a baby after her day and night of excitement, but in the early dawn she awoke and lay there listening to the regular cadence of the moving train. It was music to her. Her life had for years been a monotonous one, and every detail of the journey was a delight to her. The turning wheels seemed to sing a tune to her, "Now hath mine head been lifted up above mine enemies round about me." She tried to turn that thought out of her mind as soon as she discovered its significance, for she did not like to think that even in her heart had hid a feeling that Hiram and Nettie were her enemies, but somehow the rejoicing stayed anyway.

She began to look forward to the morning and the day that was to follow, the opening of her new life. What would it hold of good or of ill for her? Would there be trials? Yes, but there had been trials before. She would have "his strength to bear them, with his might her feet could be shod. She could find her resting-places in the promises of her God," as she had done before. And it was such delightful work before her, a prospect of making over a home and making it pleasant. Aunt Hannah took rest, too, in the thought of experienced Molly Poppleton now reposing in the berth above her. She was going on a mission at last. How good God had been to her! He had tried her for a little while, but he was bringing her out into a large place. She could see that, even though she could not know the trials that were before her. Of course there were trials, she expected that, earth was full of them; but she did not need to carry them; Christ had borne them all for her long ago. She would trust and he would bring her safely through as he had done before and was doing now. Then her thoughts dwelt in sweet reflection upon her Saviour whom she loved so much, and so communed with him and promised to try to help every person who came within that house that she was to make pleasant for him and his children, and to try to live for him before them every day. And that crowded, rushing car became a holy place, because God met her there and blessed her.

The train reached the Broad Street station at a very early hour. Celia was glad of that, for it gave her plenty of time to meet her aunt and go with her back to the house, without being late at the store. She had not had time to reflect yet as to whether she would give up her position. She was hardly ready to do so. It seemed to her that perhaps she might do more good if she retained it for the present, at least until she found some one else who needed it, and to whom she could give it with profit, both to that person and to her employers who had been very kind to her. Besides, she wished not to appear before the boarders yet as an active agent in the reforms of the house.

At exactly half past five she arrived at the Broad Street station. It was an early hour for her to be out alone, and it was still dark save for the electric lights which glared everywhere as if trying to keep off the day. But the train would come in at five minutes to six, and Celia had been too eager and too happy to sleep longer, so she paced up and down in the ladies' room until the train was almost due, watching the people come and go and wondering about them all as she was wont to do. As the time drew near for the train she went out and stood behind the gates watching the trains moving back and forth. She began to say to herself, "Oh, what if she should not come? What if something has happened to the train? Or what if Nettie and Hiram have persuaded her at the last minute not to come? Or what if she missed the train? But no, she would have telegraphed. 'Charge not thyself,'— dear me! How much I do that. I must stop worrying ahead about everything. Aunt Hannah must have seen that fault in me very glaringly. I never realized how much I do it." And then the train whistled and rolled into the station, and the passengers began to alight, and stream into the gates, looking sleepy and cold. Celia stood there in the dim greyness of the cold, foggy morning and began to tremble with the excitement and joy of watching for aunt Hannah. Suddenly she saw the ample form of Molly Poppleton loom up behind the giltbuttoned porter and she caught a glimpse of a little grey bonnet just behind and knew that aunt Hannah was come.

She took them home in the street-car, and then escorted them up to her little third story back room. She had risen early and put it in order. Molly looked around in disdain.

"Well, Miss Celia, you don't have things as fine in the city as I expected," she said. "The idea of their putting you up in such a room as this! Why, Celia, it ain't as good as the kitchen chamber at Cloverdale. I always heard a city was a dreadful place to live, but I never thought it was this bad. The wonder to me is anybody that don't have to, stays in 'em. But we'll have it *clean* pretty soon anyway, don't you worry." And she stalked to the window and surveyed the narrow court below, where she surmised she would be obliged to dry her clothes. She sniffed to herself, but Celia could see her practical eye already planning how she would change the position of the ash bucket and the garbage pail. She gave a sigh of relief at the thought of Molly Poppleton's ability, and turned to aunt Hannah, fairly smothering her in kisses. The she put a hand on each soft, loved cheek, held her off at arm's length and looked into her face.

"Now, you dear, good auntie, tell me just what you think of me? Am I a wild, impractical girl, full of crazy schemes? Tell me right away."

"Well," said aunt Hannah, a queer little twinkle in her eyes, "that's what Hiram thinks."

"Oh, he does, does he? Well, I don't really suppose it will matter much, do you? But I mustn't stop now to talk. I have to be at that store in an hour, and it takes half of that to get there. We must talk business. Do you think you can get along to-day by yourself, with Molly? That is, I mean without my worthy advice and assistance? Of course I'll be home at half-past six, and I'll give in my resignation there if you think best, but I hardly like to do it quite so soon after Mrs. Green was so kind about getting it for me. It doesn't seem quite fair to the firm either to stop now, after they have had all the trouble of teaching me. Mrs. Morris is to leave on the noon train. She is ready, except that her faith hasn't been quite equal to believing that you were really coming to take her place. She told the boarders this morning that she was going away for her health, and that she had secured a woman to take her place for a while. She guessed they would like it just as well. She wasn't sure when she should return. The clerk promptly gave notice that he should leave, and I'm glad of it. Some of the others said that if things didn't go better than they had been doing for a week they would have to follow his example, but I think they will change their minds when they see the difference. I amused myself going to market last evening. I bought a great big roast, one of the finest cuts, and some fine potatoes and apples and yeast and flour. I know Mrs. Morris' flour isn't good, for she can't make anything out of it fit to eat. I also got some spinach and celery and sweet potatoes, canned tomatoes and a few other things. I want to have a regular treat the first night regardless of the cost. You can figure things down afterwards, but I thought we'd have enough for once to make up for the days of starvation. That Maggie, down in the kitchen, is a slouch and a bear. She gets in a towering rage whenever you go near her. I have not said anything about her, except to ask what contract Mrs. Morris had with her. I find it is on a day to day basis, so you can do as you please. If you and Molly want her, and can get the right kind of help out of her, keep her. If not, get rid of her and we'll find a second girl who knows how to do things right. Now, shall we go down and see Mrs. Morris? And are you sure you are equal to all this, and not too tired to begin to-day? I suppose Mrs. Morris would wait till you are rested, if you want her to."

But aunt Hannah smiled and said no, she was eager to begin. Then she took off her bonnet and smoothed her grey hair and went down.

Mrs. Morris had on the inevitable old calico wrapper. Celia wondered if she meant to travel in it. Her hair had evidently not been combed that morning, only twisted in a knot. She seemed embarrassed by aunt Hannah in her trim grey travelling dress, and hardly knew on what footing to meet her.

"For the land sake!" she exclaimed, wiping her hands, from custom perhaps, on the side of her wrapper before shaking hands. "So you've come! And you're really willing to undertake it, and think you can succeed? I'm afraid you'll be disappointed. It's a hard life! You look too good for such a life. They're an awful torment, boarders are! Me heart has just been broke time an' again with the troubles I've been through with them. I'll show you all around, and if you feel you can't do it, *yet*, I shouldn't feel you was bound in any way to stick to your bargain. Miss Murray she seemed to be so sure, but I wouldn't want you to be took at no disadvantage. You see I am afraid, if I get away, I shan't want to come back again, and I don't want to go off and feel I left you dissatisfied.''

They went down to breakfast soon, and Celia saw her aunt seated before the uninviting meal. She felt sorry for her, and yet she thought she would enjoy the meal with the prospect of the one she would give the boarders later in the day. But she was scarcely prepared for the look of horror that gradually overspread the good woman's face, as she tasted dish after dish and found them alike unpalatable. There was oatmeal that morning. It was thick and lumpy, and only half cooked. Besides the salt had been forgotten. There was pork and greasy fried potatoes, but they were both cold, and unseasoned. The coffee was weak and muddy. Celia swallowed a few bites. She felt that she could go hungry for one day. Then she said a soft good-bye to aunt Hannah, squeezing her hand under her napkin so the boarders would not see and slipped away.

Aunt Hannah finished all she cared to of her meal and went back to Mrs. Morris. Molly Poppleton sat down to her breakfast in undisguised disgust. Nothing but the prospect of the power that was to be hers held her tongue from expressing her mind on the subject of good food decently cooked. She did not even pretend to eat much, and she looked at the slatternly form of Maggie as she lounged in to gather some plates, with animosity in her eye. She spent most of her time in the dining-room counting the fly specks and finger marks on the wall and windows. She made up her mind that she would get time for those windows somehow before dinner, if possible. If not, they should be done before another dawn of light and breakfast anyway.

Meantime Mrs. Morris was showing aunt Hannah the house. This room brought so much a week, and that one only so much, and so on, and at each room she had a tale to tell of its various inmates during the years she had kept a boarding-house. Aunt Hannah listened quietly, mentally making notes of what she would and would not do. She saw, without seeming to do so, the worn furniture, the need of a patch on a carpet, or a turning of furniture to hide it, the need of a wardrobe, or bureau in some cases. She set down in her mind the number of window shades torn, or worn out or lacking, and thought how much some cheap muslin curtains would improve things. She felt like a rich fairy, as she went from room to room seeing its needs, and knowing that she could wave a wand and change it all. Sometimes the bareness or the attempt at decoration by the boarder was pitiful. She paused a moment before a picture of a quiet sweet-faced woman, in a dark velvet frame on Harry Knowles' bureau, and wondered who she was, and if the young man whom Mrs. Morris said roomed there was worthy of a mother with such a face as that. Then she went at Mrs. Morris' request with her to her room and sat there during an hour of conversation, in which Mrs. Morris, with many sighs and tears, detailed her entire life and troubles for her benefit. Aunt Hannah's quiet, respectful attention and sympathy led her on until she had unburdened all her heart. Then was the Christian woman's opportunity, and she spoke the word in season to the other woman, that word which cannot fail to bear fruit in due time. Mrs. Morris, with her empty life and joyless spirit, while she received the words with tears and some gratitude, but gave no outward sign that they had more than touched the surface of her life, yet remembered what had been said to her, and as she sat in the train that afternoon, speeding far away from the scene of her disappointments and disheartening, her fare paid by one Christian, her house taken and managed by another whom she saw must be a true saint, pondered all these things in her heart.

Mrs. Morris was gone, and aunt Hannah descended to the kitchen, bidding the impatient Molly Poppleton wait until she called her.

Just before Mrs. Morris' departure, she had informed the sullen-looking Maggie that Miss Grant was the woman who was to take her place. Maggie had responded with a significant look, which did not promise much for taking the new mistress into her favor. She met Miss Grant in the middle of the dining-room during her progress to the kitchen. Her hair was frowsy, her dress soiled and torn, and her arms akimbo. Altogether she would have furnished a formidable encounter to a woman who was not used to managing servants and holding the reins of her household well in her own hands.

"I just came to see what you wanted fer dinner," she announced. "There's some things come from a new place where we never deal. I thought I'd let you know."

Aunt Hannah thought a minute. Then she said:

"Yes, Maggie, I'll be out in the kitchen soon to attend to dinner, but meantime it is only one o'clock and there is time enough to get this room in order first. I think you would better wash those windows."

Maggie stood aghast.

"And what's the matter with this room, I'd like to know?" she said in a loud, belligerent tone. "It's just the same as it always is, and what's good enough fer Mis' Morris ought to be good enough fer you. Indeed I'll wash no windows to-day. I've got me afternoon's work all planned out. This room'll be swep' when I sets the table fer dinner, an' that's all it'll get to-day. And you needn't trouble your self about comin' in the kitchen. I never like to have the missus in the kitchen, it flusters me. I know me business and I 'tend to it, and I likes to have them as I live with attend to theirs. If you've got any orders, give 'em, and I'll get dinner on time, you needn't worry about that."

Maggie had backed up against the kitchen door, her arms still akimbo, and stood as if to defend the fortress of her domain.

Aunt Hannah waited till she had drawn down a crooked shade and rolled it straight again, pinning the torn edge, before she answered. Then she turned and calmly faced the irate Maggie.

"I always manage my own kitchen, Maggie," she said, in a quiet voice, "and I intend to do so still. I want this dining-room put in order first, before anything else is attended to. Get some cloths and hot water right away, please."

There was a dignity about aunt Hannah that was new in Maggie's experience. She had been accustomed to intimidate Mrs. Morris by such conversation as she had just used, and she supposed she could do the same by her new mistress. She never expected to have it treated with such calm indifference. She was forced to her last resort.

"I can't stay in a house where things are managed that way. No lady goes into the kitchen. I know me business, and I don't like to be interfered with. If you ain't suited with me doing as I think best, I can find plenty of places."

"Oh, certainly, if you prefer," said aunt Hannah, pulling down the other shade and fixing it neatly.

"Well, if I do, I'll go right away, and then what'll you do?" burst out the astonished Maggie. "There's all them boarders got to have their dinner. You can't fool with boarders, you know. They'll all leave you."

"I shall do very well," answered aunt Hannah. "I brought one of my home servants with me, and I can get others very easily. If you choose to stay and do as I say I would like to have those windows washed at once, otherwise you may go."

Poor Maggie! She was crestfallen. This was new treatment. The mistresses she was used to had to cater to the desires of their servants. She did a great deal of work, and she preferred to do it her way. But aunt Hannah was firm. Molly at that moment, too impatient to begin to be able to wait any longer, put her head in at the door and asked if Miss Hannah was ready for her. That was enough. Maggie tossed her head and declared she would not do another stroke of work in that house, and demanded back pay. Miss Hannah settled up with her, and she departed, leaving Molly monarch of the kitchen and scornfully surveying her new realm.

11

It's just a pigpen! That's what it is!'' declared Molly Poppleton, holding up her ample calico skirts and clean gingham apron in a gingerly way. "I don't know where to begin. I didn't suppose a human being *could* be so dirty!'' Then she plunged into work. The range got such a cleaning as it had not had in years. The ashes were cleaned out, and the soot removed from all its little doors and traps and openings. Molly was not used to a city range with all its numerous appliances, but she had very keen common sense and she used it. She knew dirt and ashes could not help a fire to burn, so she removed them. While she was about it, she gave it a good washing inside and out, for she found the oven encrusted with burned sugar and juice of some sort, and the top was covered with grease. Then, in the most scientific manner, she started a fire, and before very long it was glowing, and the water in the old tank was steaming hot.

It appeared there really was no time for those dining-room windows that day, after all. With skirts tucked together and sleeves rolled high Molly generously used the hot water and soap in the kitchen. She unceremoniously took the old ragged cloths which must have been Maggie's wiping towels for scrubbing rags, trusting to Miss Hannah's sense of the fitness of things to provide others in some way. The kitchen table and shelves and windows and paint and sink were scrubbed, and even the floor, and then Molly stood back and surveyed the room now pervaded with a damp atmosphere redolent of soap.

"There! I guess it'll do fer over night, and the fust chance I get I'll give it a good cleaning. I never saw the like in my life! How them poor boarders stood it eating out of a dirty hole like this I don't see. Now, what's to do? That sink was a caution! The water and dust was all in a mess underneath and the top was slimy! I wonder what the creature that called herself Maggie thought she was made for.''

Meanwhile Miss Hannah had gone to her trunk and arrayed herself in an old grey gingham and a dark apron that enveloped her completely. She had discovered that they must begin at the very foundation before they could hope to do anything toward getting dinner. She investigated Celia's stores and found they were ample for present needs. Celia's training had not been for nothing. She knew by intuition that her aunt Hannah would enquire for soap and yeast and baking powder among the first things. She had thought of the little things that might not be in stock in Mrs. Morris' kitchen and had a supply for the present. The stores in the pantry were not very full. There was a plate with a pile of sour white-looking pancakes, another with some lumpy oatmeal, a few boiled potatoes, a bowl of watery soup and two or three ends of bakers' loaves. Miss Hannah applied her nose to one of these and then laid it down again and said, "Bah!"

After looking at the array a few minutes, she gathered them all into a pan and dumped them into the garbage pail. A heavy, lifeless pie on a higher shelf also met the same fate. Then she got the dishpan and some clean hot water and washed a few dishes for her immediate use. Having done this she prepared to set some bread. It was late in the day, but it would not take long, and it could rise while she was doing other things and be baked after the dinner was cooked. Then she could hurry up part of it by making it into pulled rolls so that they could be used for dinner. The bread done she started on a searching expedition for bread cloths and clean rags. She could not work without tools. In one of her trunks was a roll of old rags and linen; with Molly's help she unstrapped the trunk and searched it out. It was a great satisfaction to have that bread covered with a clean cloth and feel that so much of her work was going on right. She decided that the dishes must all be washed. She and Molly both worked at this, Molly washing off the shelves while she wiped the dishes. By that time it was four o'clock.

"It's high time we was seeing about the dinner," said Molly, as she thumped the last pile of plates upon the clean shelf. "What are you going to do for a tablecloth? That one in there ain't fit, an' there ain't a clean one about the drawer anywhere. There's a pile of dirty ones behind the door in the back stairway. I reckon I'll have to wash one. As for napkins I should suppose they didn't use 'em. I can't find any."

Miss Hannah went on another hunt, and discovered more soiled table-cloths and a stack of soiled napkins. There was nothing for it but to wash some. Molly already had the washtub going and was working as if her life depended upon it. Well for Miss Hannah's plans and Celia's hopes that Molly was equal to emergencies, nay delighted in them, and that she was a swift worker. By the time Miss Hannah had the tablecloth and dishes off the table and the dining-room swept and dusted that linen was swinging in a brisk breeze in the back yard and the irons were growing hot on the range.

"Five o'clock and the table not set yet!" commented Molly. She was working on time and the pleasure of the race depended upon her getting done before Miss Celia should arrive, and being able to ring that dinner bell exactly on time. "Well, I reckon we'll get through somehow. You can't turn a pigpen into a parlor in one day, you know. I declare, Miss Hannah, it was a pity to turn that girl loose on the community. We ought to have kept her by main force and taught her how to scrub, before we let her go. The things that wasn't too filthy dirty to be burned or rusted is burned and rusted, and the things that had anything about them to get lost and broken has got that the matter with them. I reckon we'll have a few things to buy 'fore we get fixed out for comfort."

But Molly was working swiftly all the while she talked. She had filled the little salts and peppers, and rubbed up the knives. The careful Celia had not forgotten bath brick nor silver polish, though there was very little that had any pretension to silver to clean. The dishes and table appointments were of the plainest. Many would have said it was impossible to make any difference in that table without spending a lot of money. Miss Hannah did not think so. She knew the subtle difference between order and disorder, and the startling contrast between cleanliness and dirt. Cleanliness was next to godliness and she was practicing that to-day. The godliness she hoped would follow hard after. While she pulled the little cushions of responsive velvety dough for the rolls, she prayed a rich blessing on that first meal in the house under her care. Then she let her mind wander for a moment to the home she had left which had been no more of a home to her than this was yet to its inmates. She wondered how they were getting on, and if the baby was well. The only drawback to the joy of leaving Nettie's had been the baby. Aunt Hannah could not help loving babies, and enjoying the clinging of their soft dimpling arms about her neck and their apple blossom breath upon her cheek. The babies always loved aunt Hannah. It was only after they grew older and began to imitate the grown-up people that they began to be saucy, impertinent, and unloving. Even then, Johnnie and Lily had always come to aunt Hannah with a burn or a bump to be comforted, for somehow her motherly arms knew just how best to gather in the troubled little ones and comfort it. But aunt Hannah had no time to think of duties past, and troubles. She gave the last little jerk to the puffy roll and tucked it in the pan to rise for the last time, and then hastened in to set the table. Molly had laid the crisp tablecloth which she had literally forced to dry quickly with her hot irons, on the table and was ironing away for dear life at the napkins. Molly and aunt Hannah had high ideals, brought from comfortable private homes, and they wished this house they had come to take care of to be a home in the best sense of the word. They worked faster now, for the clock was warning them that it was getting late. The roast beef well seared in the most scientific way was roasting away in the oven with a good supply of sweet and Irish potatoes on the grate below, grouped about a huge baked apple dumpling which Molly had hastily concocted, and Molly was straining the spinach and subjecting it to a rubbing through the colander, after which it went back on the stove to keep hot before its butter and last peppering were applied. She looked doubtfully at the water the spinach was cooked in and then with a daring glance at the clock rushed about to carry out another resolution, calling to Miss Hannah:

"You ken put on the soup plates ef your a mine to. I've found I can make a taste of spinach soup with the water and some milk and flour and butter. It'll make things seem nicer I guess for the first night, and don't take a minute. That'll give the rolls time to get a little browner before they're needed, you know." Then she began to sing at the top of her voice:

"Am I a soldier of the cross,—"

Molly Poppleton always sang at the top of her lungs when she had some important work to do or was in an unusual hurry with her work. It made her very happy to have a good deal of work, and hard work at that.

Celia, opening the front door with her latch-key just then, heard the singing and rejoiced. There was the old Molly. She had not become discouraged and gone home, but was at work with heart and voice as in their old kitchen at home. She ran out into the dining-room to see how things were getting on before she went upstairs. But she stopped in the doorway astounded. Even her highest hopes had not realized the change there would be. What made it? Was it the shining tablecloth, or the glistening glasses, or the knives and forks laid straight, or what? A nice square cake of butter was in each butter-plate at the ends of the table. The salts were smoothed off and stamped with the bottom of the salt-cellars. The plates were in a pile on one end of the table instead of being upside down on the napkins at each place. Where were the plates of crackers and gingersnaps which had not failed to appear at every dinner since she had been boarding there? Where was the inevitable dish of prunes? Gone, and in its place a dish of translucent cranberry jelly which Molly had found time somehow to fix. It was all very wonderful. Even the gas had a clean globe on it. Celia wondered that so much had been accomplished in one short afternoon. She heard the door being opened from the outside and hurried into the kitchen, closing the dining-room door behind her first. This must burst upon them all at once when they entered the dining-room.

Aunt Hannah was taking the brown balls from the roll pan and piling them on a plate, when she went into the kitchen, and she greeted her with:

"Celia, go upstairs and wash your hands and then come down and fix the celery. Molly and I haven't a second to do it, and it is time to ring the bell in five minutes. Have the boarders come yet?"

Celia rushed away and was soon back, bearing aunt Hannah's white apron and a brush to smooth her hair that she might not be delayed from coming to dinner on account of her appearance, and at last the dinner was ready and it was time to ring the bell. She put the two glasses of celery on the table, and handing Molly the bell went into the parlor. She did not wish anybody yet to know she had a right in the kitchen. She was just the ribbon girl from Dobson and Co.'s. There were things she wanted to accomplish first which could better be done that way, she thought.

The bell rang and the boarders trooped down. The little old lady from upstairs was first and interrupted the advance of the others, for a moment. She walked into the dining-room followed by Miss Burns. Both stopped blinking in the doorway and staring around, before they slowly walked in a dazed way to their respective places. The two girls from the three-cent store became embarrassed, and stood back awkwardly against the wall staring undisguisedly. The three young men came after, Harry Knowles ahead.

He drew a long whistle, and turning on his heel, started back into the hall again. "Whew! this is great!" he said as he went. "I'm going to wash my hands and comb my hair. I don't fit in there."

Aunt Hannah with her grey hair and placid face and grey dress with its white apron presided well over that table. The dishes might be thick and the tablecloth coarse, but no dinner on any rich man's table was ever cooked or served better, nor more thoroughly enjoyed. After they were seated Miss Burns began with her nervous little giggle:

"Oh really, now, this is simply, — simply — simply *fine*, don't you know. This is quite a change, isn't it, dear?" and she looked across the table at Celia who was passing celery and handing soup plates as aunt Hannah ladled out the pale green tempting soup. Her guests ate of it in wonder. They were not acquainted with puree of spinach. They wondered how it got colored, and what it was anyway, and the most of them ate every drop in their plates, some of them tilting the plates to accomplish it. The three-cent store girls and the university student asked for more and got it, and then Molly, her sleeves rolled decorously down and a white apron over her dark one, took out the soup and brought in the platter with that great brown perfectly cooked roast, and brought potatoes and spinach and hot plates, while aunt Hannah with experienced hand and keen knife, sharpened by herself, cut great juicy slices in generous plenty and filled the plates.

They were a rather silent table that first night. They were embarrassed to a degree by their surroundings which were so familiar and yet so unfamiliar. And then the dinner was absorbing. It absorbed their thoughts and they absorbed it.

When it came time for the dessert they sat back satisfied, and feelings that perhaps it were as well that the inevitable pie, which they always had for dessert, did not come to spoil this ideal repast. But they forgot such feeling when that great pudding was brought in, its crust browned to a nicety on the top, and light as feathers when it was cut, its luscious quarters of amber apples in the bottom, and a dressing of some sweet transparent syrup with just a dash of cinnamon.

"I tell you what!" said Harry Knowles, leaning back in his chair to fold his napkin and talking in an aside to Celia, "that was the best dinner I have tasted since I left home. I feel as if I had been invited out, don't you? I don't know what it means, do you? She certainly can't keep it up. I suppose she's just standing treat for the first night, but I declare, if I could have meals like that, I'm not sure but I might be a different kind of a fellow and amount to something. How's our lamp getting on? I thought of a way to fix the spring in that sofa the other night. I believe I'll stay in and try it to-night."

Aunt Hannah, as they were leaving the table, apologized for not having the rooms in order that day. She had only been in power, she said, since one o'clock, and there had not been time to do everything. She hoped to have things in better shape very soon if they would all be patient. Then the boarders went into the parlor to whisper with one another about that good dinner, and Celia slipped unseen out to the kitchen to exult and to help.

12

Out in the street, not far from that boarding-house, two young men met. "How are you, Horace? Glad to see you, old fellow! You look as thin as a rail. What do they feed you on down in that miserable hole where you hide yourself? I say, Horace, you ought to have either a new boarding-place or a wife."

The other man laughed. "I'm hunting one," he said, "that is, a new boarding-house, not a wife."

"Well, you may find the one while in search of the other, you know. They always used to say, when we were children, that if you lost a thing you never could find it till you lost something else and went to hunting that. Now you haven't exactly lost a wife, you know, because you never had one. So that's just as bad, but maybe you'll find her. However, I fear that any one you'd find in hunting a boarding-house wouldn't be worth her salt. That's my experience. Say, old fellow, why don't you come up our way and live? It isn't much further, and you are a good walker. You could walk to that blessed church of yours, if you still hold to your puritanical ideas about not riding on the trolley on Sunday. Now there's the place Royce boards; that would be first-rate, and I happen to know there's a vacant room there now, second story front, fine sunny room, all conveniences and splendid board."

"But I can't afford second story fronts, Roger; my salary has mostly to be paid by myself yet. You know we are building and the church is just struggling to live. It is all made up of poor people."

"Well, what in the world did you go down there for? You might have had a church in Germantown if you would have taken it, and you also had a chance out in West Philadelphia. I heard. Why, you've friends enough to have got you hearings in several big churches down in the heart of the city where they pay big salaries. I'm sure I don't see any virtue in your hiding your light under a bushel. For my part, I think you are as good, if not better, than any preacher I've ever heard in the city, if you only would consent to let go of a few high and impossible views you have about social equality. However, I suppose that's neither here nor there. You're here and the churches are there, and so it will continue to be, I presume, in spite of all I can say, and there'll be nothing for me but to tend you in your last sickness and pay the funeral expenses, if you go on at this rate. I must see what I can do about getting our church to help that mission of yours, if you persist in your folly."

"I wish you would, Roger, for they need help, and a church in this neighborhood is much more needed than in the quarters you have mentioned, where there is a church of some sort every two blocks almost. But I must go on, for I have a meeting this evening, and I want to go to one more place before I go to church.''

They parted, the young man Roger wishing the other would reconsider, and come higher up in town to board, and thus be near his friends. Then Horace Stafford went on his way, and having consulted a list of addresses in his notebook, in a moment more paused at a door and rang a bell and the door was opened by Celia.

Now Celia was very happy over the successful dinner. She had lingered about the halls catching words that the boarders had dropped, and she knew that they were intensely pleased and surprised. When she was happy or excited a clear red color came into her cheeks and a brightness into her deep, grey-blue eyes which made her very beautiful. She was not always beautiful, although she was always pleasant to look at; certain conditions, however, had the power of making this charm bloom into beauty. To-night the color and the shine were there, and she seemed a charming picture to the young man who had spent the afternoon in calling at boarding-houses, and had begun to know just what to expect to see when the door opened. He was agreeably surprised, therefore, as he stepped into the hall and waited while Celia called aunt Hannah, for he had said he wanted to see Mrs. Morris, having been directed there for board. He glanced into the parlor and sighed. It was the same grade of parlor he had grown to expect, a dreary enough place, but he did not know what was the matter with it, and as he should have to spend very little time in it, it did not make great difference. He heard a low cultured voice upstairs saying: ''Tell Molly I will send her some in a moment,'' and then Miss Grant appeared before him.

It is true she did not know much about taking new boarders, but she did the best she could. She told him there was one room left vacant that day, that it was not in order yet, but if he cared to see it, he might come upstairs and do so. He followed her to the room. It happened to be the second story front. It was not large, for economy of space had been exercised to a great degree in the building of that house, but it had a sunny exposure, and the young man knew by an uncomfortable experience in a dark room that that was a great advantage in a room. The bed did not look very soft nor inviting, and the two chairs in the room were rather dilapidated. The bureau was a cheap one with a rheumatic castor, which gave it a reeling appearance. The bed clothing was tumbled in a heap on the bed, as the clerk had left it. Altogether it was not just what one would call luxury. But it was so much better than some the weary man had seen that he ventured to ask timidly, ''Could I have some sort of a table to write on?''

Miss Hannah thought a moment and told him that she thought he could. He asked the price and it proved to be not much more than he was now paying. After a little reflection he said he would take it. Afterward, when he had gone downstairs to the parlor to wait for the supper which she had said he might have, in response to his question if it was too late for the evening meal, he wondered why he had done so. What power had been upon him upstairs to make him determine to cast his lot in here? It was not that room, even though it was a second story front, for that was very forlorn in the dim flickering gaslight. It was not the general look of the house, for that certainly was not attractive. And now as he sat in the dimness of the shadow of the front window, and watched some of the boarders at the further end of the room, he felt that same sense of desolation steal over him which he had felt in so many boarding-houses that afternoon. He could not hope to find many congenial spirits here. He sighed. It was hard not to have some pleasant friends about one who could talk of the things one knew and loved, when one came in at night after a hard day's work. But as Miss Hannah came back through the hall and in that quiet sweet voice of hers that made one feel as if a benediction had been pronounced upon one, told him that he could come to the dining-room now, he followed her and knew that it was his landlady who had drawn him to select this as his temporary home. She seated him and poured his coffee, and then excused herself and left him. He looked about him after he was left alone, and had bowed his head a moment, more in supplication that the Lord would give him rest and strength for his work, than in thankfulness for his food, for he had learned that there were kinds of food which were as hard to eat as they were to digest. With pleased surprise he saw the tablecloth was clean and free from crumbs. The plate before him held food as appetizing as any he could remember in pleasanter homes than those he had occupied lately. Of course the potatoes had been heated over and were not so nice as when first served, but the meat was tender and juicy, and he ate it with a relish, for he was weary and had not had anything to really tempt his appetite for six weeks, that being the length of time since he had gone to his friend Roger's, to dinner. Those delicious rolls and that coffee were enough in themselves to satisfy a hungry man, and he began to feel that he had not chosen his home amiss. Then the kitchen door opened, and Celia entered bringing a bounteous plate of apple dumpling covered with plenty of sauce. She put it down beside his place and began to remove the empty dishes, asking him if he would have anything more.

"Thank you," he said, looking up and smiling, "I have had plenty and it has been so good. I have been boarding where they had miserable fare, and I did not know how hungry I was. This meal has tasted like my mother's cooking."

Celia's eyes danced as she said demurely she was very glad. As she went back to the kitchen with the dishes, she could not help thinking what handsome eyes that man had, and how they were lit up by his smile. He was tall and thin with an intellectual face which many persons would have called homely, but of the style which Celia always designed to herself and aunt Hannah as "homely handsome."

The new boarder went out after his meal was finished. He had told his landlady that he would bring his belongings when he returned later in the evening, and she had promised to have his room ready for him.

Celia went upstairs to see if she could do anything. She was bubbling over with delight over the house and its inmates and all she wished to do. No child in a fairy tale ever had such delightful possibilities put into her hands, she thought, as had been given to her.

"Now," said aunt Hannah, "that room must be fixed for that man, for he will come back by and by, and what shall we do with it to make it more habitable? Poor fellow! He must have been hard put to it indeed for shelter to have taken it looking like that, or perhaps he doesn't know any better. But it did look so desolate I couldn't bear to take him to it."

"Yes, he does know better, aunt Hannah," said Celia, laughing. "I know he does. He had a mother — and," she added half ashamed, "he has a smile."

"Well, I'm glad he has that," said Miss Hannah, pulling the bedclothes off in a gingerly way and extracting the sheets and pillowcases from the mass. "He'll need it to keep cheerful in this room to-night, I think. Celia, I do wish I could get into my grandmother's linen and blanket closet for a little while to-night. I should like to burn this quilt." She held it out by her finger and thumb and examined it carefully.

"Burn it, then," said Celia solemnly. "Haven't we got an allowance? We'll buy another." Then she went to work to try and make that room less dreary.

When the bed was made up with the cleanest things aunt Hannah could find, the wash bowl and pitcher and soap dish immaculate, and two copies of those flaring chromos called "Wide Awake" and "Fast Asleep" framed in varnished coffee berries had been removed from the walls, there was not much more to do. It was too late to do more at the paint than to wipe it off with a damp cloth, and the floor needed only brushing up. Aunt Hannah found a kitchen-table in Mrs. Morris' room which had done duty for a dressing-table. She had Molly carry this upstairs for a writing-table, and sighed that there was no cover for it. Celia meditated a moment, and then went up to her own back-room and took the embroidered denim cover from her trunk which she had made for a Christmas present for aunt Hannah and brought it. It was a little sacrifice but the table needed it. It wasn't too fine for use, and it would cause the bare room to look more habitable.

"There, aunt Hannah," she said, "I made it for you, but you may do what you like with it."

Then aunt Hannah took Celia's face between her hands and kissed her and said, "My dear girl!" and put the pretty cover on the table.

"I don't know as I should have done that," meditated Celia later, "if it hadn't been for that smile and his speaking about his mother."

She looked around the room once more as she was about to leave it. Aunt

Hannah had gone down to the kitchen to help Molly prepare for breakfast. Her eyes fell upon the two rickety chairs. She thought of Harry Knowles. A moment's reflection, and she ran down to the parlor and beckoned him to come into the hall.

"Harry," said she (they had already gotten well enough acquainted so that she could call him by his first name; she exercised that prerogative which a girl a little older than a young man likes to use and which the young man seems to be proud to have exercised sometimes. It was a pleasant brotherly and sisterly way to treat one another), "did you know there was a new boarder? I was passing the room just now. It looked awfully dreary before it was fixed up. The worst thing is the chairs. I wonder if you couldn't bring up your hammer and fix them a little. It seems too bad for a new boarder to find things all run down on the first night he comes."

"All right, I'm with you, Miss Murray," said Harry, interested at once. "I know how it feels myself. Besides that good dinner has given me a longing to do something for somebody else."

They went upstairs to the chairs, and as they went Harry said in a confiding tone, "Say, Miss Murray, I believe that Miss Grant is going to be great, don't you? She seems kind of like a woman who knew how, don't you know? Sometimes she makes me think of my mother just a little."

Celia smiled and said she thought so, and they went to work.

It was after the room was all in order, and some delicious cakes set rising in the yellow bowl downstairs for the morning breakfast, set with buckwheat that smelled of the waving fields it came from. The lights were out and everything quiet and Celia, lying awake to think over all that had happened, suddenly became aware that her aunt Hannah was awake also. Upon questioning her she at last ferreted out the reason for her wakefulness.

"Well, you see, Celia, I suppose I'm rather tired to-night, though I don't feel it one bit, I've been so interested in it all. But somehow I've just begun to think that maybe I ought not to have let you undertake this scheme. It is all very nice and benevolent, but what if it shouldn't succeed? If it should run behind and take a good deal of your money and you have to work hard for your living again, I should never get over blaming myself. Then too, I'm a little worried about that new man. I don't know as I ought to have taken him into the house without knowing the first thing about him, and I've always heard a city was an awful place to get taken in. He may be a robber, or some dreadful kind of a man, though to be sure he didn't look it. I must confess that I liked his looks very much, but you know, Celia dear, Satan sometimes appeared as an angel of light. I have heard that gamblers are often mistaken for ministers. I know perfectly well that I am 'green,' as the boys used to say, and perhaps I have been deceived. He was very late getting in and he looked pale. It may be he is dissipated, though I cannot really think that."

"Now, auntie dear," laughed Celia, putting her arms about her, "that isn't a bit like you. You must be over-tired or you never would talk like that.

Just remember your own words to me 'Charge not thyself with the weight of a year' and 'Bend not thine arm for to-morrow's load. Thou mayst leave that to thy gracious Lord.' Don't you fret one bit. What if he is a gambler or a robber? He can't do us any harm. We've nothing to gamble and nothing to rob. Perhaps we'll do him some good, and anyway I don't believe he's anything but good — he talked to me — that is he said he had a mother and she cooked like that, and then he smiled.''

Then they both laughed and Miss Hannah kissed her niece and thanked her for the reminder that she need not bear burdens. After that they fell asleep.

13

The minister was very weary when he went up to his new room that night, and he put down his satchel and looked around him hoping the bed would be more inviting than when last he saw it, though he had grown accustomed to sleeping soundly on any bed no matter how hard or uneven. He drew a long sigh of relief. It looked clean anyway. He turned down the covering and smoothed the sheets. They had no appearance of having been slept in before. He drew another sigh. That was one fear off his mind. He noticed next the table with its pretty cover. He was not accustomed to fancy work. He did not know whether this was done by hand or machinery. He only knew that it was a touch of beauty in his dreary room and he felt gladdened by it. He went over to the table and awkwardly felt of the material, passed his hand over the embroidery and smiled. He said to himself he would write to his mother about it and she would be pleased. Then he knelt down beside the table and bowed his head in prayer upon it asking that he might receive and give a blessing in that house where he had come to take up his abode, and that if possible, it might be such a place that he would feel it was right and best that he should remain for a time.

About that same time Harry Knowles stood before the bureau in his room and looked at his mother's picture. His face was grave and sad. He looked into the pictured eyes with a questioning longing as if he would have her with him again that he might ask her advice. He looked into her face till the tears started in his own eyes. He let them drop unheeded on the bureau and on the little velvet frame. She seemed to him to be looking into his life, and asking him what he had done with his time since she left him. At last he turned away his head and said aloud, "Well, I'm glad I didn't go to-night anyway. I s'pose the boys'll give me no end of chaff about backing out, but I've proved to myself that I can stay at home *once* when I say so. I wish mother *was* here. I'd tell her all about it, I believe, and promise her to start over again. I wonder if 'twould be any use! If a fellow only had some one to help him!" and he sighed and went to bed.

It is not quite certain what time Molly Poppleton arose the next morning. Celia told her if she had only gotten up a very little earlier, she might have met herself going to bed. The range, unused to such treatment, brightened up early too, and was soon baking and boiling away to please the most fastidious cook. The oatmeal had been cooking slowly all night, and was getting ready to be a delicious porridge, such as is found in its perfection only in the land of Scotland. Molly had coaxed the milk by all the arts she knew, till it actually gave forth a thin yellow cream for the oatmeal. True, she scoffed at it and said it wasn't as rich as skim milk in Cloverdale, but then the boarders were not used to Cloverdale milk, and they called this cream. She picked and shredded the codfish to a degree of fineness that would have made the departed Maggie stand in amaze at such a waste of labor, and then with all the skill of long experience, she mixed just the right proportion of potatoes for the most delectable codfish balls, when they should be browned to a crisp, that ever any one tasted.

"Codfish balls are good, and anybody that doesn't like 'em when they are made just right doesn't know, that's all. Besides one can't have beefsteak every day and there's plenty else to eat." So said Molly.

Then she tested the buckwheat cakes to be sure there was exactly the right amount of soda and enough milk to make them brown on both sides, and set the coffee where it would get its finishing-off, and rang the bell. Just one minute ahead of time that bell rang. Molly Poppleton did love to get ahead of time, even if it was but one minute.

"I say," said Harry Knowles, holding a golden-brown fish-ball up on his fork and admiring it, "if that is a fish ball, then I never saw one before. It is a libel on that pretty thing to call it by that name, or else all the ones I ever tried to eat were very poor imitations." Molly coming in just then with a generous supply of hot buckwheats heard the remark, and her soul swelled with joy and pride, and thereafter Harry Knowles was her favorite of all the boarders unless it was the minister who grew into her good graces by another way not long after. He had come in just a moment before, and was enjoying his dish of oatmeal and wondering what made the difference between it and all other oatmeal he had tried to eat in the weeks since he came to Philadelphia to live. Was it possible that he had at last found a place where things were really good to eat, or was he getting a good appetite from working so hard? He resolved, at any rate, to ask the cook, sometime when he was well enough acquainted, if he might take a dish of this to the old Scotch woman who was lying sick in an attic and longing for her dear home across the seas.

That breakfast was a pleasant surprise to more than one of the boarders. The brakeman, coming in a little late from his all-night run, having taken his dinner the night before at the other end of his line, and therefore not being prepared for changes except the mere fact that Mrs. Morris had gone away, and some one else was to supply her place for a while, was dumbfounded. He drew his chair up to the table with his usual familiar assurance, and then looked around in almost embarrassment a moment. He was not quite sure what made him feel so. Was it the pleasant-faced, white-haired woman at the head of the table, who smiled a good-morning to him in a tone which was cordial and yet had a note in it that made him feel she was from another world than his own? Or was it the few flowers in the tiny vase in the centre of the table? Or? But he was unable to detail the rest of the changes, they seemed to him so subtle. He turned his attention to the breakfast which certainly was good. Maggie had improved, evidently.

In short, those boarders went to their day's work well fed and comfortable for the first time in many weeks, and were therefore better workers, and better human beings in every way, because they were not all day troubled by the demands and complaints of nature in consequence of what they had eaten, or what they had not eaten.

Just as Celia was going out of the door, Miss Hannah, who had followed her, put her hand on her arm and drew her into the parlor for a moment.

"Celia, dear," she said, "we must have a talk to-night as soon after dinner as possible, and find out how this house is to be run and decide some questions. You know we cannot go ahead blindly and get into debt as Mrs. Morris did."

"I'll risk you, auntie dear," Celia said, as she kissed her behind the red chenille curtain. "But we'll have our talk, and I'll get home just as early as I can to help, if you need me. Then after dinner we'll have a cozy time and do a lot of figuring. I've done some already. Good-bye. Don't try to reform everything to-day, leave just a little for to-morrow. Do you want me to stop at some employment office and get another servant?"

"No, not yet, dear. There's too much to be done before we introduce any new elements, and besides we don't know yet whether we can afford another servant. We mustn't run behind, you know."

Then they parted with a smile of perfect understanding, and aunt Hannah went to her new duties with enthusiasm. There were a few things she meant to have radically different in some of her guests' sleeping rooms before that day drew to a close, and there was much planning and marketing to do. Molly Poppleton was in her element in the kitchen. Miss Hannah could hear her voice singing above the clatter of pots and pans,

> "What though the spicy breezes
> Blow soft o'er Ceylon's isle;
> Though every prospect pleases,
> And only man is vile;—"

Molly was cleaning out the departed Maggie's kettle closet under the back stairs, and stopped occasionally in her singing to express her mind as to some dirty corner and then went on—

"In vain with lavish kindness
    The gifts of God are strewn:
The heathen in his blindness,
    Bows down to wood and stone!"

Aunt Hannah smiled as she went upstairs. She knew that the good-hearted Molly was mingling the theme of her song with her own thoughts about the dirty house and the need of the boarders and that she would work it all out by and by.

"Shall we whose souls are lighted
    With wisdom from on high,—
Shall we to men benighted,
    The lamp of life deny?"

went on the singer, and Miss Hannah knew the hard working singer's thought was that she would make a cheerful, clean house and good food, and give the rest of them a chance to try and help save the poor city heathen boarders, for Molly Poppleton looked upon all native city boarders as heathen in the truest sense of the word, and she had taken with joy the few words Miss Hannah had spoken to her about the mission they were going to try to start, the mission of making one bright little clean home spot for a few people who had hitherto been in discomfort.

The dining-room windows were washed that morning, and several other windows, and Molly Poppleton sang a great many of Isaac Watts' hymns through before she prepared lunch for herself and Miss Hannah. She did not remember when she had been so happy. Neither, indeed, did Miss Hannah.

It had been the one great ambition of Hannah Grant's life, since she had lost the love of her youth, and had been made to see that hers was not to go on the great mission of salvation to the heathen of other nations, that she should have some spot which she could call her own, where she might exercise her powers of helping people. And now it seemed as though she was to have opportunity. She thanked her heavenly Father every hour, even for the dirt and desolation of the place, because he had given to her the sweet privilege of brightening a place that had hitherto been dark.

It was after dinner. The minister was in his room writing to his mother, before he went out to a meeting at the mission. Down in the parlor the brakeman sat at the organ accompanying himself as he sang in stentorian voice the touching ballad of

"Granny's only left to me her old armchair."

Celia smiled as she ran upstairs where her aunt was waiting for the conference.

"Just listen, auntie dear, did you ever hear the like," she said, putting her head in at the door, and the words of the chorus in decided nasal twang floated up the two flights of stairs:

> "How they tittered, how they chaffed,
> How my brothers and my sisters laughed,
> When they heard the lawyers declare,
> Granny's only left to me her old armchair."

"Do you really think, aunt Hannah, that it's any use to try to reach and help people who have that sort of taste in music, even if you try through their taste in buckwheat cakes?"

Celia's face was gay with laughter, but there was an undertone of trouble in it which Miss Hannah detected and understood.

"Dearie, Christ died for him, even if he does seem to be too coarse-grained to understand the little refining influences you are trying to weave around him. Yes, of course it is worth while. You can't expect him to turn in-to a person with the tastes of a Beethoven. You are not that yourself, remember, and it's all in the scale of life. But I know what you mean, and I do think it's worth while to try. You see if it wasn't, God wouldn't have put him just here for us to try on. You mustn't expect the same result as you would from——"

"From your new boarder, auntie? The gambler with the smile you mean!" Celia was laughing now, for both had seen with the morning light that whatever else their new boarder was, he was a man to be trusted.

"Yes," said aunt Hannah. "You mustn't expect the same results from trying to help this man that you would the other, but you'll find he will have a depth to his nature which you don't suspect, if you look for it. Listen! He is singing something else. It may give you a clue."

Again the voice rang out deeply, pathetically and nasally,

> "Lost on the Lady Elgin,
> Slumbering to wake no more,
> Numbering about three hundred,—
> Who failed to reach the shore."

"Oh, auntie, I can't stand another line," said Celia rushing into the room and throwing herself on the bed in a paroxysm of laughter. "To have those awful words in that ludicrous song roared out in that dramatic way is too, *too* funny. And he asked me if I would sing 'Where is my wandering boy to-night?' with him. How *could* I?''

"Now, dear girl," said aunt Hannah sitting down on the bed beside her, "perhaps that is just your chance. Sing 'Where is my wandering boy to-night?' with him some time. You may be able to help him to higher, more refining things in some way, even if he does continue to amuse you with his music. If you want to help all the people, you will have to do as Paul did and be all things to all men, that you may by all means save some."

Celia sobered down at once.

"Yes, I know, aunt Hannah, but somehow I never could be that, unless I was interested in people. It troubles me sometimes, but this black-eyebrowed, smiling, conceited brakeman isn't in the least attractive. Now that boy Harry Knowles is. I feel sorry for him. He misses his mother, and I'm afraid he goes with a wild set. I got him to fix some chairs last night and he seemed interested and stayed at home. But to-night he slipped out just before I came up, and looked the other way when I came down the hall, as if he didn't want me to see him and ask him to stay in, at least I fancy that was the reason, because I've asked him to stay once or twice. It worries me to think he is going wrong, and I feel as if I could pray all night that God would save him. I can't get away from that look in the eyes of his mother's picture. He brought it down to the parlor one night and showed it to me. And he is so young, only just eighteen. Auntie, I want to do so much for the people, do you suppose God will let me do something at least?''

"Dear child," said aunt Hannah as she bent over and kissed her, "I feel sure he will, and he will hear your prayers and help you to work in the right way and to be interested in the uninteresting, too. And now get your pencil and paper and let's go to work."

Celia sprang up and soon they were hard at work.

"What I want to do is this, aunt Hannah," said Celia. "I want to make this as pleasant a home for us all, as it can be made on the money that we pay in for our board. You and I will pay ours too, you know, that is if it can't be run without that, and then we'll just have things as nice as we can on that. If we need anything extra, why you and I can count that a gift, you know, from our allowance. But to be strictly honest as a boarding-house, and not a charitable institution, we ought to run it on what is paid in, oughtn't we? I would like to prove that a boarding-house can be comfortable as well as cheap. Do you think it can be done?"

"I do," said the elder woman, thoughtfully. "I have done some careful thinking myself, and I think it can. I shall enjoy trying, anyway."

"And auntie, there's another thing; this allowance of mine is half yours, you know. I won't have it any other way. You and I have nine hundred dollars a year to live on, besides what is not in the bank in cash, and we can do what we please with it, give it away if we want to. If we can make this house pay our board, then we will have the rest to live on. But if we can't, we'll run the house up to the full extent of what we can afford to put into it, for a few months at least, just to give these poor souls a taste of something like home. I would rather do that than give my money somewhere else, for I think they all need it. Do you think, auntie, we have enough money to start on to hope to make things go nicely at the beginning? Nine hundred dollars a year seems to me a great deal of money, but people say that money doesn't go far in the city.''

Celia's brow was clouded as she spoke.

''There goes my girl down into the cellar of despair over a thought,'' said aunt Hannah, leaning over to smooth the pucker out of her niece's brow. ''I wish you would get just a little more trust in your heavenly Father, that he will take care of the work he has put into your hands, and see that it prospers in spite of your worries. Now tell me everything you know about this house and the way it is run.''

14

Aunt Hannah and Celia had finished the last puzzling question, added up the final row of figures, and were peacefully sleeping in their beds. All the lights in the house were out, when there was heard a loud noise at the street door, as if some one was thrown, or threw himself, several times heavily against it. This was followed by voices talking loud and excitedly, and then in more muffled tones. The door knob was turned and rattled, and a latch-key clicked and half turned in the lock as if handled by clumsy or unacquainted fingers.

The minister heard the noise first, as his room was over the front of the house, and rising he opened his window and tried to speak and quiet the disturbance, but he received only curses for his interference, and he thought he recognized in one of the midnight revelers the form of one of the boarders. Closing his window, he dressed as rapidly as possible, that he might go down if his assistance was needed. By the time he was halfway down the stairs, however, and was just striking a match, the fumbling latch-key at last turned, and the door burst open, literally tumbling into the hall three young men just at Horace Stafford's feet. Miss Grant and Celia, though they slept on the third floor, were near the stair landing and had at last heard the noise. They had slipped on wrappers and slippers and stood at the head of the stairs just above Mr. Stafford, as he struck the light.

"What does this mean?" said aunt Hannah, in as stern a voice as she could muster, with Celia, bewildered and trembling, clinging to her arm and begging her to come back.

But there was too much disturbance below for her to be heard, and she and Celia could but stand and watch.

The new boarder seemed to know what to do in the present emergency. He promptly lighted the gas, turning it up to its full strength, and then extricated the three young men, who seemed to be in a helplessly tangled condition on the floor at his feet. Two of them were promptly withdrawn from the hall by their comrades outside, and the one left stood miserably against the wall and looked about him.

It was hard to recognize in this dirty, rough fellow with bloodshot eyes and white face, the gay, bright young man who always looked so neat, and whom everybody liked and called "Harry."

"Oh, auntie, that is Harry Knowles," said Celia, in horrified tones, and then the young man looked up.

77

"Hulloa, Celia," he called, in a pitifully bright voice, "is that you? Yes, I'm here all right, only I've been out on a lark and the lark's gone to my head. Come down, and talk to a fellow a while, just fer a change, you know."

Celia shrank back in dismay, as she saw the poor fellow stagger toward the stairs and heard him say, "Can't you get down? Well, I'll come up and get you. Awful shaky stairs, I know, but I'll manage 'em yet, don't you be afraid."

And then a strong hand grasped his arm and a clear, commanding voice said,

"Stand right where you are! Don't stir a step, and don't speak another word to those ladies." Then the minister turned to the frightened women and said in low tones,

"Don't be afraid, go to your rooms and I will take care of him."

Harry had sat stupidly down on the stairs saying meekly,

"All right, cap'n, jes's you say. You're boss, an' I'm sleepy."

Miss Hannah took assurance from the calm face and powerful frame of her new boarder and led Celia away, while the minister carefully and even tenderly helped the young man to his room and took care of him as if he had been his own brother.

Miss Hannah had her hands full with Celia. The young girl had thrown herself on the bed in a violent fit of weeping, and it required all her aunt's persuasive powers to quiet her and try to soothe her to sleep. Celia had not been accustomed to young men who drank. Her cousins had been steady, whatever else they might not have been. She had never seen a man come home at night drunk, and she had never been spoken to by one.

The familiar tone and the vacant, silly stare with which the young man had looked up at her had given her a shock she could not forget. Whenever she tried to be quiet and sit up and listen to aunt Hannah, she would shudder again at the thought of the scene she had just witnessed. By and by, when she was calmer she wailed out,

"Now we shall have to give up the whole thing, auntie. We can't have people getting drunk," and she shuddered again.

"Now, child! Don't get into your cellar of despair again. It's like some people's cyclone cellars out West, always there ready for you, and you fly down the stairs at sign of the first little cloud that appears in your sky. Can't you remember we have a heavenly Father who is looking out for us? Get a little more trust, dear. No, of course we shall not have to give up, just for one boarder who has gone wrong. We are not obliged to keep him, you know, if he makes a disturbance. But I'd not be the first one to turn him out without another trial. What are we here for but to try to help such as he? Maybe he never was really drunk before. He is young and doesn't look to be bad. He'll be sorry enough for it all to-morrow, I'm sure, or I've mistaken the face of that picture of his mother on his bureau. A boy who has had a mother like that can't go wrong all at once. We'll do what we can for him. You have some work to do for him, dear, and you must try and forget to-night for Christ's sake!''

"Oh, aunt Hannah!'' groaned Celia, "how can I ever speak to him again, after his talking that way to me, and calling me by my name, too, as if I was a little girl? The idea of his taking the liberty of speaking that way. Oh, I feel as if I never could try to help anybody again.''

"Now, Celia!'' said aunt Hannah, speaking rather sharply for her, "you must *not* talk that way. That wasn't Harry Knowles that spoke to you to-night. It was a demon that he had swallowed that had taken entire possession, and put out for a time the light of reason in him. You told me yourself that he has always been respectful, and he's nothing but a boy in years, much younger than you. And Celia, he is very dear to your Saviour.''

Aunt Hannah's heart had gone out to the poor motherless boy, and she longed to save him from the awful destruction that she saw yawning in front of the path he was treading. Celia knew her aunt was right, and by degrees she regained her composure, and began to mount up into the first story at least of her faith, and believe that everything was not gone to destruction yet. However, she went to the store the next morning with a heavy heart. She had so great a horror of drunkards and drunkenness, and so strong a belief in the power of appetite, that she felt little or no hope of trying to save any one from the awful end of a drunkard, who had once commenced to tread that downward path. She went about all day, feeling as deep sadness as if she had witnessed the terrible death of some friend.

Miss Hannah had spent a long time in prayer that night, after she heard once more the regular breathing of Celia, and knew she was asleep. She asked God's grace to help her do what was best for this poor homeless boy, and if it might be that he would honor her with bearing the message of salvation to his soul, she would give God all the glory. Her soul longed for the soul of the boy whose feet were astray, and she was filled with a kind of divine compassion for him, such as Jesus would have us feel, such as he felt, for those for whom he died.

The minister, meantime, had put the poor boy to bed. He was docile enough, and almost grateful in a maudlin sort of way, for the help given him, and he sank at once into a deep sleep. Horace Stafford turned the gas low, and established himself by the bedside for some time, until he felt certain that there was nothing else the matter with the slumberer. Then he knelt beside the boy, and asked God's mercy for him and went to his own room.

It was not until far into the afternoon that the sleeper roused. Horace Stafford had found out by judicious questioning, and without revealing his condition to the other boarders (who fortunately had none of them heard the disturbance in the night), where the young man worked. He had then gone himself to the store, and asked for the head of the firm, giving his own card and explaining that the young salesman was ill, and unable to come to work that day. The head of the firm had been very kind. He had recognized the name of the minister as well as that of the mission chapel which he mentioned in introducing himself, thinking the word of a minister might go further toward excusing the absence of the young man, and asked kindly how the work was getting on. He said he had meant to send in a contribution to that work, but he had let it slip by without attention, and he handed the minister a crisp ten dollar bill. Then he promised to see that young Knowles' place for the day was supplied, and asked to be notified if the illness should prove serious, and there was anything he could do for him. He said he liked the young man, though of course he knew but little of him, but he feared he had not good health, as he looked frail. When Horace Stafford left the store, he had a better opinion of employers than he had been led to hold from some reading he had been doing lately.

When Harry Knowles awoke that afternoon, he was conscious first of his physical condition. His head ached miserably, and he could not bear to stir. His throat burned as with fire, and all things seemed full of a ghastly horror. He opened his eyes, and the first thing he saw was his mother's picture. It stood on the bureau opposite his bed. Miss Hannah had been softly going about the room that morning, putting things to rights, and putting a touch of home here and there where she could do it in a few minutes. She had wiped the dust from the velvet and polished the glass of the frame with a damp cloth, and the clear sweet eyes of Harry's mother looked straight into his, so full of love and compassion and motherly tenderness, that Harry felt it all and suddenly realized his present condition and what had caused it. He could not bear his mother's tender love. She seemed to be looking through into his very soul. He closed his eyes to shut hers out. As he did so, all his experiences of last night came swiftly and stood before him one by one, and passed before his mother's eyes too. He seemed to know at every instant what she would be feeling about it all. He recalled his resolve to stay in, and how the boys called for him before he had settled down to doing anything, and asked him to just come out for a while; how they had coaxed him away from his resolves, and interested him in their plans for the evening. They had planned an evening at the theatre and a supper afterward, and they made him feel that he was being considered mean not to join in and help with the expenses, since they had taken his coming as a matter of course, and ordered a seat and a plate for him. They joked him unmercifully, and said they believed he had been going to Sunday-school again, and had promised his nice little teacher that he would be good. They called him a "dear little fellow," and said they wouldn't bother him any more, he should have a stick of pink and white candy so he should, and one of them actually bought it and presented it to him. He had knocked it into the street, and declared he had no intention of not joining them and bearing his share of the expenses, and then they all seemed glad and turned his mind to enjoyment. "We didn't really believe you were getting to be a sissy boy," they said. His conscience had had no time to reproach him. They had not mentioned going in to any of their favorite haunts for a game — that game which he had begun to fear on account of the way it reduced his always scanty funds. They only seemed bent on having an innocent good time. Oh, they had known well how to get him into the thing. They knew they could touch something that he called his sense of honor, when they said he had left them in a tight place, as they had ordered supper for him, and if he didn't pay for it they would have to do it. And they took him to a play that was *very* funny. He enjoyed fun. There were one or two things toward the end that had brought a warm flush to his cheeks at the time, because he couldn't help thinking how ashamed his mother would be to know he was listening to and laughing at such things. But he wouldn't have had the fellows know that for anything. He had gone to that supper and been as jolly as any of them after it. But he had resolved, when he gave in to them, that he would not drink. That had been the great reason why he had tried to decline. When people offered him drink, he could always hear his mother's voice saying, "Harry dear, mother hopes you will always have courage to say no, if you are ever asked to drink wine or any strong drink." He tried to make it right with his conscience when he turned to go with the boys, by saying that he would not drink a drop. He knew they would ask him, and it would be uncomfortable to refuse, but he had done it heretofore, and he would do it to-night. After to-night, he would try to gradually drift away from that set. It would not do to break off all of a sudden, but he would try to do it gradually. Of course he could. Had he not stayed at home that evening when Miss Murray fixed the lamp, and then again last night? Both of these times he had promised to go with the boys. He felt strong with the sense of having conquered once before. He did not remember a Bible verse then that his mother used often to quote him, "Let him that thinketh he standeth take heed lest he fall," he only told himself that he had proved to himself that he was fully able to break off going with those boys whenever he chose, and therefore he had a right to go with them for a little innocent fun just once more.

Ah, but he did not know even now, as he lay in his bed with shame in his heart, and the tears of repentance overflowing his eyes and tickling between the tightly closed lashes, that Satan had leagued against him last night, and that those boys had vowed to conquer his foolish protests once and for all, and get him gloriously drunk. Once let him break down that silly shame, they said, and he would be a jolly fellow, for Harry was bright and quick-witted. Why they wanted to do it is not quite certain. Perhaps some of them were fiendish enough to want to drag him down as low as themselves, just for very love of deviltry. Others, perhaps, felt rebuke by his shrinking back at daring things which were proposed, and still others, older in their sin, liked him for his gay words and witty sayings, and were resolved to make of him a thoroughly good bad-fellow whom they could enjoy. Their experience had taught them that when one such once goes astray, he will dare more than some who never had any scruples.

Harry only knew that they had passed some cider first. They declared they had ordered it for his sake as they knew his temperance principles, and they laughed and nudged one another as it was passed and winked, and Harry felt goaded to do almost anything to prove that he was just as good, or as bad, as they were.

Now Harry was not fond of sweet cider. The few times he had tasted it, it had seemed insipid to him. He knew, indeed, that there were some people who went so far as to object to cider drinking. In a general way, he knew that there was a difference between sweet cider and hard cider, and it would have been well for him that night, if he had been possessed of a few decided opinions on the subject himself. He hesitated and then took some, but his hesitation was noticed and the boys had asked him if he were afraid of that too. He had flushed crimson and declared that he was not, and they had unmercifully passed his glass for more, and watched to see if he drank that. Then something else had been brought on, Harry did not just know what, whether wine or beer or something else. The cider had been by no means sweet and must have gone to his head. When they passed by his chair with the wine glasses, he had caught the whispered words and laughs of his companions over him, and turning quick without a thought for anything than to prove his — what? — cowardice? he ordered the waiter to give him some. A tremendous cheer had arisen from the boys, so loud it almost brought him to his senses. He drank that glass and another, and then he felt a feverish desire to swallow more, and they filled his glass again and again, he not asking or caring what it contained. That was the story. He did not know now, or stop to ask himself how he got here, to what he called home. He supposed it was in the same shameful way that some of the others were taken sometimes, the way that had hitherto been a strong barrier in the way of his joining in their drinking festivities. Whether any one saw or knew, he did not dare to ask. He only knew that he lay here, and that his mother's eyes were over there, and that God always seemed to be near his mother, and that he did not dare to open his eyes again. He heard the soft movement of a woman's dress, and a light step. It seemed like his mother's. He could almost think as he lay here that this was his home once more, and his mother was nursing him from some dreadful illness. Only this bed was so hard. Oh, the shame and horror if this had happened at his dear old home with his mother in it. It would have killed her. He groaned aloud, and then he heard that soft step again and wondered. Was he dead? Was this the — where? the judgment seat — perhaps? For his mother surely was there and God! Oh! —

15

Some one stood beside him and put a large cool hand on his aching brow, and a woman's voice, gentle and low, said "Drink this."

Then, although his very being was filled with disgust at the thought of eating or drinking anything, he let himself be raised from the pillow and swallow down the hot steaming coffee that was held for him. Miss Hannah gave his pillows a shake, and he settled back again with his eyes closed. He did not care for the coffee; he wondered that he could have drunk it, and yet he knew by the aroma of it that it was unlike any coffee he had ever drunk in that house before, and there gradually crept over him a sense of relief from the drinking of it. It was not that the throbbing in his temples was any less, but perhaps he felt a little better able to bear it. Miss Hannah brought a clean linen cloth and a large soft towel, and washed his hot face and hands, just as his mother used to do when he was sick, and gently smoothed his tumbled hair. He did not look at her. His eyes were closed tight, and he was trying with all his might to force back the hot tears that were surely burning their way out beneath his lashes. The tears came and Miss Hannah saw them. She stooped and kissed him softly on his forehead and said in that gentle pitying voice again, "Poor boy!" and then she slipped away and left him alone.

If Hiram Bartlett had been there he would have said that aunt Hannah was encouraging drunkenness by giving the young man so much attention; that pity was not what such a fellow needed, he ought to be soundly thrashed. He would get an idea that it was a fine thing to come home drunk, if he were petted and taken care of for it. But Hiram Bartlett was not there, and aunt Hannah was glad. She did what she felt in her inmost soul Jesus Christ would have her do, if she could hear his voice telling her.

When she slipped away and left Harry alone, it was to tap lightly on the minister's door and tell him Harry was awake.

It was not the first time that day she had been to the minister's room. She had resolved in the watches of the night that she would discover for herself what sort of a man was the stranger whom she had taken in the first night she came. He seemed to be all right, and he had helped nobly in this emergency. Now, if he only were a Christian, how much help he might be with this young man. She thought she knew a way to discover for herself without asking him, so instead of letting Molly "do his room" the next morning, she attended to that hall herself. She knew, if he were a Christian, she would be likely to find evidence of it somewhere about his room. It therefore gave her

83

much pleasure and some surprise, when she found on entering to make the bed, not only the Bible in full view, but also a number of what appeared to be theological books. She glanced them over. There was a row of old familiar ones, in rusty bindings, "Barnes' Notes" and a few kindred commentaries standing against the wall, on the floor. There was a soap box beside them containing other volumes yet unpacked, not many, but at the top lay two of F. B. Meyer's, and Andrew Murray's "With Christ in the School of Prayer." These were dear favorites and friends of hers, and she began to hope that perhaps she was entertaining a minister. This hope was confirmed a few minutes afterward when the postman came and brought several letters for the Rev. Horace Stafford. She made his bed and set in order that room with a light in her face then, for was she not serving one of his Master's high messengers? When Mr. Stafford came in later, she had a short conference about young Mr. Knowles, and they agreed that he should go to the store, and after the young man awoke he should have a little talk with him.

Harry lay still for some minutes reviewing his miserable existence, and going over the last few months of mistakes and sins. Suddenly it occurred to him that it must be late and he ought to get up and go to his work. With a moan, he turned over and tried to get out of bed, but he was dizzy and sick, and he had to sit still and cover his eyes. He was not yet so used to dissipation that he could rise and go about like any one else the next day, and the dissipation had been deeper than he knew. What mixed or drugged glasses were given him, after he began to drink, he did not remember. Therefore, he could scarcely account for the effect they had had.

Just then there came a knock at his door and Mr. Stafford entered. He had been listening for some sound, and was ready. He wanted to help the boy when he should fully come to his senses and realize his condition, and keep him, perhaps, from rushing out to drink again. Of course, he knew nothing about Harry's past life, but he judged from his appearance and from what little he could learn of his character that this was probably a first experience, or if not the first, that at least he was not yet a hardened sinner.

"Do you feel any better?" asked Mr. Stafford, in a pleasant, everyday tone, such as he would use for any illness of any one.

Harry looked up, his bloodshot eyes and white face making a pitiful picture of wretchedness.

"I feel worse than I ever felt in my life before," he answered, all the bright gaiety with which he was usually bubbling over, gone entirely out of his voice.

"Better lie down again," said the visitor. "You are hardly able to get up yet."

"But I must get up," said Harry in a despairing tone. "What time is it? It must be late. I'll get fired if I'm not on time. They're terribly particular down there."

"Never mind the time. You're not to go to the store to-day," answered the other quietly, in a tone that seemed used to commanding obedience.

"Why not!" asked Harry sharply, looking at Mr. Stafford with sudden apprehension in his eyes. "Have they found out and sent me my walking papers already? What time is it? How long have I been here? Let me up. But it's no use if they've found out. I'm done for. I might as well go to destruction first as last," and he sank back with a groan and turned his face to the wall.

"Listen, my boy," said the young minister bending over him and placing a kindly hand on his shoulder. "Don't say that. You are not going to destruction. We won't let you. And you need not feel like that. You have not been dismissed. Your place is waiting for you when you are able to go back. The firm knows nothing but that you are too ill to be at your work today. It is afternoon, and you have slept all day. You are to lie still now until you are perfectly able to get up, and I am going to take care of you. Is there anything you would like to have?"

Harry turned over and opened his eyes in astonishment.

"How do you know I'm not to be dismissed? Has anyone been there?"

"Yes, I was there this morning and had a good long talk with Mr. Prescott. He seemed very sympathetic and asked me to send him word, if you were not better to-morrow."

Harry closed his eyes and swallowed hard. He was almost overcome by the kindness that had been shown him. Suddenly, he remembered dimly the scene of the night before.

"Say," said he, huskily, "where was I, that is — how, what did I — do? Who was down there last night when I came in? How did I get here?"

"I brought you up here," answered Mr. Stafford, quietly, in a matter-of-fact tone. "Miss Grant was present." He thought it as well that Harry should not know that Celia had been there; it could do no good and would only add to his embarrassment. "You have slept ever since," he finished briefly.

"Were the boarders around? Do they know?"

"No."

There was silence a moment. Harry was trying to recall some faint memory. At last he spoke.

"Didn't I, — Wasn't Miss Murray there too? Did I talk nonsense to her?"

The minister turned about and faced the young man and said truthfully, "Yes, she was there, and you didn't speak very respectfully to her, I must own."

Harry groaned again. "Oh, she's been very kind to me," he moaned. Then after a pause. "But yet they didn't turn me out of the house. If they had turned me out I could have stood it, but I can't stand being treated this way. I haven't been treated kindly since Mother died." Then his weakened nerves gave way and he cried, as if he had been a girl.

Horace Stafford let him cry for a few minutes. He thought it might do him good. He had no mind to minimize the offence. It was grave and serious and must be realized.

Presently he began to talk in low, grave tones, and the young man on the bed ceased moaning and showed that he was listening. When he was quieter, Mr. Stafford drew from him as much of the story of the evening before as he could remember. He talked with him long and seriously about life and the true meaning of it, about the wonderful trust that God gave each one, when he put him upon the earth and gave him the responsibility of doing the best he was capable of. He drew him on to speak of his mother and his boyhood life. He did not talk too long. This man who was a fisher of men had been gifted with rare tact. He seemed to know just what to say and when to say it and, what is sometimes much more important, he knew when to keep still. He gave just the right note of warning to the young man before him, but he knew enough of human nature to see at once that here was true repentance, and deep humiliation, and that that lesson did not need to be further impressed this time. What he needed now was kindly sympathy and help to get upon his feet again.

Harry, in a pause, reverted to Celia. What should he do? He never could look her in the face again, and she had been so kind to him.

"Tell her so," said Mr. Stafford, promptly, as if it were the easiest thing in the world to do. "Just beg her pardon as manfully as you can, and then look out that you are never so placed that you will do so again."

The slender frame of the young man on the bed shook involuntarily as he said fiercely, "I should hope not."

There came Miss Grant's light tap at the door, and a dainty tray was handed in. Harry thought to himself that he could not eat, that he never could eat again, but when the tray was placed in front of him, and Mr. Stafford said in his quiet, commanding voice, "Now eat every bit of that," he found that he could.

Miss Grant knew by instinct just what to prepare for the invalid. Not dainties, and jellies and confectionery. Just a small, thin, white china bowl of very strong soup, containing much nutrition in small compass and sending forth an odor most delicious; some thin beautifully toasted slices of bread, a ball of sweet butter and more of that black aromatic coffee. The minister mentally decided that aunt Hannah must be an expert in the culinary art. So many kind women would have brought forth sour bread, muddy coffee and a piece of dyspeptic pudding or pie or cake, or perhaps tried more solid substantial foods where there was no appetite. He noted also the fineness of the napkin with which the tray was covered, the thin transparency of the china bowl, and that the spoon was apparently solid silver, old and thin as if it were an heirloom, but bright and unmistakably of aristocratic origin and pleasant withal to use. He noticed these things because they had been a part of his former existence before he had given his life up to saving souls, and because since he came to live in boarding-houses, he had sometimes missed their absence in a vague, undefined way. He had not known that he cared about these little accessories of a refined life, but he was conscious that he recognized a friendly look in that spoon and bowl and fine linen. He did not know that these things were among the very few bits of home that Miss Grant had brought with her, and that she had carefully hunted them out of a trunk that had not yet been unpacked, because she felt that perhaps these dishes might help in the work of saving that soul.

Nor was she wrong. Harry knew silver when he saw it. This lunch seemed like one his mother would have prepared for him.

"Now, sir," said Mr. Stafford, as he lighted the gas and prepared to be cheerful while the young man ate his supper, "you must forget everything about this for a while, and just eat your supper and enjoy it." He laughed pleasantly, and Harry looked up with a wan smile and thanked him in his heart for lifting the heavy burden for a few minutes. Mr. Stafford could talk, even if Harry just then could not, and he showed that he had no trouble in summoning to his command just the right thing at the right time. He began to tell in detail the story of a young man in whom he was interested, who had a wife and young family dependent upon his effort, and who was out of work, and unable to find a position. He had spent some time that day trying to find him work, unsuccessfully, and he told his various efforts describing the different employers so well, that once Harry forgot his own troubles and was beguiled into a laugh.

Celia, passing the door just then, heard them laughing and one more little wrinkle crept into her white brow of care. She thought Mr. Stafford must be a queer minister to laugh with a young man who had recently committed so grave an offence against the laws of God and of society. Poor Celia, she had had a hard day, what with doing her own work, and carrying on her heart the thought of Harry Knowles drunk. It was not that she cared more for that boy than she would have done for any other, but it was the shock to her faith in human nature to find one whom she had believed to be at least tolerably good and interesting, suddenly appear in the condition in which he had been. Young people are often prone to look upon their faith in human nature as something akin to their faith in God, something holy and religious, which if broken outrages their belief almost in the kindness of their God. Perhaps this is the reason that sometimes, sweet honest souls have to pass through the fiery trial of believing in, even to loving, some human brother or sister, only to find them utterly false. Such need to learn the lesson of quaint George Herbert, that

> "Even the greatest griefs
> May be reliefs,
> Could he but take them right, and in their ways.
> Happy is he whose heart
> Hath found the art
> To turn his double pains to double praise."

16

"It's my opinion," said Molly Poppleton, standing with her arms akimbo and facing Miss Grant as she entered the kitchen one morning shortly after breakfast, "that them three-cent girls need 'tendin' to." She set her lips firmly and then returned to the polishing of her range.

Miss Hannah went on with her work. She was rubbing pumpkin through a colander and reducing it to the velvety texture she always required in her pies. She waited calmly for Molly to go on with her reasons, as she knew she would soon. Molly finished the oven door and stood up again.

"Yes, they need 'tendin' to bad. If you'd just go up to their room once you'd find out. There's a stack of paper novils in their closet knee deep, an' there's pictures round that room of women from the-*ay*-tres, without much clo'es on, that are perfickly scand'lous. Besides, they've got a picture of them two took in a tin type down to Atlantic City with bathing suits on, an' two young fellers along side of 'em without much on but a little underclo'es. They are grinning fit to kill, and look real silly. No decent girls would have a picture took like that, let alone keep it round in sight afterward."

"Well, Molly, you know all girls have not been brought up alike," said Miss Hannah, as she measured out the cinnamon and ginger. "Molly, bring me the big yellow bowl and the molasses jug."

"I should hope not," said Molly, as she put the jug down on the table with a thump, and went back to her range. "Not like them, anyways. You don't know all. They have any amount of little pink and blue tickets lying round droppin' out of pockets and the like, an' I give that one they call Mamie one I picked up in the hall, thinkin' it was something valuable, an' she laughed an' said it was no good, just an old the-*ay*-tre ticket, been used. 'My land!' said I, not being able to keep still. 'If all them round your room is the-*ay*-tre tickets, you must've been an awful lot!' Then she giggled an' got red an' says, 'Yes, most every night now,' an' the other one, the one they call Carrie, she spoke up, and says she, 'Yes, she's got plenty of gentlemen friends, Molly, an' so have I,' an' then they both laughed and went out. Now I s'pose it ain't none of my business, but I must say them girls ought to be back with their mothers. They can't be over fifteen a day, or sixteen anyway. They ought to be in bed every night by nine o'clock. They ain't fit to sit at the same table with Miss Celia with their bangs and their dirty teeth and black finger nails. The fact is I'd like to give 'em both a good bath anyway."

Molly slammed out of the kitchen and Miss Hannah heard her sweeping the dining-room with all her might and main.

She went on measuring her milk and beating her eggs, and fashioning the flaky crust in the pie pans, and thinking. The fact was she had been troubled about those two girls herself. She felt that they needed a great deal of help and so far she had been utterly unable to approach them. They seemed shy and uncomfortable when she came near them, and had grown silent at the table, too, unless the tenor brakeman was present. Then the three carried on a bantering conversation in suppressed tones, with half glances toward the others. Miss Grant wondered why it was that there always seemed to be some people about her whose hearts she could not reach. It was just so with Nettie, she never could make any headway in training that child. As a little girl, she had been sullen and silent when she was remonstrated with by her aunt for any fault, and as a young woman she had been impertinent and cold for days after any attempt on the part of aunt Hannah to change her plans. With Hiram too, aunt Hannah had felt the same repellent influence and she wondered why it was, though she had prayerfully and conscientiously longed to be to these people what God wanted her to be, that she did not seem able to reach their hearts in any way. Now these two girls weighed heavily upon her. She had watched them for days and had determined to make some move pretty soon. She felt sure there was need of help for them, and urgent need, far beyond what Molly had bluntly expressed. And while aunt Hannah weighed and measured and baked and thought, she was making in her mind a plan for the salvation of Mamie Williams and Carrie Simmons.

She had noticed Mamie several times lately when Celia came to the table, and she knew that she watched Celia intently and admired her afar, at least she admired her in so far as outward adornments were concerned. Even during the few weeks since aunt Hannah had come to Philadelphia, she had noticed the gradual change in Mamie's dress, from gay and fussy and frivolous, to a style somewhat more subdued and neat. She had reduced the baggy bunches of frizzy hair that used to project over her forehead and loop far down over her ears, till they were more like Celia's graceful braids with a stray curl slipping out here and there. She still wore her many colored finger rings, but there were other little changes about her that showed she was to a certain extent making Celia a model just now. Aunt Hannah's brow cleared. She thought she knew a way to Mamie's heart and perhaps through hers to Carrie's. Celia had an influence and she could help. But how to bring that about in the wisest way, that was aunt Hannah's puzzle, for Celia was very much disgusted with the actions of the two "three-centers" as she called them. She never noticed them in any way, and her dignified bearing at the table was always meant to be a rebuke to them. Celia did not like those two girls, and while she was willing that their lives should be made more comfortable by their sharing in the good food that aunt Hannah now provided for Mrs. Morris' old boarders, still Celia would not have felt badly to have had them leave that their places might be occupied by more interesting people.

Celia was getting to be a sort of puzzle anyway. She did not enter into some things as her aunt had supposed she would. Instead she held aloof, and seemed troubled about something. She did not even make friends with the young minister, in whom aunt Hannah saw growing possibilities of a valued friendship for them all. He and she had talked together on the themes of mutual interest, and he had shown that he was a man of culture and education. Aunt Hannah was not a matchmaker, and did not immediately think of every young man in the light of a possible husband for her dear Celia, but she did have ambitions that Celia might have friends who would be helpful in every way to her, both spiritually and mentally, and she felt that such a friendship, though it were nothing more than occasional converse on some literary theme, would be excellent for the young girl whose ambitions and abilities were so far beyond her opportunities. But Celia only smiled, and remained quiet and distant, and told aunt Hannah that the young minister belonged to her, and she must not expect her niece to take him on faith. Nevertheless, she knew that no movement or word of Mr. Stafford's at the table escaped Celia. It was evident that she was measuring him.

Celia had not entered very heartily into the plans made for Harry Knowles. She had done what she was told, it was true, but she had not made plans herself. She seemed to have received a set-back on the night when Harry came home drunk. There had been much to do in the evening, however, and her aunt had not had time to have a good long talk with her. She felt it ought to come at once. She put the pies in the oven, closed the oven door carefully, and glancing at the clock went to her own room to kneel as was her custom in perplexity and lay her trouble all at her Master's feet. Then she came back to her work about the house with calm brow and untroubled heart, feeling sure the way would be opened and words given her, if she must speak. She would have made a good model for a study of a saint as she stood beside the moulding board soon after and patted the smooth, light loaves into shape for their last rising, bending her sweet, thoughtful face to her work, her mind busy with the problems of souls, while she worked with her hands to feed their bodies.

It was like a revelation of what God can do in a human soul through sorrow, to look at Hannah Grant and think of her past life and its buried and risen joys.

> "Methinks we do as fretful children do,
> Leaning their faces on the window pane
> To sigh the glass dim with their own breath's stain,
> And shut the sky and landscape from their view.
> And thus, alas! since God, the Maker, drew
> A mystic separation 'twixt those twain,
> The life beyond us, and our souls in pain,
> We miss the prospect which we're called unto

By grief we're fools to use. Be still and strong,
O man, my brother! hold thy sobbing breath,
And keep thy soul's large window pure from wrong,
That so, as life's appointment issueth,
Thy vision may be clear to watch along
The sunset consummation-lights of death."

"Auntie, who is the youth in the parlor so redolent of Hoyt's German cologne and cigarette smoke?" asked Celia, gaily, coming into her aunt's room just after dinner that night. "You opened the door for him, you ought to know. I do hope he is not a new boarder, for I'm morally certain he wouldn't be any help, and I think we have enough heathen to work for at present, don't you? Now don't tell me you called me up to ask my permission to take in that oily-looking youth, aunt Hannah."

Aunt Hannah laughed and then grew grave.

"No, dear, not that," she said, and then she drew the little rocker close beside her own and said "Sit down, dear, I want to talk to you."

"Why, aunt Hannah, what have I been doing that's naughty?" asked Celia, pretending to be scared. "This sounds like old times," but she settled herself comfortably and nestled her head lovingly on her aunt's shoulder.

"Well then, first of all, Celia, why do you act so strangely sometimes, and what is the matter with Mr. Stafford? You and he ought to be friends, and he could help much in the work you planned we should do together. You seem to me to have lost your interest in the house and everything in it, and I do not understand it. There is much that you could do and ought to do at once, and you do not seem to care to go about it."

"Why, aunt Hannah, what has the minister to do with it all? I am afraid you are mistaken in him as a helper. In fact I know you are. I had just come home that night — the night after Harry had been drinking, you know, — and was passing the door, and I heard Mr. Stafford's laugh, and then I heard Harry laugh, too, and I couldn't help hearing that Mr. Stafford was telling a funny story to Harry as I went on up the hall. Now just think of that after what had happened. A pretty minister he is, I think. He ought to have been preaching a sermon."

"Celia! Take care how you judge without knowing. You cannot tell what may have been the pointed moral of the funny story, and you do not know but the Lord could use a laugh just then to help that young man better than anything else, and he doubtless put it into the heart of his servant to know that. I believe that man has rare tact in winning souls. Be very careful, and be very slow ever to criticize the actions of a minister. His office brings him nearer to God than most men."

Celia's cheeks flushed a little. She was slightly annoyed to have her aunt speak in that way, but she respected the elder woman's opinion too much to resent the words or refuse the lesson. After a moment she said:

"Well, aunt Hannah, maybe I have been wrong, I'll try to be good." In her heart Celia had another reason for her dignified coldness toward the minister. She had recognized, after a few days, that he was a man of unusual education and refinement. She immediately began to wonder whether or not he looked down upon her, a saleswoman in a store, a poor girl, who had to earn her own living. She settled it in her mind that he probably did in a certain undefined way, though he probably did not confess such things to himself as that might have conflicted with certain Christian theories he felt himself bound to abide by. She told herself that he should see that she never expected anything in the way of courtesy even from him, and that she was one girl in the world, who was not ready to fling herself forward for companionship with any desirable young man that should chance to be thrown in her neighborhood. She had been still further strengthened in her determination by a little occurrence one evening a few days before this talk with her aunt.

The minister had gone to prayer meeting, having been busily engaged in his room all day, so that aunt Hannah had not been able to finish certain dusting and setting to rights there as thoroughly as she desired. The evening had found her hands full of some kitchen work, and she had requested Celia to slip up there when the halls were quiet, while the occupant of the room was in meeting and finish the dusting. Celia had been glad to help. She had turned the gas up and gone to work in earnest, glancing interestedly at the rows of books over the little table against the wall, and wishing she had opportunity to look them over, but she would not put so much as a hand upon them except to do her necessary work, in the absence of their owner. When she came to the bureau she had to remove some things to wipe the dust off beneath them. A Bible was lying there open before a painted miniature of a most lovely young woman. The pictured face was so beautiful that she could not but look at it again as she carefully wiped the dust from the velvet and gold of its case. The blue eyes and golden hair and the sweet intellectual face stayed in her memory, and from the fact that the miniature stood open before his Bible, she judged it was some one quite near and dear. Celia did not reason it out in words, but she thought it well that she should maintain a maidenly dignity. However, as her aunt talked, she saw that she had carried this feeling to an absurd extremity. What was it to her what the young man thought, or how many velvet-framed girls he carried in his pocket next his heart? She was in the same house with him and must treat him with Christian courtesy, and she need not necessarily make herself prominent before his eyes either. She would try to do differently. He should henceforth be as one of the other boarders to her.

"What else, auntie?" she asked, after a minute of thought, looking up.

"Harry, next," said her aunt. "You ought to interest him in something occasionally, as you once told me you did in a lamp. He is having a very hard struggle to keep away from those companions who are after him every day now, Mr. Stafford says. He does all he can for him, but you know his meetings occupy so many evenings that he can do very little and he hasn't thought it wise to try to take him to church yet. You know he's nothing but a boy. He wants to be interested in something.''

"Yes," said Celia, "I know. I'll try. But, auntie, I can't forget how he looked that night," and she shuddered. "But I'll try to get up something to help and that right away. Now what else? You always save the worst dose till the last, I know you of old. Which is it? Miss Burns or the tenor brakeman? Or — O *auntie,* now it *isn't* those three-centers! Don't tell me to try to do something for them, for I can't," and the girl put up her hands in mock horror.

Miss Grant detailed to her what she knew of them including an account of Molly's moralizing on the subject, and Celia laughed, and then grew grave.

There came a call to the kitchen for Miss Grant then and she left Celia thinking. When she returned a few minutes later she was greeted with "Aunt Hannah, are those boards still in the cellar? Are they of any use there? Because if they are not I'm going to make a cozy corner in the parlor if you don't object. I've thought of a beautiful way. Harry will help, I'm sure. He sat in the parlor looking glum when I came up. Do you suppose I must get the three-centers to help? Would they come, do you think? And say, by the way, auntie, who did you say that oily youth in the parlor was?"

"His name, he said, was Mr. Clarence Jones and he asked for Miss Simmons. I called her and I think she went out with him, for I don't see either of them about. I don't know whether Mamie Williams is in her room or not. I think it would be a good plan to see. By all means make as many cozy corners as you please, dear, and the boards are of no use to me."

Celia departed to find her helpers, and Miss Hannah locked the door and prayed for them before she went about darning some tablecloths.

17

"Now, Harry, where are you going?" said Celia, with dismay in her voice, as she ran down the stairs and saw that young man with his overcoat on and his hat in his hand just opening the front door.

He started and looked guilty as she spoke. In truth, he had been sitting in the parlor for an hour trying to keep himself in the house, and away from an especially alluring evening the boys had held out as bait; and one, too, which seemed, from their account of it, to be perfectly harmless.

He hesitated and stammered out:

"Nowhere, I guess," and then laughed and sat down in the hall chair. "Is there anything I can do for you, Miss Murray? The fact is I don't quite know what to do with myself tonight, for some reason."

Celia's heart filled with pity for the poor lonely fellow and with remorse that she had not sooner attempted to do something to cheer him up.

"Oh, I'm so sorry," she said, earnestly, with a true ring of her voice which he recognized at once. "But if you are lonesome and really have nothing pressing to do, why take off your coat and come and help me carry out a scheme. I'm going to make a cozy corner in the parlor. In fact, I think I'll make two, one in the bay window and one over there by the organ. Will you help? You're such a good carpenter, you know, and this parlor does look so bare and desolate."

"All right, I'm with you," answered the young man, taking off his overcoat with alacrity. "Only tell me what to do. I don't know the first thing about cozy corners, but if you know as much as you did about lamps, I'll be willing to say they'll be a success. Let's have a half-dozen of 'em if you say so. Now what'll I do first?"

"Bring that lamp and come down into the cellar. Wait, I don't know whether you can do it alone, they are pretty heavy and there are a good many. Perhaps Mr. Hartley or Mr. Osborn would help a minute in bringing up the boards. I'll show you what we want first, and then you can pick out the right boards. You see I want a good firm seat here in the bay window to fill the whole place to the edge of the window frames either side, just a foot from the floor, so, and then I want another over here, to reach from here to here, so wide, and the same height from the floor. Here is my tape measure. Now you can pick out your lumber." Celia moved about the dull uninteresting parlor, furnishing it with gesture and imagination, till the young carpenter was quite interested. He called the two young men upstairs, who came willingly and

94

helped for a few minutes showing not a little interest and curiosity in the undertaking. They all lingered with advice and offers to help, and when Celia had seen the carpentry work well started, she ran upstairs and knocked at the door of the two young girls.

"Come in," drawled the voice of some one chewing, and after a moment's hesitation she entered.

Mamie Williams lay across the foot of the bed, the two pillows and a comforter under her head, the gas turned as high as it would go, and a paper-covered volume in her hand. She was chewing gum. When she saw that it was Celia who had entered, her tone of indifference changed to one of pleased surprise. She sat up quickly and hid her book beneath the pillows. Then she put her hand up to straighten her hair.

"Why, it is you!" she exclaimed, and Celia knew that her aunt's conjecture that she was admired by this girl was true, from the evident pleasure the visit gave. This unbent Celia still more, and she tried to be winning. When Celia tried she was very winning indeed.

"We are having some fun downstairs fixing up that old barn of a parlor," she explained, still standing by the door, though her hostess had slipped from the bed and cleared a chair from a pile of clothing thrown upon it. "I thought maybe you would like to help. Is your friend here?"

"No, she ain't, she's gone out with a gentleman friend," said Mamie, with a conscious giggle. "It's a wonder you found me in. I'm mostly out when she is. Sit down, can't you? I'm really glad you come up, I was lonesome. The book I had wasn't any account either. What did you say you were doing?"

Celia essayed to explain and succeeded in interesting Mamie to the extent that she hunted out her thimble from a mass of ribbons and collars tumbled into a bureau drawer, and went downstairs to see what was going on, though she confessed she was not much used to doing things like that.

They went to work in good earnest. Celia had some printed burlap, which she had brought home from the store one night to make curtains for an improvised clothespress, in her room. It was cheap and there was plenty of it. The clothespress could wait. Those cozy corners must be finished to-night, at least as far as possible. She gave the tick of the cushions to Mamie to run the seams, while she applied herself to sewing the burlap cover for it. Meanwhile, the hammering and sawing and directing went forward, and by half-past nine when Mr. Stafford opened the front door and came in there were two very solid looking rough wooden shelves a foot from the floor, in the parlor, one occupying the entire bay window space in the front of the room, the other one being at the further end of the room. To the sides of this Harry Knowles was just nailing some more boards to serve as ends, under the supervision of the other two young men, while Celia and Mamie were upon their knees in front of the bay window tacking the dark blue burlap printed in a heraldic design, in a pleated valance. A nearly completed cushion lay beside them on the floor, but not tied as yet. Mr. Stafford, attracted by the unusual noises, entered the room and stood behind them looking at the work a moment. Then, as Celia turned from the valance and attempted to thread a large needle with a cord and then vainly endeavored to pull its short proportions through the thick cushion, which had been stuffed with excelsior and a layer of cotton on the top, he said quietly:

"You need an upholsterer's needle for that, Miss Murray. I think I have one upstairs that we used in fixing up the pulpit chairs at the mission. I'll go and get it."

Celia was pleased that he entered into the work and thanked him. As he turned toward Harry, he said, "Knowles, why don't you put springs in? It would be twice as comfortable."

"Springs!" said Harry jumping up and facing round. "Do you expect us to turn into upholsterers the first night?" and he laughed good-naturedly.

"No, but indeed it isn't a difficult job," explained the minister, "you just have to tie them down firmly. I'll show you if you don't mind running out with me to that little upholsterer's around the corner. I think it's open yet. It was when I came by. The people live over the store and they don't shut up shop early."

"By all means, let us have springs," answered Celia to Harry's look of enquiry. "I didn't look for such luxury as that, but we will take what grandeur we can get." Her cheeks had grown red with excitement, and her eyes were shining. The minister, as he turned to go on his self-appointed errand, was reminded of the first evening he had come to that house. Harry and Mr. Stafford were soon back with several sets of springs and the three young men, with Celia demurely in the background, took a lesson in putting in springs, which they found to be not such a very difficult matter after all. The minister had not forgotten to get some small dark blue cotton upholstery buttons when he was out, and Mamie and Celia soon learned how to use the queer double pointed needle and tie the cushion with the little buttons. Altogether it looked very pretty, and quite like real upholsterer's work when it was finished.

In spite of the proverbial "many hands" and "light work," it was nearly eleven o'clock when the two seats were finished, and a light frame work over the seat in the back end of the parlor erected. Miss Hannah had come down to send them all to bed, but found them in a state of childish enthusiasm to see their work completed. Celia had remembered that she had upstairs two or three pieces of plain and printed denim and some turkey red calico. Mounted on the stepladder beside the canopy frame, she deftly draped the rough wood, being materially assisted by Mr. Stafford who seemed to understand what she wanted to do, and to be able to drape a graceful fold of cloth, if he *was* only a man, and that a minister. He, by way of contribution, brought down a Chinese sword made of coins which the Chinese use as a talisman, for the purpose of frightening away evil spirits, and hung it above the drapery. This roused the others to emulate his example. The university student thought he knew where he could get a couple of Arabic spears to help out that canopy drapery, and Harry Knowles declared he would hunt around and find one of those dull old filigree bull's-eye lanterns that hang by long chains from the centre. Mamie said her contribution should be a couple of sofa pillows, and Celia promised to make some more. Miss Burns, coming in just then looking weary and worn, brightened as she came into the parlor and exclaimed over the new furnishings, "They are simply, — now — simply — *fine* — aren't they, Miss Grant? Indeed they *are!* What *wonderful* taste and *skill* have been exhibited here! I declare it is *simply marvelous! Simply fine!* Indeed — *indeed* — it is!" she giggled wearily. She asked permission to contribute a pillow also.

"Now we need a low bookcase running along that wall and turning that corner," said the minister, as they turned to go to their rooms. "Can't you manage that, Knowles?" and Celia's eyes sparkled over the idea. The minister evidently understood esthetics anyway. The bookcase would be a great addition. She went upstairs so excited over her new work she could hardly sleep. She had almost forgotten her three-cent protégée, till Mamie squeezed her hand over the stair railing and said, "Good-night, Miss Murray, I've enjoyed myself ever so much. And say, would you mind coming into my room a few minutes tomorrow night? I want to ask you some questions very particular."

Celia promised readily enough, though the prospect was not a pleasant one, but she had made up her mind to try to help this girl, so she might as well accept the situation and the opportunity together.

But aunt Hannah sat up that night till nearly one o'clock, and looked over the stair railing till she heard the night key click, and saw the befeathered hat of Carrie Simmons as she came airily in.

"Poor child!" murmured the watcher, as she turned out the hall light and went to bed, "something must be done! Out till one o'clock and with that kind of a young man!"

The next morning she noticed that Carrie had dark rings under her eyes, and was developing thin, sharp lines about her nose and mouth, which did not add beauty to her pert, weak face.

The next evening as Celia started for Mamie Williams' room, Carrie having again departed with the aforementioned youth, aunt Hannah called her. "Celia dear, two things," she said, with her hand on Celia's arm. "Don't forget to pray before you go, and if you get a chance mention soap and water. Don't forget that cleanliness is next to godliness. Perhaps in this case it comes first." Celia laughed and said, "All right, auntie," and went back to her room to take the first advice given.

Reinforced by a turning of her heart to her heavenly Father for guidance, she went to her unpleasant task, her mind more than half full of the new bookcase and some other plans she had for the adornment of the parlor. The minister seemed to have taken Harry Knowles away with him immediately after dinner, so she had no one to help her carry out any parlor schemes just at present, and she could not help being disappointed that she must turn aside to another piece of work.

Mamie was evidently expecting her this time. She had given the room some semblance of a cleaning up: that is, she had picked up Carrie's old store dress from the floor where she left it, and tumbled everything that was out of place on the bureau and table into a drawer, for the confusion of some future hour of need.

She seemed to be in earnest, and plunged at once into her subject when she had seated Celia.

"Say, I thought maybe you wouldn't mind telling me how you do it. You see I thought you wasn't any more pretty than I, and you haven't got expensive clo'es, but you manage somehow to look awful stylish and pretty in spite of it. I know it takes a knack, but don't you think I could learn? I've been trying ever since you came here to do my hair the way you do, but I can't make it act right. I thought maybe you wouldn't mind doing it a few times for me, to get me started, and perhaps you could tell me what the difference is between you and me. I know it ain't very polite to ask you things like this, but I thought you was so kind last night asking me to help that I'd just be bold and ask you. You ain't mad, are you?"

Celia ignored the doubtful compliments and tried to smile, albeit her very soul shrank within her. What, handle the coarse greasy hair of that girl who seemed actually dirty to her? How could she? Surely the Lord did not require that sacrifice. Why had she undertaken this task anyway? It was *dreadful*. She half rose from her chair, as she began to foresee the magnitude of the possible proportions of this proposition. What might she not be asked to do? Then she remembered whose she was and whom she served, and sank back again in her chair, putting up a petition for help to her heavenly Father.

> "What is prayer? ...
> 'Tis the telegraphic cord,
> Holding converse with the Lord;
> 'Tis the key of promise given
> Turning in the lock of heaven."

18

"Do you think I'm too homely to fix up?" anxiously asked Mamie, as her visitor did not at once respond.

"Oh no, indeed!" said Celia, laughing, "I was only trying to think how to answer you, and it's so funny for you to want to copy me. I have never tried to be 'pretty' as you call it. I only tried to be clean and neat, and have things look as nice as I could without spending much money. But now that you've asked me, if you really want to know how you could improve your appearance, in my eyes at least, I'll try to tell you a few things. What is it that troubles you most? We'll begin with that."

"Oh my sakes!" giggled Mamie. "There's so many things. Well, my hands and my feet. They're so big, and in the way. My hands are red and rough and bony, and my face is always breaking out in little ugly black pimples, and my hair won't get into any shape I want it to, and my teeth aren't pretty, and then of course my clothes, and I just *wish* I could walk across a room like you," she finished with a sigh.

Celia laughed and began.

"Your hands," she said, "let me see them." She turned up the gas and surveyed them critically a moment, while Mamie waited in breathless anxiety comparing her red, beringed fingers to Celia's small white ones.

"Well, if I were you I would take all those rings off first," said Celia, decidedly. "They look gaudy and out of place, except perhaps on a woman in society, and even then I should prefer to see just one or two at a time, and not a whole jewelry store at once."

Mamie looked disappointed. She drew them off slowly. "I thought they were pretty," she said, the least bit of dismay in her voice. "Don't you like any rings?"

"Not for young girls, — unless they mean something. Have you any that have tender associations?"

"Some," simpered Mamie looking self-conscious.

Celia ignored or did not understand this answer. "Which one?" she asked. "Did your mother, or father, or brother, or sister give it to you?"

Mamie blushed. "Well, yes, I have got one Ma give me, but it isn't any of them. It's a little plain gold thing, looks kind of out of style now. I don't wear it any more."

"I'd wear that one," said the oracle, "and put the others all away. You're too young to have rings given you to wear by strangers. Now about training those hands, I can give you some little exercises that they gave me when I was taking music lessons, which I think help the hands to be graceful. First, if I were you, I would go into the bathroom and give them a good washing in hot soap suds, finishing off with cold water. That will make them more pliable. Have you a nail brush? You ought to have one. There is nothing like it for making the nails look rosy. I suppose you find great trouble in keeping them clean, working all day, don't you? I do. But a nail brush makes the work much easier. I would cut the nails more in this shape if I were you, see?" Celia held out one seashell tipped hand to be inspected.

When the hands were duly scrubbed, Celia gave her a short lesson in Delsarte, an exercise for each joint of the finger and hand. Mamie's eyes sparkled and she proved herself an apt pupil. "Now," said Celia, "practice that, but be sure you never do it where any one can see you. It will have its effect on your movements in time, but never practice in public. Don't think about your hands. That's the best way to do. If they are clean they will take care of themselves, and the more you think about them and think how awkward they are, the more awkward they become. Did you never try making people stop staring at you by looking hard at their feet in the street cars? Well, try it some time. It is very funny. I have been annoyed once or twice by somebody staring at me till I was very uncomfortable. I remembered what I had read somewhere, and looked down at their feet as if I was very much interested in them. They very soon took their eyes from me and began to draw their feet back out of sight and to fidget around and wonder what was the matter with their shoes."

Mamie laughed and looked at her new teacher with admiration. She began to think she had made a mistake in saying Celia was not pretty.

"Now the complexion," began Celia again in a businesslike tone. "Your general health will affect that. You ought not to eat much fat or sweets for one thing, and you ought to bathe all over every day and rub your skin till it's all in a glow. That will make a great difference in the complexion. How often do you bathe?"

"Oh my!" gasped Mamie, "I do hate to take a bath. Why, Ma used always to scrub us children all around once a week, and I s'pose I'd ought to keep that up, but sometimes I do skip a week, it's so dreadful cold in the morning."

"Well, if I were you I would bathe every day, for a while anyway. You don't know what a lot of good it will do you, and after a while you will get to love it. Once a week you ought to have a thorough wash with warm water and plenty of soap, and finish off with a cold dash, and a good hard rub, and then every morning take a sponge off in cold water and a good rubbing. That you will find will make your complexion very different. Then I would give the face some treatment of hot and cold water. Wash it in water just as hot as you can stand it every morning and then in very cold. That will make your cheeks have some color, too, I think. As for your teeth, let me see them. Oh,

Mamie, it's too bad to let such nice even teeth get into such a condition. They are hopelessly black, and you can't get them white yourself. Do you brush them every day, after every meal?"

"My land, no!" exclaimed Mamie. "What an awful nuisance that would be! I never had a tooth brush but once, and then Carrie used it to scrub the ink off her fingers when she was going to the theatre."

Celia could scarcely repress the exclamation of disgust that rose to her lips on this announcement, but Mamie was luckily too interested in her own words to hear.

"Don't you think I could ever do anything with my teeth?"

"Why yes, you must go to a dentist at once and have them attended to. They need a good cleaning, and while you are there you ought to have him go over your teeth and put them in first-class order. It doesn't pay to let your teeth go before you are a woman yet. He will tell you how to take care of them. You ought not to eat much candy or to chew gum. That injures the teeth."

"Oh!" said Mamie, in a sort of despair. "You don't have much fun, do you, if you try to do all them things? But I don't mind, for I do want to look pretty, an' I'm willin' for it all, if it'll do any good."

Celia's pulses quickened, for she thought if this girl would do so much for the outward adorning, perhaps she might be able some time to persuade her to do as much for the beautiful inward adorning of a meek and quiet spirit which is in the sight of God of great price.

"Then your hair," went on Celia, "needs to be washed often. I would wash it first with powdered borax in the water. It isn't good to use borax often, for it makes the hair so brittle it breaks, but it will take out the extra oil now, and that is what you need. Then it will need to be thoroughly rinsed, and dried and combed. After that you can do almost anything you want to with it. I'll let you watch me do mine once, and then you will see how it is done. That is the best way to learn. And then about your dress, why that is a long subject. You will need to take a lot of time for that. You'll have to decide things one at a time. One rule I go by, in buying. I never buy a thing that is in the very extreme of fashion, because for one reason it will look queer very soon, and for another it is sure to be poor material, or else it is very expensive. It is always best to get good material. The plainer things are the better, you can be sure, as a general rule. Then you ought to study your complexion and eyes and buy things to become you. You will excuse me, if I mention the necktie you have on. I don't think you ought ever to wear that color. Cerise may be becoming to some people with dark eyes and a very clear complexion, but it ought not to be worn by blue-eyed people with light brown hair. Dark blue would be more becoming to you. Then too, I think a necktie is an unbecoming thing on you anyway. You would look much better in a close, round collar."

Mamie looked down at her cherished silk scarf, to be able to buy which she had gone without new stockings for some time. Her mind was something akin to the maiden's about whom our grandmothers used to tell, who said: "I ken wear my palm-leaf and go bare-footed, but I *must* have a buzzom pin."

Celia's zeal was perhaps on the eve of getting the better of her wisdom. She was growing interested in making over this girl as her aunt was interested in making over Mrs. Morris' boarding-house, and she forgot that there were probably a long line of prejudices to be overcome before the girl would be willing to walk in the way laid out for her, even though she had asked to be directed in that path. It would look thorny to her at first.

"Mamie," she said, seeing the downcast expression on the young girl's face, "don't get discouraged with all these new things. You can't do every one of them right at first, but, do you know, I think it makes a great difference when people try to be and look the best that is in them. You must not think you are a homely looking girl. You are not. You were meant to be a pretty one, and I think you can make yourself look ever so much prettier, I do indeed. Now I wonder if you would be willing to do something just to please me."

"Why of course I would!" said Mamie, readily enough and brightening up at the encouraging words. "What is it? You've been awful kind to me and I sha'n't forget it, Miss Murray," she added.

"Well then, it is this. You see out in Cloverdale, where I used to live, I belonged to a little society of girls. We were each pledged to read one verse of the Bible every day, and to pray every day, and when some of us left the home and the society, we each promised to try and get up another band where we were going, even if we could get but one other person to join it. Now I was wondering if you wouldn't join it to start my new circle? We called ourselves the Bible Band. I believe there are a good many such bands all over the country. We have this little gold badge. Isn't it pretty?" and Celia held out a tiny scarf pin with a pendant gold heart, on which were the letters engraved B. B. "If you will join us, I'll give you this pin of mine, and I can send and get another."

Mamie grew interested as soon as she saw the pin. Jewelry of all sorts was attractive to her. It would be quite delightful to appear in the store with a new pin on, engraved with mysterious letters, and let the girls and the young men there try to guess what they meant. Of course she didn't need to tell them if she didn't want to. She asked again what would be required of her, though Mamie belonged to the class, from which are derived so many untrue members of the Christian Endeavor societies, and, sad to say, also of the church; that class who are eager and willing to join anything, and care very little what obligations they thus take upon themselves; as little as they care when they break these solemn vows. To such, indeed, might apply the many and various arguments against pledge taking, not because pledge taking is bad, but because the pledgers themselves are not made to understand the solemnity of the pledge they take. Mamie cared very little what pledge she took, so long as the performing of it might be done in private and at her own discretion. She did not stop to think long, but accepted the pledge card and donned the pin with pride, thanking Celia.

"Though I ain't much of a hand at prayin', Miss Murray, I never could think of anything to say when I was a little girl, and Ma used to make us say our prayers every Saturday night. I guess I could learn a prayer and say the same one every time, if that would do. You write me out one, can't you? 'Course I'll do it to please you, you've been so good to me, and I'm awfully obliged for this pin. It's a beauty, and won't I have fun to-morrow at the store with it? Say, I don't mind telling you why I want all this fixin' up to be pretty, you know. You won't tell Carrie, will you? I wouldn't have her know, for the first you'd see her settin' up to the same thing. Why, you see it's this way. There's a new boss to our store. The head of the firm's going out to Chicago, and he's put this feller, Mr. Adams, Harold Adams his name is, in at the head. He's only just nineteen or twenty, though he made them think he was twenty-one, but he's dreadful smart. His father's been at the head of a three-cent store in Baltimore for a long time, and he kind of growed up in the business. He's handsome, too, and everybody likes him, and the girls will just stand on their heads to please him, and you see he's been payin' me attention for four weeks now, takin' me to theatres, and gettin' me flowers and candy, and all the other girls was hoppin' mad. They've just done everything they could to get him to look at them, but he never did till there came a new girl to the china teacup counter. She has gold hair and I believe she paints her cheeks, and she's awful stylish, and has the littlest mite of a waist, and he's just gone clean crazy over her. He's nice to me yet, but she gets half the flowers now, and I want to get him back. You see, I don't mind telling you I'm in love with him myself, and of course I ain't willin' to just give him up without tryin', so I made up my mind if I could get to be good lookin' an' stylish, maybe I could do something."

Before Celia had time to collect her thoughts and say something in response to this startling disclosure, there came a hurried knock at the door, and Molly Poppleton's strong voice demanded, "Is Miss Celia there? Miss Hannah, she wants her right away bad. That old lady upstairs's got a fainting spell. She says to come right away."

Celia dropped everything and ran. She wondered afterward if the heavenly Father arranged that call to her for just that moment on purpose to prevent her saying anything to Mamie, for she felt sure if she had spoken then she would have expressed her mind in what might have proved, for the sake of her influence on the girl, the wrong words.

> "Blind unbelief is sure to err,
>   And scan his work in vain;
> God is his own interpreter,
>   And he will make it plain."

19

Old Mrs. Belden was made comfortable at last. It appeared that she had worked too hard for the last three weeks, sitting up far into the night to finish an order. She was a knitter of fancy hoods, sacques, socks and mittens. Miss Hannah, while she ministered to her, heard a feeble account of the poor soul's life. Her husband and her children were all dead, except one boy who was a sailor, and who, perhaps, might be dead, too, for she had not heard from him for over four years. She resorted to the only thing she knew how to do to earn her living, and it had been pretty hard work sometimes, though, perhaps, no harder than many another woman had to do. She was very thankful for the good food which had come in with the advent of Miss Grant. She murmured her gratitude in an apologetic way for everything that was done for her, and said she did not see why they made so much trouble, they might just as well have let her slip quietly away, if it had been the Lord's will. Her life wasn't worth much anyway, and she was only making a lot of trouble that would all have to be done over again pretty soon, maybe. Miss Hannah and Celia had looked around the room and resolved that there should be more comforts there before another night, and when she was at last ready for sleep, and they felt sure that all she needed to restore her to her usual health was a good rest, they left her, with a promise from Molly Poppleton, whose room was next to Mrs. Belden's, that she would sleep with one ear open and step in occasionally to see that she was all right and give her anything she needed.

Celia sat down on the bed and rested her forehead on the footboard, after she and her aunt had gone to their room for the night.

"Aunt Hannah," she said, "I'm just discouraged. There are so many things to worry about in the world I don't see how I can keep from it."

"Celia! Celia!" said aunt Hannah, laying her hand on the brown head bent on the footboard, "is my little girl questioning the wisdom of God? You sound like a little child, to-night, who thinks his parents cruel that they will not give him fire to play with. Remember that God knows all, and that he does all for good. It may be that old lady needs just the kind of thing she is going through now to fit her for heaven. I do not know whether she is getting ready for heaven or not. Maybe God had to call her to himself by taking all her dear ones first, or maybe she is set to be a help to some one else, — perhaps you. Does my little girl doubt him because she cannot see and understand? Oh, Celia! You will grieve him."

"Well, auntie, I did not mean all that, of course, only I am so tired and disheartened. I meant to try to plan a grill work for the parlor to-night, and I couldn't find Harry at all. I am afraid he has gone out again with those dreadful fellows. What is the use in trying to do anything with setbacks all the time?"

"But your heavenly Father had another plan for you to-night, and the parlor can wait, you know. As for Harry, I think he is safe in his room by this time. He went out with the minister, and while you were up with Mrs. Belden they came in with a lot of boards and screws and a saw and hammer and a pot of varnish, and they went to work in good earnest. The other young men went down and helped, and in the morning I think you will find something new in the parlor. Didn't you smell new varnish? They asked for you before they began, but I told them how you were occupied and said I was sure you would want them to go ahead and not wait for you."

Celia sat up and smiled through her tears.

"Did they really, auntie? How nice! What did they make? A bookcase? I am sure it must have been that, for Mr. Stafford spoke of it, and asked me if I did not like the low kind running around the room. I am so glad. And Harry stayed in! I was afraid he was with those awful young men again."

She brushed away the tears and began to take down her hair, when she remembered another discouragement.

"Oh, aunt Hannah," she said, "but you don't know what an utter failure my three-cent enterprise was," and she gave a detailed account of her interview with Mamie Williams.

Miss Grant listened intently, sometimes laughing with Celia, and sometimes looking grave over possibilities of danger for the girl, which perhaps the younger woman hardly understood. When she had finished, Miss Grant's face was very serious.

"Celia, dear, you have made a good beginning. Your first trial was by no means a failure, and I do not believe you half understand in what great need of help that young girl stands. She has revealed volumes in her few frank sentences. Be careful that you keep her confidence, and ask to be guided in what you shall say, that you may be both wise as a serpent and harmless as a dove. That is one of the greatest gifts God gives to his workers, and it needs to be carefully watched and tended daily to keep it fit for work, — that mixture of wisdom and gentleness."

"But, auntie," said Celia, doubtfully, "do you believe I can ever accomplish anything? What is the good of getting such a girl to read a verse every day in the Bible? As likely as not, she will choose one among the minor prophets, which won't mean anything to her, and as for praying, she said she did not know how. What good will it do her to pray. 'Now I lay me down to sleep' for instance, every night, not meaning a word of it, nor scarcely knowing what she is saying?"

"Remember, Celia, it is his work. You have not to do with the end of it, nor are any results in your hand. Don't you know he says, 'Ye have not chosen me, but *I* have chosen *you*, and ordained you, that ye should go and bring forth fruit, and that your fruit should *remain:* that whatsoever ye shall ask of the Father in my name, he may give it you.' After I read that verse I always feel comforted to do the work without seeing the results, knowing that God has planned all that out from the beginning, and all I have to do is to execute the little part of the plan which he has entrusted to my hand. As for saying that such a girl will not get any good out of the Bible, you talk as if you did not believe in the Holy Spirit, Celia. Will he not guide her to the right words that will help her? And do you not remember that the Bible says about itself, that it is written so plainly that 'he who runs may read' and that the way of life is made so plain that the 'wayfaring man, though a fool, need not err therein'? Then even if her heart and her lips do not know how to pray, if she truly tries to kneel and present herself every day before her Maker, don't you believe he can find ways and means to speak to her heart and teach her lips the right phrases? It is a great thing to have a habit of prayer, even though your heart is not always in it, for you at least bring your body to the trysting-place with God, and give him a little chance to call to the inattentive heart. Don't you know how Daniel had a habit three times a day of praying with his face toward Jerusalem?''

"Oh yes, aunt Hannah, I see it all. You always have a Bible verse ready for every one of my doubts and murmurs. I wish I had the Bible all labeled and put away in the cabinets of my brain the way you have, ready to put my hand on the verse I need at the right time,'' interrupted Celia, laughing, and putting her arms around aunt Hannah's neck to kiss her. "Come now, it's late and you look tired. I'll be good and go to bed without fretting any more, and to-morrow I'll try to think up some ways of helping that feather-headed girl.''

Meantime, up in the third story room of the "three-cent" girls, quiet and darkness reigned. Miss Simmons had come in a few moments before, tired and cross. Her mind was wrought up by a play she had just witnessed, and she had been quarreling with her escort about something which she did not deign to explain to her roommate, so they had gone to bed at last without the usual giggling confidences, and Mamie lay there in the darkness thinking over her evening and the advice given her, and wondering what the adorable Mr. Harold Adams would think of the changes in her when she had been fully made over to suit her new guide. Suddenly she sat straight up in bed with a jerk, which threw the clothes off Miss Simmons' shoulders, and exclaimed:

"My land alive! If I didn't forget the very first night,'' and with that she flung herself out of bed, and striking a match, relit the gas.

"What in the world is the matter with you, Mamie?'' said Miss Simmons, pulling the bed clothes up angrily. "I was fast asleep and you woke me up! Turn that gas out and come back to bed! Come! We won't be fit to get up in the morning, if you keep rampaging around all night.''

But Mamie imperturbably proceeded with what she was doing. She tumbled two great piles of paper-covered books over in the closet, searched among a motley collection of boxes, old hats and odds and ends on the closet shelf, and then began hunting in the bottom of her trunk. It was some minutes before she succeeded in finding what she wanted, and by that time Miss Simmons was asleep. Mamie drew forth from an entanglement of soiled ribbons and worn-out garments a small, fine-print red Bible with an old-fashioned gilt clasp. It was stained on one side and blistered as if a tumbler of water had been left standing wet upon it. Mamie remained seated on the floor beside her trunk while she turned over the leaves rapidly, intent upon keeping the letter of her promise in as short a time as possible, for the furnace fire was low for the night and she was beginning to feel cold. She opened near the beginning of the book and chanced upon a list of long, hard names which she could not pronounce. Perhaps her conscience would have been eased as well by a verse there as anywhere, but it was too much trouble for her unaccustomed mind to pronounce the words to herself, so she opened again at random toward the end, and letting her eye run down the page in search of something attractive and brief, she was caught by this verse:

"And to her was granted that she should be arrayed in fine linen, clean and white: for the linen is the righteousness of saints."

"Well now, ain't that funny!" she said to herself, as she paused to read it over before she turned out the gas again. "That seems kind of like her talk. Dressed in fine linen! It would be kind of nice and pretty, and real stylish, too, if it was tailor-made. I saw a girl on Chestnut Street last summer in a tailor-made white linen that was awful pretty. It sort of rustled as if there was silk underneath, and her hair was all gold and fluffy under a big white hat with chiffon on it. She looked real elegant. It would take an awful lot of washing though, to keep her in fine linen 'clean and white.' "

She glanced at the verse again with her hand outstretched to turn out the gas, and read it over once more, and then got into bed. "For the fine linen is the righteousness of the saints!" "Well, it does seem a sort o' saint-like dress, now that's so, and come to think of it, Miss Murray, she's got a sort of saint face. I knew it was something kind o' strikin', and I couldn't think what, 'cause you wouldn't exactly call her pretty, and yet she ain't the other thing, and some folks — most folks maybe — would like it better than to have her pretty. Maybe it's because she's got the righteousness this talks about. She does look like a saint, that's certain. Anyway, she will when she's as old as Miss Grant. Miss Grant, now, she's a saint sure! And she would look nice in a fine linen dress all white, too. I wish she'd put one on some time, so I could see. How funny it is to have the Bible talk about dress. I supposed the Bible thought clo'es was wicked. I'm sure the Sunday-school teachers always say you mustn't think about 'em. Well, that's a pretty verse anyhow. I wonder who it was that had the fine linen dress granted to her, and if she wore it all the time, that is, clean ones every day, all fresh and crisp! My! I wish 'twas me! Wouldn't I be happy though! I guess this reading's going to be real interesting, maybe. I never thought there could be any verse in it like that. Most things I've read before was about sinning and dying and heaven, and scarey things like that. Anyhow, I've kept my promise. Why, no I haven't either!'' she exclaimed aloud, and suddenly bounced out of bed again, to the detriment of her bed-fellow's temper.

She knelt down beside the bed, and her thoughts paused a brief moment, while she tried to put her mind in praying frame. She tried to think how to pray aright. She wanted to feel the satisfaction of having performed this duty that she had felt in her Bible reading. She must ask for something. She was conscious of a vague wish in her heart that she were good enough and had friends great enough that this that she had read of might be granted to her, to be arrayed in spotless, neat apparel, beautiful, and given by the love of some one who cared for her above others. How to put such a thought into fitting phrase, or even if this were done, whether it would be a proper wish to express in prayer she did not know. At last she whispered, ''Oh God —'' and paused, and waited and tried to collect some better words, and then murmured again. ''Oh God —'' and then — ''Amen.''

When she lay down to rest again, it was with a sense of awe upon her which would not let her sleep for some time. She had been near to the great God, and touched as it were the hem of his garment, with curious perfunctory fingers, like a child who had been dared to do a certain thing, and coming, curious, unthinking, heedless, had touched and suddenly felt the power and greatness and beauty of that which he had touched, and had stolen away ashamed.

Altogether Mamie Williams was not as satisfied with her first effort at prayer as she had been with her Bible reading. But yet in heaven it was recorded, ''Behold, she prayeth!''

20

The next day was Sunday.

Celia had wakened early, in spite of the fact that she was up late the night before. She lay thinking over the changes that had come into her life, and wondered how things were going to work out. Somehow there seemed a cloud over what she had been trying to do. She had not accomplished much with Harry. She had kept him in the house a few evenings, it is true, and interested him in a few good books, but nothing really to much purpose after all. To be safe from all the temptations that beset his path every day, he needed to be anchored on the Rock of Christ. She did not feel that she knew how to help him in that way, he was such a bright fellow, so ready to laugh. She thought of the minister and the influence he seemed to have over the young man, and felt half indignant at him for not exercising it in a religious way, instead of merely a personal one, and then she realized that she knew nothing at all about what influences he was using, and ought not to judge him. For aught she knew, he had spoken to him many times. How unjust she had been! Then she remembered what her aunt had told her about the improvements made last evening in the parlor, and jumped up to dress and run down to see them. Aunt Hannah had already completed her toilet and gone down to the kitchen to help Molly Poppleton, and to direct the new waitress who had been in the house but three days.

Celia was delighted with the bookcase. Somebody had an artistic eye and constructive ability. The bookcase was exactly the right height, and filled the long bare wall on one side of the room beautifully. It was finished with a neat molding of natural wood, and the whole nicely oiled. There were a few books piled on the floor beside it, waiting till the shelves should be perfectly dry to receive them, evidently contributions to the new case. She stooped to read their titles, and was astonished and pleased to find among them several new books by best authors, which she had been longing to read, but had as yet not seen. They were nearly all in new bindings as if fresh from the bookstore, though one or two had the names written inside in fine, strong handwriting "Horace L. Stafford."

Celia drew back, a slight flush creeping over her face. She was grateful for the books thus loaned or donated. The newcomer was evidently bound to be helpful, and seemed to know how to do it. Now if they could have a few games under the lighted lamp on the table, perhaps some of the young people might be kept in evenings. Would such things reach Mamie Williams and her friend, she wondered? And she sighed and feared that Mamie was too much interested in other things to be reached so simply. She remembered that Mamie had been reading the other night. Perhaps some of these delightful stories would reach her. There were one or two religious books, small and danitily bound, which looked attractive. Celia picked them up and turned the pages, her expressive face kindling with a thought she read here and there. Then she went to the small cozy corner by the organ and sat down. She looked about her at the few changes they had made, and remembered the night when she had looked around in that parlor waiting for the postman. How much difference a few little things had made! She could see other changes that might be made to improve matters, and she resolved to try them as soon as possible. Then she sat down at the organ. She had never tried that whining instrument, since she had been in the house. It had pained her some times to hear it groaning and wheezing under the bold touch of the tenor brakeman as he ground out an accompaniment to some of his solos. Celia did not like a cabinet organ. She longed for a piano, but there was no piano, and here was this organ. What could be made of it? Perhaps it might be tuned and answer for singing occasionally. Certainly, if it was to stay there and be used, it would conduce to her own comfort to have it put in order. She touched the keys softly to see how bad it was, and went on playing chords gently. She was not a finished musician, but she had learned to play a little for the home pleasure, and now instinctively her fingers sought out some of the old favorite tunes.

> "Safely through another week,
>   God has brought us on our way,
> Let us now a blessing seek,
>   Waiting in his courts to-day."

Her conscience pricked her, as the words rang themselves over in her mind. She had not been going to church very regularly since she came to the city. She had wandered around from one church to another, feeling forlorn and lonely at all, not going often enough to one place to become noticed as a stranger and welcomed, even if the people had had the disposition to welcome her. Since aunt Hannah had been there, she had made an excuse to stay at home with her if she was not able to go out, and at such times when her aunt could go, she had taken her to the different churches near by in rotation, that she might choose where they should go. The elder lady had not as yet made any choice, nor indeed, had she expressed her mind concerning the places of worship they had visited. Celia thought of it now, and wished their dear old church from Cloverdale could be transplanted bodily. It was so desolate to go among strangers and not have any place or work in the church home. She sighed and made up her mind that she must go more regularly and perhaps offer to take a class in Sunday-school or something of the sort. Of course it was not right to live this way; but her heart was not in her resolve. She played on, not realizing what tune she had started till she began to hum the words in a low sweet voice:

"The day of rest once more comes round,
    A day to all believers dear;
The silver trumpets seem to sound,
    That call the tribes of Israel near;
            Ye people all,
            Obey the call,
And in Jehovah's courts appear —"

She broke off suddenly and played a few stray chords. She knew that the next verse began:

"Obedient to thy summons, Lord,
    We to thy sanctuary come";

It was strange that all the words were on that subject. She would choose something else. She thought a moment, her fingers lingering on the keys. Then she began to sing:

"Father in thy mysterious presence kneeling,
    Fain would our souls feel all thy kindling love;
For we are weak, and need some deep revealing
    Of trust, and strength, and calmness from above."

She felt the beauty of the words and the depth of meaning, and sang with her heart, each word as a prayer. Her voice grew fuller and sweeter as she went on.

"Lord! We have wandered forth through doubt and sorrow,
    And thou hast made each step an onward one;
And we will ever trust each unknown morrow;
    Thou wilt sustain us till its work is done."

She had not heard the step upon the stairs and did not know that some one entered the parlor and sat down on the divan near by, until, as she commenced the third verse, a rich, sweet tenor, full of cultivation and feeling, joined with her in the words:

"Now, Father! now in thy dear presence kneeling,
    Our spirits yearned to feel thy kindling love;
Now make us strong; we need thy deep revealing
    Of trust, and strength, and calmness from above."

Celia's voice trembled at first, but the stronger one sustained the tune and she kept on, the pink color stealing up her cheeks and to the tips of her ears. If the other singer saw her embarrassment, he did not notice it. When the last note died slowly away and Celia was wondering what she should do and how she should get away from the room, he said quite in a matter-of-fact voice, as if he and she were accustomed to singing together early on Sabbath mornings: "Will you play 'Lead Kindly Light' please?" And she had played on, glad that she knew it well enough to do so, and they sang together.

"Thank you!" he said simply, when the last verse was finished. "That has helped me for the work that I have to do to-day. In fact that song always helps me. Do you, sometimes, come to a place where you want to look ahead and see whether things are coming out as you wish? Isn't it blessed to think he leads the way, and makes the gloom for our sakes that we shall not fear for what is to come, while perhaps if we could look and see the blessings — in disguise — sometimes we might turn and flee. You belong to him, do you not, Miss Murray? I thought I could not be mistaken. I want to thank you for this pleasant bit of morning praise. It has been like home."

Celia had raised her eyes in one swift glad glance of recognition of their kindred discipleship, when he asked her if she was a Christian and had answered, low and earnestly, "Yes, I do," feeling in her heart how very wrong she had been in calling this man unspiritual. Her heart longed to reach that high plane of trustful living where he seemed to move. She lifted her eyes again and timidly asked:

"Do you think it is possible for every one to feel that perfect assurance where they cannot see the way? I wish I knew how to trust that way and not worry over things."

"It is hard sometimes, isn't it, to just lay down the burdens at the Father's feet and realize that we need not carry them? But isn't it strange that it is hard?" And he looked at her with that peculiarly bright smile which she had noticed the first night he came to the house. "One would think that we would be only too glad to get rid of the burden and the worry, when he, so strong and willing, offers to take it. Perhaps that is one reason why I like that hymn. It seems to help me to remember whose I am and who is my Saviour. I am prone to forget when I think, for instance, of some dear one whom I see fading day by day and know cannot be long upon this earth, that the night ever will be gone.

> " 'And with the morn, those angel faces smile
> Which I have loved long since, and lost awhile!' "

A deep sadness had settled over his face, as he looked up to her and repeated the lines of the hymn they had just sung, and her heart was filled with pity for some sorrow she felt he was bearing. Instinctively she remembered the sweet beautiful face in the velvet case, and while he seemed set apart and sacred in her thought of his sorrow, she let a shade of her old dignity creep back into her voice, which had fallen from it for a few moments. The breakfast bell had sounded, and the boarders were coming downstairs. With one accord the two rose and went toward the dining-room, feeling that they did not care to have the quiet confidences of the few moments they had spent together intruded upon or misunderstood. Celia thanked Mr. Stafford for his words a little stiffly, as one, as a matter of form, might thank any strange minister for a good sermon, and perhaps the young man wondered a little at her seemingly variable moods.

It was after breakfast, and the church bells were sending their various calls to worship through the clear cold air of the city. Celia stood ready dressed for church, waiting for her aunt in the front hall. Miss Grant had been called back by Molly Poppleton, just as they were starting out the door, and Celia tapped her foot impatiently on the hall oilcloth and wished aunt Hannah would hurry. Not that she was anxious to go to church, but she wanted to get the duty done with and come back, for Mr. Stafford had slipped a most inviting little book into her hand, as he passed her in the upper hall after breakfast, saying, "Have you read Daniel Quorm? If not, it will interest you, perhaps. It is along the line of our talk this morning, and it has helped me to trust him where I couldn't trace him."

She had read a few pages while aunt Hannah tied her bonnet and put on her gloves, and had already grown deeply interested in the quaint phrases of Daniel in his story of his little maid. She wanted to get back to it. She stilled her conscience when it pricked her for not caring to go to church, by telling it that the book would probably do her more good than a sermon in a strange church, but her conscience was too well trained to let her forget that God had promised to meet her in the church.

Some one was standing in the shadow of the parlor curtains, Celia did not know who. She thought that perhaps it was the brakeman. He had returned the night before, and was off duty for the day. She unfastened the door and breathed in the clear sunny air with delight, then glanced up the stairs to see if aunt Hannah was coming. But just then came Miss Grant's voice, as she leaned over the stair railing, and Celia saw that her gloves were off and her bonnet untied again.

"Celia, don't wait for me. I am not going this morning. I have made up my mind my duty is with Mrs. Belden. She is feeling very despondent. Go on without me. Isn't there some one else you can go with?" she asked, as she saw the look of dismay on Celia's face and heard her exclaim, "Oh auntie!"

Then the figure that had been standing in the shadow of the window curtain in the parlor moved forward and Harry Knowles stepped out.

"Miss Murray, would *I* do?" he asked humbly, "or — would you rather not go with me?" There was a hesitancy and shamefacedness about him which was not like his usual manner, and he seemed anxious to have her accept. While Celia hesitated, Miss Grant said: — "Why, yes, Celia, that is very nice. You and Mr. Knowles go together. I am so glad he is going," and then slipped away from the stairs pleased in her heart, both for Celia's sake that she would not be alone, and for the young man that he was willing to go to the house of the Lord!

As Celia turned to go with him, she reflected that she had been wishing he would go to church, or wishing she might say some word to help him, and now he had himself opened the way by inviting her to go. She felt reproached, that she had never invited him before. But Harry seemed uncomfortable, and when he had closed the door, he stopped on the upper step and asked again, "You are sure you are willing to go with me? You aren't afraid or anything?" and Celia looked up in surprise, and saw the earnest, eager, shamed face and said, "Why surely, Harry, I am willing. Why should I be afraid?"

"Well, I thought, — I was afraid you — after that night — you know —" he said, growing red and grinding his heel into the stone on which he stood, "I can't forgive myself, Miss Murray, that's all, and I thought you didn't like me asking you." He looked up bravely through his embarrassment with his sorry, boyish eyes asking forgiveness.

"Harry," said Celia, turning her clear, honest gaze full upon him, "I was truly glad, and was only being ashamed myself because *I* had not asked *you* before, for I have been wishing you would go to church, and — I have been praying for you."

She spoke the words low and embarrassedly, for she was not used to talking much about such things to strangers, but the young man's eyes filled with moisture, and he said, "Thank you," in such hearty tones that she knew he meant it. Then he added, "So is the minister, and maybe I'll amount to something, after all."

Celia was surprised to find that she suddenly felt a sense of satisfaction in what he had told her about the minister. She did not understand all her feelings to-day. She must sit down and analyze them when she reached home.

"But where are we to go, Harry?" she asked, pausing on the sidewalk a moment. "Have you any choice? I have not put my letter into any church yet, though I ought to have done so before this."

She tried to remember in her mind which of the churches she had attended would be the most likely to help the young man, but could not remember any of them definitely, and concluded that since she had been in the city she had taken her body to the church and left her soul at home, or wandering in fields of other thoughts than those presented for her deliberation at the sanctuary.

Harry's face grew eager again.

"Well, then, that's nice. Maybe you wouldn't mind going to hear Mr. Stafford, because I've half promised him that I would come there this morning, you see."

"Oh, of course we will," said Celia, wondering why it was she had never thought to go and hear him before, and why it was that the thought of hearing him preach had suddenly become so pleasant.

She wondered again as she listened to his opening prayer. Every word seemed to be prayed for her, and to fit her needs exactly and she pulled herself up sharply when she found that she was actually imagining that he remembered their talk before breakfast, and was praying thus for her. The hymn just before the sermon was wonderful, and again she reprimanded herself severely, for thinking he looked at her while he read that last verse, so perfectly did it appeal to her need. He read it exquisitely and tenderly, and as he reached the last line he looked at her again, and it gave her a strange pleasure to feel those words spoken so to her, even as if the Father himself had sent her an especial message that morning, and by a noble messenger.

> "Take my soul, thy full salvation!
>   Rise from sin, and fear, and care.
> Joy to find in every station
>   Something still to do or dare.
> Think what Spirit dwells within thee.
>   Think what Father's smiles are thine!
> Think what Saviour died to win thee!
>   Child of heaven, shouldst thou repine?"

21

That Sabbath afternoon was one of deep thought and soul searching for Celia. The sermon she had heard, the hymns she had sung, the prayer she had listened to, the book she had partly read, all seemed to bring her the one thought, that of the possibility of a life beyond anything she had known heretofore, a life whose every breath was trust, and whose joy was unalloyed because there was no care in it to break the deep, sweet peace. The longing for some change of this sort in her own heart did not take her interest from the work she had just begun around her. Instead it seemed to deepen her interest in all in the house, and to make her heart throb anew with love to her Saviour.

With the little book in her hand which Mr. Stafford had loaned her she passed through the hall that afternoon on some errand for her aunt, and returning saw Harry Knowles hovering restlessly about the parlor. It came to her that perhaps she might say something to help him, but what could it be? She felt hardly ready yet without more thought and preparation. She might do more harm than good. Following an impulse she offered him the book to read awhile, and then went back to her room, half sorry that she had deprived herself of the pleasure of finishing it. However, she had read enough to remember, and there lay her Bible. She took it up and read. Somehow the words seemed to fit all the other circumstances of the day, and to help her on to the one great desire that was growing deeper in her heart, that she might forget to fret and worry and learn to trust Jesus entirely for all that was to come. She read a chapter and part of another. The words seemed especially fresh and new to her. She began to wonder if she had been giving her whole mind to her Bible reading of late. Then suddenly from out the printed page there came a command. It was not so very marked, not more than other verses she had read, and yet it seemed to her to have a special significance for her, and to remind her that there was a young girl of nearly her own age upstairs, over whom she had been shown her own influence, who was perhaps needing help from her at this very moment. She felt that she must go, though she could scarcely tell why, and she laid aside her Bible and knelt to ask God's help before she went.

As she knocked at Mamie Williams' door she wondered at herself for coming, and how she was to explain her visit. She decided that if any one answered she would say she had come to ask them to go out to church with her that evening, though she had hardly made up her mind before that to go herself. She felt much embarrassed at herself in that one minute after she had knocked, and heartily wished herself back to her own room. But she had not long to wait. The door was thrown open after a moment of what sounded like scuffling inside, by Mamie herself, this time without gum in her mouth, but with rather red cheeks and her hair floating in wet strings down her back over a towel. Her face and hands were a brilliant, tender pink, giving strong evidence of a severe scrubbing Celia had recommended the night before. She instantly recognized what it meant, and her heart sank that in her advice this girl was spending her Sunday afternoon in such a way. Perhaps the angels knew that by making herself sweet and clean, she was coming nearer to the kingdom of God than she had ever yet been.

The other roommate occupied a comfortable lounging spot on the bed. Her hair was tumbled and her dress loosened, and in her hand was a paper covered book. Celia had opportunity afterward to observe that it was the same one that Miss Williams had been reading the day before.

Miss Simmons did not rise from the bed, but she greeted the intruder with a languid surprise, and withal a show of pleasure that made Celia feel she was not unwelcome, and told her to sit down. She was munching cheap candy from a box which lay beside her on the bed, and she held it out at once to the guest saying:

"Sit down. Have some candy, do. I had it give to me last night." This with a significant giggle interpolated into her natural drawl. Then looking at her roommate, she said, apologetically,

"You must excuse Mamie. She's took an awful fit of cleanin' up. I don't know what she's getting ready for, but she's made herself a sight. Her nose's as red's a beet. Did you want something or did you just come in to kill time?"

Celia accepted the chair, declining the candy as graciously as possible, saying she seldom ate it, and made known her request that they would go with her that evening to meeting. She bethought herself to the service she had attended that morning, and that possibly it might interest these two to go and hear the minister who lived under the same roof with them, and urged that as an incentive, describing the pleasant room, the good singing, and perfect friendliness she had met, with an enthusiasm that surprised herself.

"I can't go," said Miss Simmons, promptly, "I'm expecting company." There was the same conscious drawing in of the breath when she said this, evidently meant to express a certain and especial kind of company, that Celia had noticed in Mamie's talk the night before. It made her heart sink with the uttere uselessness of trying to work against such odds, till she remembered her new half-formed resolves, not to look ahead for results, but to do the work trusting the rest to God.

Mamie's cheeks had grown redder, if that was possible. She was sitting on the edge of a chair with the hair brush in her hand. She seemed a trifle shy.

"It's awful nice of you to ask us," she said, "but I don't know but perhaps I'm going to have company, too. It wouldn't do to be away, though I ain't just positive, you know."

"Couldn't you bring them along?" said Celia, promptly, as if it would be the most natural thing in the world to do, though her heart misgave her at the idea of taking the oily youth she had seen in the parlor waiting for Miss Simmons not long before.

"Oh, no indeed!" snickered Miss Simmons, "he wouldn't go a step. He ain't that kind. And besides he'd be mad, for he said he might be going to bring another fellow along he wants me specially to meet. He wants to see me very perticular to-night anyway, so I couldn't think of going out," and Miss Simmons retired behind her book.

Mamie had meantime been puzzling over the problem of how to please herself and her new object of adoration at the same time, and seemed to have arrived at a solution.

"I don't know but I *might* go after all," she said, slowly, looking down at the toe of her shoes. "Say, Carrie, if he should come would you be sure and tell him I had gone out with somebody *else?* — you could tell him it was a *very special* friend who had invited me, you know, and he would think it was another fellah. That might have a good effect on him, you know. I believe I'll try it this time anyway. I'll go, Miss Murray, if you want it so much. It's a good thing to get people jealous once in a while, don't you think? Say, was that you down in the parlor singing this morning early? It was awful sweet! Who else was there? It didn't sound quite like Mr. Yates, but I didn't know any of the others sang. It wasn't Harry Knowles, was it? He's too young for you anyway. You don't say it was the minister! My! He's awful talented, ain't he? Wouldn't it be romantic if it should turn out you was to marry him some time? Did you ever know him before? I've heard of stories like that lots of times."

Celia's cheeks rivaled Mamie's in hue, and her anger had risen rapidly. She did not dare trust herself to rebuke this girl, for her desire to do her good was still strong. She quickly looked about for a turn to the conversation.

"Are you fond of singing? Then come downstairs and let us sing now. I think some of the others are down there. We can have a very pleasant time, I'm sure. I have some Gospel song books. Put up your hair and come." She walked to the door trying to steady her fluttering nerves, and still that queer beating of her heart, half indignation, half something else which she did not understand, and which she did not wish to countenance.

"My land!" said Mamie, beaming, "I'd come in a minute, only what'll I do with my hair? It's about dry, but it'll take me an hour to do it all up after washing, it's so tangled and slippery. Perhaps you will fix it for me. Do, that'll be nice. Then you can show me how to do it like yours."

Celia was dismayed. She would scarcely have chosen Sunday afternoon for a lesson in hair-dressing, but how could she refuse on that score, as the request had been put in answer to one of her own? To handle another person's hair at any time was to her a sore trial. She shrank from contact with any one except her nearest and dearest. But how was she to refuse? How was she to get an influence over Mamie if she let her see she was unwilling to do what she asked of her? For a minute her repugnance of the coarse girl, with her coarse hair, red face and loud, grating words was so intense that she almost yielded to her desire to turn and flee from the room and shake the dust from her feet, and tell her aunt Hannah to take her away from the horrible boarders and never let her see any of them again. Then she gained control of herself, and though her cheeks were still red at memory of the careless words of the girl, she consented to undertake the hair; and even the deeply absorbed Carrie on the bed, who had been furtively watching the stranger during all, never suspected what a trial she had quietly taken upon herself.

Having undertaken the task, she did it well. She had a naturally artistic eye and hand and there was some pleasure, after the dislike had been overcome, in making Mamie's hair look as she had often thought it ought to look. Quickly and deftly she twisted it, smoothed it here and there, and fastened it firmly, and after it was accomplished Mamie stood and surveyed herself.

"It looks awful plain," she said, hesitatingly, and it makes me seem queer, 'cause I ain't used to it, but I guess I like it. Don't you, Carrie?"

"It looks real stylish," answered that young woman, enviously, mentally resolving to try her own that way as soon as the others had left the room.

Celia went to wash her hands, with a heavy heart. She must certainly have mistaken that voice which she thought called her to go to that room. What had she accomplished by teaching the fashions this afternoon? How was she ever to know whether a thing was a duty or not? She went down to the parlor with her singing books, and found Mamie there before her looking pretty and a trifle shy in consciousness of her new coiffure. She was talking to the tenor brakeman who was evidently lost in admiration of her charms. She went at once to the organ and started the singing, but she found that the brakeman's tenor was not quite so pleasant as that which had blended with her own voice earlier in the day. The other boarders heard the music, and one by one dropped in, all joining in the words when they were familiar until even Miss Burns was there. Mr. Stafford had come in also. The minister joined in the singing, though he sat in a shaded corner of the room for the most part and sang softly, as if he were weary. Celia found that her thoughts kept wandering to him and wondering what was the matter, and she grew exceedingly annoyed over this fact, as she remembered Mamie Williams' careless words a little while before. She was glad when the tea bell rang and called them from the organ.

The church party was larger than she had expected. Mamie had wheedled Mr. Yates into being one of the number. She was the kind of girl who always wants a young man along when she goes anywhere. The other three young men joined the group also, perhaps at Harry's solicitation, or it might be out of interest in the minister who had been singing with them.

They were starting out of the door. Aunt Hannah was behind with Harry

Knowles. Mrs. Burns had volunteered to stay with Mrs. Belden during the evening. Celia stepped down to the pavement beside Mamie and walked on.

"Say, he's awful nice. I like him. I wish he *would* marry you, 'cause I like you both," said romantic Mamie, in a confidential whisper.

"What do you mean? Who?" said Celia, startled, and having a vague idea of the tenor brakeman.

"Why, Mr. Stafford, the minister!" said the other girl.

"You must never say anything like that again," she said, in a suddenly chilling tone which almost froze Mamie's eager enthusiasm for a minute. "It is utterly absurd and ridiculous."

She wished afterward that she could have turned it off with a laugh, and let the girl see that she had no notion of any such thing, without making such a tragic thing of it, but indeed she had felt so annoyed at the second bold intimacy of the girl, which seemed to her like the handling and mixing up of sacred things by clumsy hands untaught and unknowing what they did, that she had almost stopped in her walk and gone back to the house. However, she managed to steady her voice and her steps and keep on.

"Why?" asked Mamie, half timidly, "don't you like him?"

"Certainly, I don't dislike him. But neither of us have any idea of any such thing. It is very annoying to have it suggested. He is simply a boarder." She said it freezingly.

"Oh," said Mamie, in a frightened tone, "I didn't mean any harm. I just thought it would be nice, that was all." After that she dropped behind with Bob Yates who had come up, and Celia walked with aunt Hannah and Harry Knowles.

"She's an awful queer girl in some ways," confided Mamie to her escort a few minutes later. "I just said she and the minister would make a nice match, and she got just as mad as a hornet. My! She scared me so I didn't know but I'd cry!" and then she giggled in a way Bob Yates much admired.

Celia sat in the meeting too much annoyed to rally her spirits and enjoy what was going on. She scarcely heard the hymns or realized the sermon. The voice of the minister, cultured, earnest, tender, loving toward his people, awakened in her the knowledge that she was more interested in this man than she wanted to be. She did not wish to hear his voice and like it, and his sermon she knew she would enjoy and therefore tormented herself with her annoyance, so that she did not hear it, and saw between the lines in her hymn book, ever and anon, a sweet pictured face in a velvet frame. She called herself a fool, and wondered that there was anything about a man whom she had so short a time ago not even heard of, to make her feel so uncomfortable. Then she turned to watch Mamie's face and her heart sank again as she reflected how useless it had been to try to do anything for her. True, her hair was becoming and neatly arranged, and the black eyes of the young man beside her were admiringly turned toward her occasionally, but perhaps that was only another source of harm to the poor girl. After all Celia's resolves, her day seemed to be ending most miserably.

How could she know that at that very moment the young girl beside her was listening to the minister with undisguised amaze, as he read the words of his text, "And to her was granted that she should be arrayed in fine linen, clean and white: for the fine linen is the righteousness of saints." She did not know about the hurried getting out of bed to read the promised verse the night before, nor how the verse itself had impressed itself upon the young girl's mind, perhaps the more because it was about dress, and one great theme of all themes of interest to her mind; — unless perhaps one might except those of love, courtship and marriage. If Celia had been told all this, it might only have discouraged her the more that the Bible itself meant no more to Mamie than a fashion book might have done, and so it was a wise thing that Celia could not see and know until all God's plan was worked out to the finish, and she was given eyes perfected through his teaching to understand the whys and wherefores.

The sermon which followed was simplicity itself. If Celia had not been so taken up with her own uneasy heart, she would have recognized the skill of the preacher, as he plainly and simply drew the meaning from what might have otherwise been to many minds before him an empty and meaningless passage. Even the feather-brained Mamie was able to understand and to carry away with her the few facts she had wished to know when she first read the words, together with their deep spiritual meaning. She had felt a pang of disappointment when she heard that this incomparable person, this child of luxury spoken of, was the church, Christ's bride, and she told herself, half enviously that she had nothing to do with the verse at all, of course. But, immediately, the preacher made it plain to every one in the house that he and she individually did belong, ought to belong, by right were, members of that church for whom Christ died, and that it was only through their own wills that they deliberately put themselves outside its pale, that really, to every one present, it had been granted as a privilege, and it was their own fault that they did not accept and wear it. He spoke at length of the difficulty of keeping such garments white and pure in the midst of a world of work and constant contact with that which would soil, how only the children of the rich could afford to dress in a color which would so easily soil, and how only those who could go and have such garments washed in the blood of the Lamb could keep them pure and white. Then he talked about that righteousness of the saints until even Bob Yates dropped his eyes from the earnest, eloquent face of the speaker, and began to look into his own heart and wish that he might some way be different, and Mamie's cheeks glowed and her heart beat fast. She had forgotten, for the time, Mr. Harold Adams, and even the admiring glances of her escort to church that night. She even forgot the new arrangement of her hair, and ceased to feel the back of her head, to discover how perchance it might be affecting those who looked upon her from the rear. She resolved, in some way, to discover for herself how she might wear this fine linen, and when the closing hymn was announced, she stood up with the others, and sang in a loud voice the words, meaning them in her heart more than any words she had ever sung before. She felt a strange sweet thrill of longing, new and faint, but real, as the hymn went on.

> "O Jesus Christ the righteous! live in me,
> That, when in glory I thy face shall see,
> Within the Father's house, my glorious dress
> May be the garment of thy righteousness."

Mamie felt for the first time in her life that night, that she had really a strong determination to go to heaven when she died. The white linen could be worn then, if not before. The minister had said it might be worn now also. Well, perhaps —

Her heart was softened, and on the way home she confided the coincidence of her verse the night before and the minister's text to Mr. Yates, who was deeply interested and impressed. Celia would have been surprised, perhaps, if she could have heard the brakeman telling Mamie at the door that she had helped him, that he wanted to be better than he had been and he was glad she was that kind of a girl.

As for Celia, the minister himself had walked home with her. She hoped that Mamie had not seen, and her cheeks burned red and her embarrassment did not lessen during the entire walk. He asked her to help him in his Sunday-school work, and she accepted the class he offered her, after much hesitation, but she was stiff and unlike herself, and aunt Hannah wondered greatly why Celia seemed so cold and uninterested in things. She sighed as she went about preparing for the night, and wished that Celia's mother had lived; nobody could understand a girl like her own mother, she thought. Then she knelt as she always did, and laid her care at her Master's feet, and rested with an unburdened heart for the next day's work.

22

One morning, about eleven o'clock, Molly Poppleton was up in the third-story hall attending to the rooms on that floor. The chambermaid was not well, and Molly had been put back in her work a good deal, so that it was late and she was in a hurry. She thumped the water pitchers down hard, slammed the doors, and punched the pillows into shape with extra vigor on this account, but, suddenly, in the midst of making up the University student's bed, she came to a sharp halt and straightened up to listen. She was not mistaken. She certainly had heard sounds of distress. They grew clearer now as she went to the hall door, and she quickly located them. They were low, half-suppressed sobs, following quickly upon one another, as thought the weeper were in deep distress. After listening, she marched down the hall, and without more ceremony threw open the door of a room. There lay Mamie Williams across the foot of her unmade bed crying bitterly and shaking with sobs. Molly Poppleton was at all times a straightforward maiden, and she believed in coming to the point at once; it was the way she had been brought up. So, without apology for intruding into the young girl's trouble, she demanded what was the matter.

Mamie raised her head long enough to show a red nose and blurred eyes, and to see who had come in without knocking. Then she went on crying harder than ever.

Molly shut the door with a slam and said:

"For mercy's sake, do tell me what's the matter? Are you hurt? Do you want a doctor? Or are some of your friends dead?"

Mamie shook her head and finally controlled herself sufficiently to sob out:

"No, M-m-molly. It's my heart! It's broken!"

"Oh, well, if that's all, you'll get over it! They always do! I've been there myself, and I know that state don't last long. You better get up and wash your face while I make the bed." And Molly proceeded energetically to throw open the window and shake up the pillows.

"Oh Molly! You don't know. You never was crossed in love!" wailed the miserable girl, without stirring, and then she sobbed the harder.

Molly turned irately from the bureau where she had begun to dust.

"Crossed in fiddlesticks!" she said, sharply. "You'll find you ain't near so hard hurt as you think for. And as for me, I've had my chances in my time like other girls, and plenty of 'em at that, an' I preferred to live single. It's

123

much more independent. It's my opinion you ain't old enough to be away from home anyway. You better go back to your ma if you've got one.''

But as this only set Miss Mamie to crying the harder, the perplexed Molly marched down to find Miss Grant and report the case.

"Miss Grant, you're needed up there in that three-cent room. That silly thing is actin' like a fool over some poor sickly fellow, that couldn't support her ef she got him, I s'pose. She says she's been crossed in love an' her heart's broke, an' she's cryin' fer dear life. It's my opinion she better be crossed with a good spankin', an' I wouldn't feel sorry to be the one to give it to her neither.''

But the latter part of this sentiment was lost upon her hearer who had already started with swift steps for the third story.

A moment later Mamie felt a cool hand on her hot forehead, and Miss Grant stooped down and took her in her arms and kissed her. She was so surprised to be kissed, that she stopped crying for a minute. Then the sympathy of the eyes that met hers started her tears afresh, and she buried her head in the motherly arms held out to her and cried like a hurt child who had found a comforter. After she had cried a few minutes and been soothed by the woman who seemed to have the gift of soothing from above, as others have a gift for music or painting, she was able to tell her poor little sad, commonplace story.

"It was Mr. Harold Adams at the store. And he was awful handsome. The girls all thought so. I fell in love with him the first time I saw him. Yes ma'am, he was the head clerk there, all this winter he had charge. The owner went to New York and left him here to run the business. He was awful smart, they said. He used to pay me lots of attention at first, and he's told me many a time he loved me better than any one else'' — here she broke into fresh sobs — ''and it was only when that ugly girl with bleached hair and a pretty face came, he got to going with her, and now I'd planned a way to look nicer than her and get him back, and he's been real nice to me for a whole week — she was away — they all said she was sick, but now it turns out she was getting ready to be married, and he's to be sent to have full charge of a three-cent store up in Ohio, and they say she's going along. The girls had it all ready to tell me this morning when I went in to the store, and they just couldn't laugh enough at me, till I nearly sank through the floor. They was always jealous of me. First one twitted me an' then another, till I got so mad and felt so bad I just come home. He's a goin' to marry her, they say, an' it's all been no use after all, an' oh, my heart's just broke!''

It is commonly supposed that women who do not marry and have no children cannot enter into the feelings of young people, and are not able to sympathize with them. But God had somehow given this woman a sweet insight into natures in distress, which helped her to be able to give comfort wherever she went, to say the right word and do the right action. She bent down now and kissed the tear-wet face.

"You're awful kind," moaned poor Mamie. "But you don't know how it is yourself. You ain't never been crossed in love."

A shadow of the passing of a great dark cloud, tipped with brilliant light, went across Miss Grant's face, leaving the reflection of the light there, ere she spoke again.

"Listen! Mamie," she said, and her voice was very sweet and tender, and her eyes looked soft and dewy, as though she saw things beyond the range of human vision, "I want to tell you a story all about myself."

Yes, she actually went back to those dear, bright days so long ago, when she had found a kindred spirit and had lived in a sweet elysium of hope, and dreamed those rose-colored visions of youth. Some women would have counted it a desecration to the memory of her dead hopes and sacred love before the eyes of a vulgar girl who wept over a man a hundredfold more vulgar; would have thought it an evidence of lack of good taste and delicacy to do so. Not so this woman. Had she not sent swift petitions to the throne as she came up the stairs asking for guidance? She felt in her heart that this story of hers, which had never before passed her lips to mortal ear, told here, might help this poor, friendless, untaught girl: might, perhaps, lead her to see life in a different way, and to begin to try to live it for the God above, instead of for her own selfish pleasure. And she knew the man she had loved, who had been in heaven these years, well enough to be certain he would be glad also to have her tell the story, if it could in any wise help a soul to find comfort. And so she told it, simply and eloquently. She even let herself dwell on the tender passages, the little things that make such a story beautiful in the eyes of a girl. She spoke about the flowers he had sent her, the pretty, simple gowns she had worn that he admired, and the ribbon he stooped and kissed, as it floated from her throat, that last time he parted from her, saying she would soon be with him now to stay; and how she treasured it yet.

Before she was half way through the story, Mamie had dried her eyes and sat up on the bed, her face expressing intense interest. She had forgotten her own troubles in the trouble of another. Her tears, which were dried on her own sorrows soon flowed silently for Miss Grant. She wondered at that peaceful face, which shone bright even through the mist that would gather in her eyes, as she told of the dark days when her hopes were taken from her, and of the time when she wandered about forlorn, until the Lord spoke to her and comforted her. When the story was finished, Mamie found she could look up and talk. She seemed to have risen above her recent grief. There was a longing for something in her heart, she scarcely knew what.

"I always thought it would be an awful thing to be an old maid," she said bluntly, "but if I could look like you, and be like you, I wouldn't mind it — not much!" There was a look of admiration on her face. It was not much encouragement, but Miss Grant was not one who let her work depend upon results. She went steadily on talking, cheering, advising, drawing out the girl, until she had a pretty thorough understanding of what her life had been hitherto. She did not wonder that the heart seemed broken, nor that what seemed to the poor girl to be the life love had been freely given to an unworthy object. What better had been set before the girl? She had been untaught and unguided. Before she left her, Mamie had confided to her the story of her Bible reading and of all her thoughts about the garments of fine linen, and this missionary of the Most High had sifted out from the chaff of foolish talk and worldly longings the grain of earnest desire after better things and found joy, the joy of encouragement in it. She even knelt beside the girl with her arm about her waist, and prayed for her as Mamie had never heard herself prayed for before, and then, instead of sending her back to the atmosphere of selfish strivings and silly thoughts of what should be noble things, she advised her to stay away from the three-cent store, at least for that day, and come down in the kitchen, as she had some work for her there which might take her mind off her trouble for a little while.

It is true that Molly sniffed when she saw her come into the kitchen with her red eyes washed and a white apron on, but Miss Grant wisely sent Molly to work in another part of the house, and herself carefully inducted the awkward novice into the mysteries of making some most delectable cake, to be used in the celebration of Miss Burns' birthday that evening. It spoke well for Miss Grant's ability to read human nature, that she chose cake to teach Mamie. If it had been a lesson in bread-making or how to cook potatoes, it is doubtful if the girl would have been interested. Cake, now, somehow, seemed "sort of stylish," and belonged to the festive side of eating; therefore, she enjoyed learning how to make it nicely, and she came to the dinner-table that evening beaming with satisfaction over the cake which she had iced and decorated with smilax and candles herself. She told them all that she made the cake, and it received much praise, especially from Bob Yates, who asked for a second piece and said some low words of commendation that brought a smile and a bright flush into the girl's face, just as Molly passed the ice cream which was also a part of the evening's celebration.

"H'm!" said that worthy woman coming out into the kitchen the better to converse with herself. "I thought so! She's got over it sooner than most of 'em. It generally takes over night at least just to let the glue dry, but she must have used some lightnin' stuff. Her heart ain't more'n skin deep anyway."

23

The days that followed were filled with new things for Mamie Williams. However shallow her hurt had been, it was deep enough to make her shrink decidedly from returning to the store. The young man whose charms had fascinated her was not yet gone, and Miss Simmons brought word from day to day that there had been delay in sending him away. The yellow haired girl seemed to have returned to her place behind the candy counter. After this report had gone on for about a week, Mamie suddenly manifested a desire to return to her position, with the express hope that she might still win her lover back, but Miss Hannah, feeling that this might be the turning point in her life, had a long talk with her, the result of which was that she appeared in the kitchen an hour after, with red eyes, a meek air and a clean gingham apron and made herself generally useful. Molly, who had kept herself informed of the state of the case nodded approval and announced to Miss Grant at the first opportunity that she didn't know but that girl had some chance of growing a little sense after all.

It is doubtful whether Mamie's resolution would have outlasted the next day, however, had not several things occurred to strengthen what Miss Grant had said to her during that long earnest talk. The first was the announcement that the charming Mr. Harold Adams had departed from the city to parts unknown, taking with him a goodly portion of the profits of the three-cent business, which he had, by a careful system of bookkeeping, been laying up for himself against this day. Neither had the yellow-haired girl shared in his booty. She seemed to be as happy as ever, and as the days went by was reported to be "making up" to the new head of the business, who had come to straighten out affairs.

Mamie, on the announcement of this news, betook herself to her room for a whole morning, where she cried and was angry alternately, and from whence she came out a wiser and meeker maiden, quite ready to do what Miss Grant should ask of her, and to look for another position. But that lady was in no haste to urge the girl to apply for another position. Life in such a store, as Mamie would be likely in her present stage of development to get into, was too dangerous and risky a thing for the unformed girl, who seemed to be hesitating on the brink of better things. After careful thought, and much discussion with Celia, Miss Grant told Mamie that she would like it very much, if she would be willing to help her for two or three weeks, with upstairs work, sweeping and table setting, until she could find another second girl who suited her. She told her she would give her what she had been paying to the second girl who had just left, and that she would of course have her board, so that she might be able to look about her leisurely for the right place, and still lose nothing by being out of work. Mamie, after a struggle with her pride, and reiterating many times to her roommate that she only did this for a few days as a favor to Miss Grant, finally accepted, and was somewhat surprised that she was not scoffed at by Miss Simmons for "doing housework," which to the minds of both girls had always been menial service quite beneath them.

But it turned out that Miss Simmons had other things to think of than Mamie Williams' affairs. It was scarcely three weeks after Mamie had left the three-cent store, when it was discovered that the said Miss Simmons had "eloped" with the friend of the oily youth who had been visiting her. Just what she had eloped from, as she had no friends or kindred in the city who seemed in the least interested in her welfare, it was perhaps hard to make out, but she left a note in Mamie's Sunday dress pocket stating that she had eloped, and bidding an affectionate farewell. It was no more than was to have been expected, Miss Grant thought afterward, as she turned over pile after pile of romantic, third-class, sensational novels in the closet, after the departure of the young girl, but she sighed and brushed away a tear, that she had not been permitted to help this girl also. She had by this time some hopes of Mamie. The affair of Miss Simmons, she feared, might perhaps upset her, and excite her desire for some romance herself, but happily it worked the other way, rather frightening her, and making her cling close to Miss Grant, asking her advice daily and almost hourly. This effect became still more salutary when it was learned some days after that the young man with whom Miss Simmons had eloped had already a wife in another state. During the passage of these events Mamie cried a good deal, but there was growing in her face the shadow of a sweet womanliness which gave promise of what might be in the future if all things went well. She had not even the brakeman to brighten this hard time for her, for he had been sent out West on some special work by one of the heads of the road, and would not return for a month. Mamie learned to efface herself somewhat, and gradually seemed to be cultivating some of Celia's quietness and repose of manner. Celia, on her part, was much interested in the girl. She kept her in mind daily, and was always trying to help her, and praying for her.

"I'm not sure, auntie, after all, but she may develop enough to become a ribbon girl some time," she said one night, when Mamie had left them.

Aunt Hannah smiled dreamily. She was beginning to have much hope of her young protegee herself.

"Yes," she said, with her far-away look in her eyes, "she may be fit for the white linen dress some day. Who knows?"

"You mean the tailor-made one?" asked Celia, mischievously.

"The heavenly-made one, anyway, dear. She told me to-night that she was beginning to feel as if she really prayed like other people now."

There were other influences at work also. Mr. Stafford was holding meetings every night in the new chapel, and the boarders had as a family adopted that church as their own. It was becoming a regular thing now for every one who was able, to attend service morning and evening on Sunday, and several of them had dropped in to the special meetings. Miss Hannah, Celia, and Mamie Williams had been there every night. Harry Knowles had joined the choir, and his friends rejoiced that at last all his evenings were securely filled for him. His face was bright and interested. He was enthusiastic in sounding the praises of Mr. Stafford, and ready to do anything to help in the church work, though as yet he did not seem to have made any move to number himself among the Christians. Celia was deeply interested in a class of big boys who were most of them beginning to attend the services. She kept herself in the background with them as much as possible. No one could say of her that she was trying to get the attention of the minister. She tried with all her might to keep away from him, insomuch, sometimes, that he noticed it and was puzzled and troubled. He sometimes sat with his eyes shaded by his hand up in his room when he was weary with his work, and thought about it. Did she dislike him? Or was there some one else who so filled her life that she had no desire to have other friends? More and more her sweet, womanly face, and her pleasant ways were making their impression upon his mind. He began to confess it to himself by and by, and he thought of what his friend Roger Houston had said about finding a wife that night he had met him in search of a boarding-place. His heart told him that there was more possibility of such a thing happening than he would care to confess to his friend just yet. In fact, Mr. Houston had visited Mr. Stafford several times, and once had remained to dinner with him, since which time he had unreservedly gone over in favor of the new boarding-house, declaring that the cooking was as good as they had at his own home, though perhaps not quite so stylishly served. He had laughed, it is true, at Bob Yates, who that evening favored the house with one of his high-keyed solos, while Roger and Mr. Stafford tried to talk in the latter's room directly over the organ; and he had mimicked Miss Burns' laugh — for he was a born mimic — and had denominated Mamie Williams and Carrie Simmons as "giggling kids," but he admired Miss Grant, and declared Celia to be artistic in the extreme. He kept talking about her after they came upstairs. He was an artist by profession, and he begged his friend to ask her to sit as a model for him, and was surprised at the prompt way the suggestion was squelched. He asked if Celia's character was as fine as her face, and pondered much afterward over the slow thoughtful answer of his host, "Yes, I think it is." He was so possessed of the idea of catching Celia's expression on canvas for a picture he had it in mind to paint, that he asked again as he was leaving, "And you don't think you can ask that girl to sit for me, Horace? I like that style of face awfully, and I don't know just where else to turn for it.

"I don't think there *is* another face anywhere just like hers," answered the minister slowly again.

"Now look here, Horace, you talk as if you were personally interested in her. Don't go so far as that, I beg of you. You ought to marry a rich girl, for you never will allow yourself to get money any other way, unless you fall dead in love with it. Well, I suppose I may ask her myself. It won't hurt my feelings, if she does refuse, you know. Where can I find her?"

A firm line came around the minister's mouth, as he said, decidedly:

"I would rather you would not do that, Roger. She is not that kind of a girl."

Afterward, the young artist remembered his friend's face, and whistled on his way home as he thought it over.

But though Mr. Stafford had watched Celia for several months now, had seen her under varying and trying circumstances sometimes; had shown her little attentions, which were the outcome of a frank talk he had within himself, wherein he confessed a deep interest in her, she still held aloof from him. Miss Grant had given up trying to make it out. Celia was too deep for her.

Meantime Bob Yates came home from the West. He had been working hard and was glad to get back again. He had been promoted to an engineer's position, and was off duty every evening now. He seemed much struck with the change in Mamie Williams. Miss Grant noticed it the first evening at dinner. There was a deference about his manner when he addressed her that was new. She noticed also its reflex influence on Mamie. Had she taken a lesson from Celia's reserve, or were the influences of prayer and daily life about her, and her new hopes and resolves making the change? Miss Grant wondered. Mamie flushed a little, but she drooped her eyes modestly, and was quite unobstrusive during the entire meal, a thing so unlike the old Mamie Williams that the contrast was marked. Bob Yates admired it evidently, for he cast many glances across the table at her, and his own loud, jolly voice seemed somewhat toned down, in harmony.

Celia passed through the hall behind them after dinner and heard Mamie shyly decline an invitation to the theatre. "I'd like awful well to go, but we all go to meetin' every night now," she was saying. "I promised in the meeting last night I'd bring somebody along to-night and I don't just like to break my promise. Mebbe you'd just as soon go to meetin' as the theatre to-night, then I'd have somebody to take to keep my promise with. The minister's awful good, and the singin' is fine. They'd like your voice in the choir, I know."

And so Bob Yates willingly gave up the theatre to go to meeting. He was not greatly concerned where he took his amusement. The theatre had no special attraction for him, but he had thought of it because Mamie had once told him she would rather go to the theatre than anywhere else in the world. In fact, the prospect of a "good sing" was rather more enticing in itself than sitting still and listening to the singing of other people.

That night the minister was very much in earnest. He preached a soul searching sermon. Some of Celia's boys arose, when at the close of the sermon the invitation was given for all who would like to belong to Christ to stand with those who were Christians during the singing of a hymn. Mamie sat quite still, her cheeks pink and her eyes downcast during the singing of the first verse and part of the second. She held one side of the hymn book with Bob Yates and her hand trembled a little. He was singing with his usual fervor the deep, heart-stirring words, but Mamie did not sing. Just as the second verse was nearly finished, she suddenly rose with a jerk and an embarrassed countenance, leaving the singing book in the hands of the man by her side. He looked up astonished, and went on singing, but not quite so loud as before, and his words seemed to be getting mixed up. He fidgeted on his chair, and when they began to sing the next verse, he arose also and stood beside Mamie, offering her again the book. She took it, looking down, her heart fluttering gladly that he had arisen too, and kept her company, and so they stood until the benediction was pronounced.

"Say," said Mamie, softly, when they had walked half of the way home in an embarrassed silence, "what did you mean by that? Did you mean what the minister said? What made you do it?"

"Mean it? 'Course I did!" answered Bob, heartily. "My mother used to be a good woman, an' I've always meant to turn that way some time myself. The first time I ever heard Mr. Stafford, I made out he was more'n half-way right, an' to-night I thought so again. I don't know as I should 'a' said so out'n out fer folks to see, ef you hadn't, but I calculated I wanted to be on that side ef you was, so I stood up. Why?"

"Well, I didn't know," said Mamie, embarrassedly, "I was afraid mebbe you just did it outo' politeness. But I'm real glad you meant it."

"Are you? Sure?" He looked at her searchingly by the light of the next street lamp, and then added, "Well, I don't mind tellin' you 'twas you that did it. That what you said about wearin' a white dress got me to thinkin'. You seem most's if you was wearin' it yourself since I come home. I didn't know but 'twas my 'magination, but when I see you get up in meetin', I knew it was that there white dress in the Bible you was wearin'. I mostly made up my mind while I was out to Ohio, I wanted to be fit to walk along side o' you."

Mamie's heart fairly stood still with a joy she had not known before and only half understood. It was the joy of having helped another immortal soul to find the Light.

"I'm only just startin' myself," she murmured low. "I ain't half fit for that white dress yet, but I'm goin' to try, an' I'm awful glad you think I helped you."

"Well, then, let's start out together, and mebbe we can help each other," he said, and she murmured with downcast eyes, "All right," as he grasped her hand in a hearty clasp, and then helped her up the steps into the house.

Other young men had, on occasion, clasped Mamie's hand in more or less hearty grasp on the way home from places of amusement, but no hand ever touched in her the chord of such true, heartful, honest friendship, and purpose to do right. She felt as though she had been uplifted in some way and yet she knew not how nor why.

A little later Harry Knowles sat in Miss Grant's little private sitting-room, his head leaning on his hand, his whole attitude indicative of deep thoughts.

"I tell you, Miss Grant," he had been saying, "it was that three-cent girl. When I saw her stand up there all by herself, right in the middle of a hymn, too, when no one else was rising, it made me ashamed. Here was I who had been brought up to pray and read the Bible and know how to be good, and had a good mother, sitting still; and that girl, who never had any bringing up to amount to much I guess, *coming,* right away as soon as she was asked. I can't stand it any longer, and I wanted to talk to somebody about it, so I came to you. I knew you would help me, and it would seem some like having Mother to tell it to. I've made up my mind to be a Christian. Yes, I'll tell the minister by and by, but I wanted to talk to you first, and he was busy anyway. But I don't know as I'd ever have done it, if it hadn't been for Mamie Williams to-night."

Verily the mysteries of influence in this world are great, and past understanding, and we cannot tell if our actions may not affect the eternal welfare of some one whom we have never seen.

Certainly, Mamie Williams, as she sat reading her Bible that night, did not dream that she had helped to bring Harry Knowles to Christ.

> "Hast thou not garnered many fruits
> Of other's sowing, whom then knowest not?
> Canst tell how many struggles, sufferings, tears,
> All unrecorded, unremembered all,
> Have gone to build up what thou has of good?"

24

Celia Murray had gone to her room and locked the door. It was just after church, and aunt Hannah was busy in the kitchen. It was the only time during the day when she might hope to have entire possession undisturbed, of the room she shared with her aunt. She could not remember a time in her life before, when she would have cared whether her aunt came in upon her, or came to the door and found it locked, or not, but this time she did. She wanted to be entirely alone and face her own heart.

The winter had passed by on rapid feet, and they were well on into the spring. The meetings which had been held in the little chapel had continued for several weeks, and during that time Harry Knowles and Mamie Williams and Bob Yates had professed publicly their faith in Jesus Christ. The University student had taken his church letter out of its hiding-place in his trunk and put it into Mr. Stafford's church, and the school-teacher had sent to his far-away home for his and both were working hard for the salvation of others. Family worship had been established daily in the boarding-house, not in the morning, because the coming and going of the boarders was at such different hours that it would scarcely have been possible to get them all together, but in the early evening, just after the six o'clock dinner, while they still sat about the table. No one was obliged to stay, but all chose to, unless called away by something urgent. Mr. Stafford conducted it, and read a very few verses and prayed. Once or twice, when he had been absent for a day, Miss Grant had read part of a chapter, and asked Harry Knowles once, and once the brakeman to pray, and they had each done so; stumblingly and with few words, it is true, but Miss Hannah had been glad and gone about her daily work feeling joy at the place in which the Lord had set her.

They had grown to be a very pleasant family, in spite of the various elements of character and up-bringing which they represented. They talked about their abiding-place as HOME, and each one felt it to be that in the true sense of the word. Miss Grant had taken care to observe each birthday with some little unusual festivity in the way of eatables, and at Christmas and other holidays they made merry enough to forget, most of them, that they were away from their own kindred.

Mr. Stafford had grown to be a part of the household so fully that it would have brought dismay to each one if there had been a thought of his leaving. Even Celia had unbent, and he and she had become good comrades in a way, though there was always a dignified barrier which Celia kept up,

133

which prevented his showing her any of the ordinary attentions which young men like to show to the young women whom they admire. Having quieted her conscience by keeping up this wall of conventionality and excusing herself from anything of a social nature which he offered her, she shut her eyes to consequences and enjoyed his presence in the house. How could she do otherwise? She read the books he loaned her, and conversed about them with him afterward, and she visited the poor and sick for him sometimes and took them little delicacies. There had been times, it is true, when it troubled her that she let herself enjoy his society as much as she did, but she had been learning during the winter months to put this aside and think no more about it. Occasionally she prayed to be delivered from a trouble which she sometimes saw hovering like a shadowy cloud over her own life, and looking at aunt Hannah resolved to trust the Lord to make her what he would have her to be, even if it must be in spite of sorrow, as he had done with her aunt. But now a time had come when Celia must face her heart and understand herself. If it was to be that she must come out of the ordeal bowed in spirit, then she must face it and accept it, but she must understand herself now.

It had come to a sudden crisis in this way.

Mr. Stafford had been away for nearly two weeks. A telegram had come to him, when Miss Grant was out. Molly had taken it up to him and a little while afterward had been surprised to see him standing in the kitchen door, his grip and umbrella in hand, and a drawn, anxious look upon his face. He told Molly to tell Miss Grant he had been called away by tidings of sudden illness and did not know how long he would be gone. They had heard nothing from him until Saturday evening of that week, when his friend Roger Houston had called to get some church notices from Mr. Stafford's room to hand to the minister who was to supply the pulpit the next day.

It was Celia who opened the door for him and showed him to the second story front room. With a possible view to prosecuting his petition that she would give him a sitting some time, he lingered a moment.

"It is very sad indeed," he remarked to Celia, as though she knew all about the matter. "You knew there was no hope of her life? Oh, haven't you heard? Well, I suppose Stafford has had his hands too full of other things to think of writing. He gave me no particulars, only said all hope was gone and she could linger but a few days longer at most. He asked me to get this man to preach, and arrange everything for him. It will be very hard for him, he depended upon her so much. There was a peculiarly close relationship between them. He never missed writing to her regularly and some of her letters were wonderful. He read bits of them to me once or twice. She was a wonderful character. He will miss her immeasurably."

Then Mr. Houston looked up from the papers he had selected from the minister's table, to the face of the girl who stood silent in the doorway. He was wondering whether he dared venture to ask her to let him sketch her face some time, but when he looked at her he remembered his friend's words,

"She is not that kind of a girl," and concluded that his friend had been right, and it would be better not to ask her this time. He wondered what it was about her that made it seem impossible for him to speak to her about it, as he would to many another pretty girl just as nice and refined as she was. He fancied as he looked again that she was white about the mouth, but, of course, that must have been all his fancy.

It was not until late the next Saturday night, after all the house had retired, that Horace Stafford returned to Philadelphia, and letting himself quietly in with his latch-key, went to his room. They did not know he had returned the next morning at breakfast time, for one and another were wondering who would preach, and saying they wished their own minister was back, that they did not know whether they cared to go to church or not, and all those other things people will say when they love a minister, just as if he was their God, that they went to church to worship him, and when he was absent they had no object for worship. He had called to Molly, as she passed through the hall early in the morning, and asked her for a cup of coffee, and told her not to mind if he did not come to breakfast, as he needed all his time for preparation, having been away so long. He had gone to church early, while those who were going out were dressing, so that it was not until she was seated in church and saw the little study door open, and the minister walk out and into the pulpit, that Celia knew that Horace Stafford was back with them again.

She had gone through many changes of feelings since the night when Roger Houston had spoken those few common-place words to her. She had not asked him then what he meant, nor who it was who was lying so low, who was so dear to Mr. Stafford. Instinctively she knew. It was the young woman of the pictured face, so sweet and lovely, within that velvet frame. Something had arisen in her throat while she listened, that froze the words she would have spoken, an expression of sympathy for him, and her heart was filled with conflicting emotions. She had dreaded Mr. Stafford's return. It was as if she had had her convictions verified now, and knowing his heart was engaged she wished to put him entirely from her thoughts. It seemed impossible though, for constantly the surmises would come up among the boarders, why Mr. Stafford was away, when he would return, etc. She obliged herself to repeat a few of Mr. Houston's sentences, a very few it is true, so few that the boarders were left in doubt as to whether the one who was lying so low and keeping the minister away was man, woman or child, and when Miss Burns asked if she knew whether it was one of the family, his mother, perhaps, Celia answered briefly, "He did not say," and then wondered if she had done wrong in not telling what she was so certain of, though she silenced her conscience by saying that Mr. Stafford might not care to have them know he was engaged at all. Then Celia had tried to fill the week with earnest hard work. She had succeeded in persuading Dobson & Co. to let her induct Mamie Williams into the ribbon business, with a view to possibly succeeding her sometime in the future, and she found that she was able to keep busy. Mamie was a tractable enough pupil, and growing quick to appreciate the fine distinctions in manner and actions which Celia strove to inculcate. But there was still room for improvement, and Celia worked early and late at her chosen task, moulding the young woman's character as carefully and eagerly as though she had been an artist making a model for some marvelous statue.

"When you get her done, Celia dear, I'm afraid she will be too good for the engineer, and I can see he wants her," said Miss Hannah, with a quiet smile.

"Well, that's all right, auntie dear," said Celia, with a thoughtful sigh. "He'll make her a good husband, and I don't believe she'll be too good for him. It seems to me her influence on him has been wonderful. He seems to change as fast as she does. I never would have dreamed it last fall."

"I thought so, dear. Do you remember the talk we had about him some time ago? There is more good in most people than we suspect. You have to live with them awhile to find it out," said Miss Grant.

"You mean *you* have to live with them, auntie, and *I* have to live with *you* to find out about them. I never would have found all these boarders out in the world, if you hadn't been here with your 'saint's eyes' to read them."

Miss Hannah smiled, but she watched Celia furtively and wished that she could read *her,* and understand what made the little cloud which seemed to settle down upon her usually bright girl and make her heavy hearted these days.

But to go back to church. Celia's heart throbbed painfully when she saw the minister walk into the pulpit. She knew by his face that his dear one was dead. It was not that his face wore a look of bitter grief, it was rather one of chastened exaltation. He preached a sermon about heaven that morning that seemed as though it had been written by one who had recently been very near to the portals, seen them open and caught glimpses of friends, and of Jesus within. Celia forgot her heart throbs and listened, forgetting, too, for the time who was preaching, in the absorption of the words he spoke. She had had a struggle to keep back the tears during the closing hymn, when they sang:

"And with the morn those angels' faces smile,
Which I have loved long since, and lost awhile."

She knew why Mr. Stafford had selected it. He sat during the singing with shaded brow and bowed head. Celia could not sing. She felt as if she were choking. She turned as soon as the benediction was pronounced and the solemn hush following it broken, to hide her tears by searching for her umbrella which had rolled beneath the seat. When she rose again and turned around, the minister was standing in the aisle beside her. He put out his hand and clasped hers, and a light of joy lit up his face which looked pale and worn, as he said, "I am so glad to see you again."

They were commonplace words. He might have used them to any member of his congregation; yes, and with the same tone and look too, perhaps, she told herself as she hurried excitedly homeward, but they sent a thrill of mingled joy and sorrow through the young girl which she did not understand and could not control. One minute she was fiercely glad, and the next minute she was plunged in a whirl of shame and despair that it had affected her so. And now she was locked in her room. She took off her hat and coat and sat down, but she could not think. She could only feel the joy, and the certainty that it was not hers. She tried to face herself and shame herself with saying plainly to her heart, "Celia Murray, you have fallen in love with Mr. Stafford. Yes, and you did it when you knew he belonged to another woman. Yes, you knew it well enough, though you wanted to pretend that maybe it was not so, because no one had told you so. But now you love him and he *does not love you!* He has just buried his heart, and you know you would not consider him the noble gentleman you think he is, if he should forget that love was 'so peculiarly close in its relationship.' And you love him in the face of that! Aren't you ashamed! He does not love you, and he never will, and you must not *let* him, and oh — what shall I do?" —

The poor girl threw herself upon her knees and begged for forgiveness and help. She felt she had done wrong to let her heart grow interested so easily. She tried to remember some of God's gracious promises for help, and to remember that he would bear her trouble for her, but her head seemed in a whirl of excitement and she could not think connectedly. She heard the dinner bell ring, and she rose and bathed her face, but decided she would not go down. She wanted to be by herself. Molly came up pretty soon and asked what was the matter. She told Molly to tell aunt Hannah she had a headache, and would not come down now, and then she bathed her throbbing temples and lay down to try and grow calm before aunt Hannah should come as she felt sure she would.

Wise aunt Hannah! She knew something was amiss! She had not watched her girl in vain. She had seen the start and the change of color when the minister came into the pulpit and again when he took her hand; she had seen other things during the months which had passed. Just what the trouble was she did not understand, and she would not ask Celia yet. If Celia needed counsel, she felt certain she would confide in her sooner or later. In the meantime she could pray.

Miss Hannah did not go up to her room for some time. Instead, she arranged a dainty tray with a tempting little lunch and a fragrant cup of tea. Under the corner of the napkin she had slipped a little note which was merely a scrap of poetry with the penciled words above it, "Dear child"; written hastily. It read:

"Dear child:
" 'God's plans for thee are graciously unfolding,
    And leaf by leaf they blossom perfectly,
As yon fair rose from its soft enfolding,
    In marvelous beauty open fragrantly.
Oh, wait in patience for thy dear Lord's coming,
    For sure deliverance he'll bring to thee;
Then, how thou shalt rejoice at the fair dawning
    Of that sweet morn which ends thy long captivity.' "

    Then she laid beside it a lovely rosebud which Harry Knowles had brought her the night before, and sent the tray up by Molly. She herself went to the third story, and read to Miss Belden nearly all the afternoon.

25

Celia aroused herself from her unhappiness in time to hurry to her Sunday-school class. She purposely went late that she might not be obliged to walk with any one, and she intended to hurry home before any of the others from their house had left the chapel, but it so happened that one of her scholars had a sad tale to tell her of trouble and need, and she was obliged to linger and get the particulars. There was an address to be taken down and several items of information she would need in helping him to find work. When this was done and she glanced hurriedly round to see if the others were gone, she saw that one of her boys was lingering with an embarrassed expression, half smiling, half doubtful, as though he might wish to speak a word with her. Something told her that this heart was ready for a quiet personal word and here was the time. The other boarders were gone, the minister with hat in hand was standing by the front door talking with a man. He was evidently about to go also. There were one or two groups in earnest conversation, a teacher with two of her class, three women in a corner, and a young man and a young girl talking. "Ben," she said, "can you sit down and talk with me a few minutes?"

The hunger for souls was awakened within the young teacher. Her own heart's unrest and sadness made her long to plunge into some other interest. She put her whole soul into the words she spoke, and the young man listened intently. There was no doubt but that she had reached his heart and that he was on the point of yielding to the Holy Spirit. Celia prayed as she talked and forgot herself, forgot everything but her desire for this soul's salvation. She listened to his hesitating, low words in answer to her earnestly put questions with bated breath. She could almost hear her own heart beat while she waited for his final decision, as he sat minute after minute thoughtfully looking down at the toe of his rough, unblackened shoe and trying to fit it between two nails in the floor, where the boards were somewhat worn away by the many feet that tramped over them.

The decision was made at last, and the boy, with a furtive glance around him, drew his coat sleeve hurriedly across his eyes as he strode out the room after having murmured an incoherent good-bye.

Celia stooped to pick up her rubbers which lay under the seat, and then looked about the deserted room. The sexton was doing something to a refractory window, which refused to go up and down right. He was used to busying himself while lingerers kept the church open. Celia thought everybody else was gone, till, as she neared the door, the minister arose from one of the back seats and came toward her.

"Would you mind sitting down a few minutes longer?" he said. "I want to tell you something, and it seems to me that I can tell it better here than anywhere else."

Celia felt her heart throbbing and her knees suddenly grew weak, so that she sat down more because she felt she could not stand without tottering than because Mr. Stafford had asked her to do so. The day had been an exciting one for her, and her emotions had been stirred to their depths by the wonderful talk she had just had with the boy Ben. What could be coming now? She could not understand, and yet she felt in some way that it would have to do with the things which had been hurting her so all day, and would probably hurt her more. She passed her hand across her forehead wearily, and tried to brace herself to bear whatever might be said. Perhaps he would ask for sympathy in his sorrow, and how could she give it? She sent up a swift prayer for help.

Mr. Stafford must have seen the weary expression and the piteous baffled look in her face, for a troubled one came over his own, as he took a seat in a chair near her, and asked, anxiously,

"Are you too tired just now? Perhaps I ought to wait. I know you have been working hard, and your work is telling, too, I could see by that boy's face as he went out, that he will be a different fellow from this time forth. Now, if you would rather go right home, please say so."

But there was a note in his voice of longing to be heard now, that made Celia push aside her desire to slip out of it on the plea of weariness and assert, a little coolly perhaps, that she could hear him now just as well as to wait.

Her manner made his heart sink, but he began what he had to say with a frank, "Well, then I'll try not to keep you long.

"Miss Celia," it was the first time he had ever called her that, though several of the other boarders had adopted it from hearing Molly Poppleton address her in that way, "I do not know whether or not you know that I have been passing through deep waters during the past week; I have been by the deathbed and then by the grave of one who was very dear to me. I felt as though I wanted to tell you about her, not only because I need the sympathy which I know you can give, but because she knew all about you and your work, and was deeply interested in you."

If Mr. Stafford had not been looking down and struggling to control his voice, so that it would be steady and without the deep emotion he felt, he would have noticed that Celia's face grew swiftly white. It was worse then than she had feared. Not only was she asked to give sympathy, but this other woman had known all about her. They had talked her over together. Why this should seem so dreadful to the girl she could not quite understand, but at the time it seemed more than she could bear. It was well Mr. Stafford did not pause for a reply, for Celia would have been incapable of giving any just then.

"She had been ill for a long time," he went on, his voice breaking a little, "we knew she could not stay with us much longer, and yet, you understand that it was hard to part with her."

He told in a few words of her beautiful life of sweet patience and cheerfulness in the face of pain that had endured for years, till Celia felt ashamed of her selfish jealousy, and longed to shut herself away from sight that she might cry in quiet. The great tears filled her eyes and fell unheeded on her hands. She felt herself the meanest and smallest of mortals, and this other one beautiful and good and bright enough to be, as she was, with the angels. And yet her heart was very miserable. She longed to speak a word of sympathy, but knew that she could not, and blamed herself for it.

"I want to show you her face," he said, putting his hand in his breast pocket and bringing out a little velvet case, which Celia knew even through her blinding tears. He opened and placed it in her hands, the lovely face with its velvet-blue eyes looking into hers, as he said. "She was my only sister, you know, and she was *so good* to me." Then the strong man bowed his head on his hand and covered his eyes.

He did not see Celia start, as he said this, but he heard the difference in her startled exclamation,

"Your sister? Why! I thought!" — and then she stopped, and when he looked up, as he did at once, her face had changed from white to rosy red.

He looked at her face, lovely behind its tears and blushes, and read the dawning sympathy, and was glad, even in his sorrow.

"You thought what, — may I know?"

"Why, I —" said Celia, embarrassed and hesitating, blushing deeply, "I — I did not know you had only one sister!" she finished, desperately.

"But what was it you thought? May I not know?" he asked again, with a searching look at her face.

"No," said Celia, dropping her eyes to the picture, and trying to hide her embarrassment by wiping away the tears with her handkerchief.

"Then may I tell you and you will say whether I am right?" asked the minister, a daring light coming into his eyes. "You thought that she was some one even nearer, and dearer than a sister?"

He looked at her long and earnestly and seemed to be satisfied with the answer of her mute, drooped face.

"Oh, Celia, did you not know that you were the only one who ever had or would occupy that place in my heart? Have you not seen that I love you? Don't you know it? and don't you care, just a little, Celia?"

The front chapel door stood open, and the afternoon spring sunshine was flickering fitfully across the floor. They could see the people on the street passing, loitering and talking, some looking curiously in as they passed, but none seeming to notice them. Celia felt it all as she sat dumb in the midst of a whirl of joy and sorrow and shame, and she knew not what else. She could not answer. She could not look up. The minister's eyes were upon her, and she felt what the look in them would be, and knew she could not bear the joy of seeing it. The silence was long and could fairly be heard. The sexton who was growing hungry, came back from the little alcove where the primary class was held and where he had been straightening the chairs for the evening service and distributing hymn books. He drew quite near to them now, and slammed books and put down windows significantly. Celia, feeling that she must say something, murmured low, still with downcast eyes, "How should I know it?"

The minister laughed and then grew grave. "That is true," he said, "I never could tell you, because you would not let me. But *she* knew it, and she was glad of it, and loved you, and left her blessing for you." Then he turned suddenly to the sexton, a new tone in his voice. There was something about Celia that no longer discouraged him.

"Thomas," he said, "I am going now. Will you kindly see if I left my Bible in the primary room?"

Thomas went with alacrity to search the primary room.

The minister watched the sexton until he had disappeared, and then he stooped swiftly and picked up Celia's gloves which had fallen unheeded to the floor. As he handed them to her he reverently touched his lips to one of her little, cold, ungloved hands. She lifted her face for a moment, and in that moment he got his answer from her eyes.

The sexton was coming back without the Bible, which the minister suddenly discovered to have been lying on the floor under his chair all the time, and the two stood decorously apart, Celia trying to keep her cheeks from growing redder, as she walked to the open door and looked out into the glad spring sunshine, gladder than any sunshine her eyes had ever looked upon before.

Some little child, perhaps, had dropped a flower upon the steps, and as she stood waiting for the minister, she saw it. It was then she remembered the rose on her lunch tray and its sweet message of hope.

> "God's plans for thee are graciously unfolding,
> And leaf by leaf they blossom perfectly."

Her heart thrilled over the joy that this had come true, while she realized that her happiness was yet only in the bud, and she could see the promise of the day-by-day opening of it for her. Oh, why had she been doubting? Why could she not trust him perfectly? She lifted her heart in one swift breath of penitence and thanksgiving. She felt in that first gush of joy that she would never doubt her Lord again.

Then she turned to walk down the glorified street and gaze on the familiar surroundings under a halo of joy.

26

It was noon and it was June, and there was to be a wedding in Mrs. Morris' boarding-house that was. It was not *the* wedding, that is the wedding nearest and dearest to aunt Hannah's heart; *that* was to be later, and in the new chapel, and about it most of the boarders had not even heard, as yet. Later, when they knew, the bridegroom of the first wedding said it was a pity they had not fixed things up sooner, so they could have had a double wedding; that would have been "real nice," and Celia and Horace Stafford had looked meaningly at one another, and never hinted that such an arrangement would have been other than entirely satisfactory to them, provided "things had been fixed up" in time. They had their little quiet laugh over it, of course, and kept their secret.

Meantime, the present wedding was a source of deep interest to every member of the household. Each one contributed something to the general plans. The parlor, that used to be so dismal was itself in bridal array. The organ at the further end was literally smothered in palms. The palms and flowers were Mr. Roger Houston's contribution. He was not a boarder, but he had become a frequent visitor at the house, and seemed to be as much interested as any one in the event. But the arrangement of the palms was Celia's, and Celia was to sit behind them and play the wedding march in the softest, sweetest tones she could coax from the old organ. They made a lovely background for the bride and groom, and they completely hid the organ and the player. Under the mantelpiece and above it, where used to hang the crayoned visage of the deceased Mr. Morris, were more palms; and the imitation-marble mantelpiece, which Celia always said looked as mottled as though it were made of slices of Bologna sausage, was covered with a bank of lovely roses, white and pink and yellow and crimson. If the wedding had been Celia's, she would have preferred to have the roses all white, but the bride in this case was extravagantly fond of color, and had declared herself in favor of "lots of roses all colors" so longingly, that Roger Houston said "Let's please her for once if she wants *green* roses, even if the white would be better taste, Miss Murray. It's her first wedding, you know, and after all a rose is a rose."

But the colors were arranged with Celia's own skill, and no two colors dared but harmonize.

Out in the dining-room the long white table was dressed in trailing vines of smilax and roses; and the largest and most orthodox wedding cake that could be procured occupied the place of honor. All about it were evidences of Molly Poppleton's art, and everything spoke of readiness for the ceremony to begin.

Up in her room the bride was being arrayed. The dress was a simple white muslin plainly made, but she was to wear a veil. It would perhaps have been more sensible to have worn a traveling dress, as she was to go away at once, but Mamie (for of course you know the bride was Mamie Williams, and the groom Bob Yates) had always cried and said she shouldn't feel that she was really married if she didn't wear white, when Miss Grant counseled economy and good sense. Seeing her heart so set, they did not try to persuade her, but managed to change her purpose of purchasing a flimsy white silk which would never be of any use to her afterward, and persuaded her to take instead this simple white lawn. She had demurred, but finally consented. She was never wholly reconciled to the change, however, but was somewhat consoled by the fact that it was white and she was to have a veil.

Celia herself dressed her hair and arranged the soft folds of the veil, and kissed her, and told aunt Hannah afterward that Mamie Williams was really lovely in her pretty array. Miss Hannah thought so too as she came up to give the girl a few last words, as her mother might have done, perhaps, had she been there. She found Mamie standing by her bureau with her open Bible before her. Miss Grant did not know that the white vision of herself in the glass had prompted her to turn to that first Bible verse of hers and read it over again, "And to her was granted that she should be arrayed in fine linen, clean and white; for the fine linen is the righteousness of the saints." Nor could she know that the softened, glorified look on her face came from the thought in her heart that now, perhaps, even she might one day wear that pure heavenly dress of clean white linen, the garment of Christ's own righteousness.

Bob Yates had saved up a nice little sum, and now there was waiting for them, not many blocks away, a new, neat house of four or five rooms, as daintily furnished as a bird's nest. There Mamie was to put in practice the culinary arts she had learned from Miss Grant and Molly Poppleton, and to entertain her friends, and some of the young girls with whom she had grown intimate during her time of selling ribbons with Dobson and Co., for she had attained to that and taken Celia's place, and now in turn was to give it up to a young girl from the minister's Sunday-school class.

And they were to take a real wedding trip, too, like all the girls in the stories Mamie had read, in the days when she used to fancy Mr. Harold Adams held the key for her of all such delights. They were going to Atlantic City to a hotel for a whole delightful week, and they were going to see Mamie's mother, and all her little brothers and sisters, and her gruff, hard-working father. After that Bob Yates would take his bride to visit his married brother and sister out in Indiana — the far West, Mamie called it — and then they would come back to their little house and their new furniture, and their dear church and their respective Sunday-school classes. It was all very beautiful, and Mamie felt very happy and all the boarders felt happy for her. She went back in memory to the time when Mrs. Morris was there, and felt, rather than thought, how different her life was now, and in fact how different everything was, and thanked God for the change. She thought of Carrie Simpson with a pang, and wished that she could have done something for her. Perhaps, if Miss Grant had come sooner Carrie might have been saved. Mamie had so far forgotten her old pride that she actually felt a little glad that Carrie could not look in from all her own sorrow and misfortune and shame and misery, in which she had heard she dwelt, and see her own joy and happy surroundings.

Miss Grant had gone down to the kitchen to watch things while Molly Poppelton got on her best gown for the ceremony, and everything was progressing toward the last exciting minute, when the door-bell rang. The second girl who was setting chairs in the dining-room in the best possible way to economize room, went quietly to the door, her neat blue and white striped gingham and white waitress-apron and cap making a decided contrast to the slatternly Maggie who used to answer the door in Mrs. Morris' time.

The large, oldish-looking woman, and the tall, grizzled man, unmistakably a farmer, who stood together on the step stared at the girl when the door was opened, in undisguised amazement.

"Why!" said the woman at last, looking up at the number over the door as if mistaken in her whereabouts, "isn't this, — at least — isn't this a boarding-house?"

"Yes, it is," responded the maid, "won't you walk in? Miss Grant is busy just now, that is she will be in a minute, but I guess she can see you first. Did you want to get board?"

She had ushered them into the bedecked parlor, which happened at the moment to be entirely uninhabited, as the boarders were all in their rooms donning their gala attire.

But she saw that they had evidently not heard her question, so telling them to be seated, she went for Miss Grant.

The strangers, however, did not sit down. Instead, they stood staring around.

"For the land sake!" ejaculated the woman at last, looking around her more and more bewildered.

"Wal, it's pretty nice, 'pon honor, M'ria, I wonder now you ever give it up fer an ole fellow like me," and he looked at her quizzically.

But the look was lost this time. She was taking in the familiar pattern of the carpet, which somehow looked strangely bright, and noting all things new and old about the room.

Then came Miss Grant with her soft grey cashmere, made more lovely by the cloud of white tulle she wore about her neck, which seemed to blend so tenderly with the creamy white of her hair.

She stood a moment looking doubtfully at the visitors, seeing something familiar about the woman's face, but for an instant not recognizing her.

"Miss Grant, don't you know me? I'm Mrs. Morris — leastways that used to be me name. I'm Mrs. Sparks now. I married out there in Ohio, and I'm real comfortably fixed. He" — nodding her head toward the man — "has a farm and a nice house, and owns several houses in the town besides. But I couldn't rest comfortably noways, a-thinkin' of you an' the hole I left you in, an' at last me husband found out what was the matter, an' he just brought me on to see how you was gettin' along, and to say he'd help you out of it, if you got badly stuck and pay some of the bills I left behind me, but when we got here everything looked so kind of different, somehow I couldn't think 'twas me own house. You don't look as if you was hard up. What's the meanin' of it all ennyway, an' what's goin' on? Are you expectin' company?"

Miss Grant's face shone with welcome and her greeting was cordial, even in the midst of this busy time.

"We're going to have a wedding in half an hour," she said, "and you're just in time. They will both be delighted to have you here for they are two of your old boarders. And you can relieve your mind about me, for I'm not in any hole at all, and coming here was the best thing that ever happened to me in some ways. I'm grateful to you for giving me a full fledged boarding-house. I find every month that I am getting on a little more financially. It isn't great riches, but it is sure."

"A wedding! For the land sake!" said Mrs. Morris-Sparks, sententiously.

After Miss Grant had excused herself in haste, to answer a call from Molly, the guest called after her.

"It must be that nice niece of yours, Miss Murray, but I didn't never think she'd take Bob Yates, she used to be so awful stiff with him, but land alive, you never can tell!"

Miss Grant smiled to herself as she hurried down the hall. She would not explain now, as the visitor would soon see for herself.

That evening, after all the guests were gone, and the bridal pair had departed, Miss Grant took Mrs. Morris-Sparks, and slipped out the front door, let her in by a latchkey to the adjoining house which had for months been closed, with a "For Rent" sign in the window. This however, had disappeared. She carefully locked the door behind her, and turned up the gas, pointed out the place where wide, double doors had been roughly drafted on the wall between the two houses. She also enlarged upon some other improvements, among them a wide bay window to be added in both first and second stories of the front of the houses. Then she took her upstairs, and showed a suite of rooms beautifully furnished, and told the story of how the minister had bought this house and furnished these rooms for himself and Celia, and that the houses were to be connected, and the remainder of the room used to enlarge the boarding-house, in which scheme their hearts were deeply interested. She told her, too, how with careful looking to the little details she had been enabled not only to make both ends meet, but to have a trifle over, and how she hoped in the coming year with the enlargements and her present experience actually to make it a paying business.

And Mrs. Morris-Sparks looked and listened, and shook her head, but all she could say was, "For the land sake! Who would 'a' thought it!"

27

Hiram and Nettie Bartlett had been talking a good deal lately about running down to Philadelphia to see aunt Hannah and Celia. Hiram was feeling that a little ready money in his business would enable him to get through a hard time which he saw ahead. Nettie was missing aunt Hannah dreadfully, as the hot days grew longer. They had decided that it would be a good thing to forget and forgive, and open their home and as much of their hearts as was necessary to their relatives. Aunt Hannah would manage the kitchen, and Celia would manage the children, and Hiram would manage Celia's money. Having decided matters thus, and having made some changes in the arrangements of the rooms, to suit the new order of things, they began to feel very sure that it was to be. Of course aunt Hannah and Celia were thoroughly tired of living in a boarding-house by this time, and would welcome the change, and they had but to speak the word and they would fly back to Cloverdale. But before they came, it would be a pleasant change to take the children to Philadelphia for a visit.

No sooner had they decided this than Nettie wrote to aunt Hannah.

The letter reached Philadelphia in the midst of plans for Celia's wedding. They read it together, Celia and aunt Hannah, and looked at one another in dismay. Somehow, in the joy of the life they were living, they had forgotten to write Nettie anything about Celia's proposed marriage. Perhaps it was but natural, as Nettie very seldom answered aunt Hannah's long letters, which had been written at regular intervals at first, until she began to feel that they were not desired. But now they both felt that Nettie must be invited.

Celia summoned all the cousinly feeling she had ever possessed for Nettie, and wrote her a nice letter, putting into it a little touch of her sweet girlish joy over the happiness that had come to her. She finished with a cordial invitation to them all to come on, though the addition to the family at this time would be extremely inconvenient.

Celia did fret a little over their coming. Hiram would be disagreeable and Nettie would want to manage everything, and the children would be always about when they were not wanted.

She was sitting one evening thinking about it, with brow knit in troubled thought, when Mr. Stafford came in. He watched her a moment, and then taking both his hands he placed them over her ruffled brow and smoothed the wrinkles out. Then he bent and kissed her forehead fondly.

"What is the matter dearest?" he said. "I mean to make it my business

148

always to keep that troubled look away from your dear face."

"Oh, Horace! How can I help it? I have tried and tried, but I do not seem to be able to conquer the habit. Indeed, I am ashamed of it. Can you not tell me how I can conquer it?"

"Only by casting all your care upon him, who careth for you. Listen Celia, have you ever heard this?

> " 'Wherefore should we do ourselves this wrong,
> Or others, that we are not always strong;
> That we are ever overborne with care,
>   That we should ever weak or heartless be,
> Anxious or troubled, when with us is prayer,
>   And joy and strength and courage are with thee?"

Then Celia opened her heart to him and told him the story of her winter, beginning with her birthday and the little bookmark aunt Hannah had sent.

"And I thought then, Horace," she went on, "after that money came to me, my 'daily rate' for 'all the days of my life' that I would never doubt any more because I had money, and with that I would be able to relieve most of the other anxieties. But I found it wasn't so. I began to fret about other things, and then after I got money, I wanted love, and now I have that, I find I'm still fretting."

"It's because you don't remember that it's 'for every day,' dear, and that means for every need of every day. You trust from one set of things, but you think you have to worry along and look out for another set. Here is a quaint old poem I came across the other day that I cut out and put in my pocket-book to read to you some time. It fits in right here, let me read it.

> " 'I have a never-failing bank,
>   My more than golden store;
> No earthly bank is half so rich,
>   How, then, can I be poor?

> " 'Tis when my stock is spent and gone,
>   And I not worth a groat;
> I'm glad to hasten to my bank,
>   And beg a little note.

> " 'Sometimes my banker smiling says,
>   Why don't you oftener come?
> And when you draw a little note,
>   Why not a larger sum?

" 'Why live so niggardly and poor,
  My bank contains a plenty;
Why come and take a one-pound note,
  When you can have a twenty?

" 'Nay, twenty thousand ten times told
  Is but a trifling sum,
To what my Father has laid up
  For me in God and Son

" 'Since, then, my banker is so rich,
  I have no need to borrow,
But live upon my notes to-day,
  And draw again to-morrow.' "

Nettie Bartlett settled herself for the homeward trip from Philadelphia with a discontented look. She slapped Johnnie when he went to get a drink — which he did the first fifteen minutes of the journey — because he stepped on her toes. She jerked the baby up who was endeavoring to pick a piece of orange peel out of a pool of tobacco juice on the floor, and then settled into her discontented silence again. She was thinking about the fall sewing and house cleaning, and the endless darning and baking and cleaning, with no aunt Hannah to fall back upon. Occasionally, she reflected upon the bride's pretty dress, or had visions of Celia in her cloud-like veil looking up with happy eyes into her husband's face, and a half jealous feeling shot through her heart. She knew how Celia felt, or thought she did. She had felt so herself, but of course all such nonsense was passed. She looked gloomily across at Hiram, who was staring stolidly out of the window, with his inevitable newspaper lying across his knees. Then she curled her lip and told herself that Celia would soon have the sentiment taken out of her by the prose of everyday life.

"You made a great mistake by not cultivating that minister-cousin-in-law, Nettie," remarked Hiram, snappily. "I talked to him every chance I got, but it takes women and compliments and that sort of thing to work on men, and especially ministers, I guess. You ought to have invited them to our house for part of their wedding trip. I'm dead certain he's rich. Did you see all that furniture he's fixed out for Celia? He'll spoil her the first thing off."

"You made a great mistake yourself, when you let aunt Hannah, and Celia, too, go away from our house, and you can't ever undo it. Yes, I saw the furniture, but his mother sent it, for Celia said so. We might have had a few blessings, and our children would have been brought up right, if aunt Hannah had been with us. She always brings a blessing wherever she goes, and we've had nothing but ill-luck since she left us," and Nettie put her handkerchief to her eyes and wept while the train sped rapidly through the darkness.

Some weeks later, Celia seated in the pleasant study of the suite of rooms which were her new home, and yet her old home, engaged in the delightful task of classifying and placing in a cabinet the various clippings which her minister husband had gathered about him during his bachelor years, came upon this poem. She paused to read it and smiled with a little echo of the peace it spoke in her heart, and bent her head to thank her Father it was true.

"The child leans on its parent's breast,
Leaves there its cares and is at rest;
The bird sits singing by his nest,
   And tells aloud
His trust in God, and so is blest
   'Neath every cloud.
He has no store, he sows no seed;
Yet sings aloud, and doth not heed;
By flowing stream of grassy mead,
   He sings to shame
Men, who forget, in fear of need,
   A Father's name.
The heart that trusts, forever sings,
And feels as light as it had wings;
A well of peace within its springs;
   Come good or ill,
Whate'er to-day, to-morrow brings,
   It is his will."

A
CHAUTAUQUA
IDYL

A CHAUTAUQUA IDYL

Down in a rocky pasture, on the edge of a wood, ran a little brook, tinkle, tinkle, over the bright pebbles of its bed. Close to the water's edge grew delicate ferns, and higher up the mossy bank nestled violets, blue and white and yellow.

Later in the fall the rocky pasture would grow with golden-rod and brilliant sumach, and ripe milk-weed pods would burst and fill the golden autumn sunshine with fleecy clouds. But now the nodding buttercups and smiling daisies held sway, with here and there a tall mullein standing sentinel.

It was a lovely place: off in the distance one could see the shimmering lake, to whose loving embrace the brook was forever hastening, framed by beautiful wooded hills, with a hazy purple mountain back of all.

But the day was not lovely. The clouds came down to the earth as near as they dared, scowling ominously. It was clear they had been drinking deeply. A sticky, misty rain filled the air, and the earth looked sad, very sad.

The violets had put on their gossamers and drawn the hoods up over their heads, the ferns looked sadly drabbled, and the buttercups and daisies on the opposite bank, didn't even lean across to speak to their neighbors, but drew their yellow caps and white bonnets further over their faces, drooped their heads and wished for the rain to be over. The wild roses that grew on a bush near the bank hid under their leaves. The ferns went to sleep; even the trees leaned disconsolately over the brook and wished for the long, rainy afternoon to be over, while little tired wet birds in their branches never stirred, nor even spoke to each other, but stood hour after hour on one foot, with their shoulders hunched up, and one eye shut.

At last a little white violet broke the damp stillness.

"O dear!" she sighed, "this is so tiresome, I wish we could do something nice. Won't some one please talk a little?"

No one spoke, and some of the older ferns even scowled at her, but little violet was not to be put down. She turned her hooded face on a tall pink bachelor button growing by her side.

This same pink button was a new-comer among them. He had been brought, a little brown seed, by a fat robin, early in the spring, and dropped down close by this sweet violet.

"Mr. Button," she said, "you have been a great traveller. Won't you tell us some of your experiences?"

1

"Yes, yes; tell, tell, tell," babbled the brook.

The warm wind clapped him on the shoulder, and shook him gently, crying, — "Tell them, old fellow, and I'll fan them a bit while you do it."

"Tell, tell," chirped the birds overhead.

"O yes!" chorused the buttercups and daisies.

The little birds opened one eye and perked their heads in a listening attitude, and all the violets put their gossamer hoods behind their ears so that they might hear better.

"Well, I might tell you about Chautauqua," said pink bachelor thoughtfully.

"And what is a Chautauqua?" questioned a saucy little fish who had stopped on his way to the lake to listen.

"Chautauqua is a place, my young friend, a beautiful place, where I spent last summer with my family," said the bachelor in a very patronizing tone.

"Oh! you don't say so," said the naughty little fish with a grimace, and sped on his way to the lake, to laugh with all the other fishes at the queer new word.

"Go on, go on, go on," sang the brook.

"We lived in a garden by a house just outside the gates," began Bachelor.

"What gates?" interrupted the eager daisies.

"Why, the gates of the grounds."

"What grounds?"

"Why, the grounds of Chautauqua."

"But who is Chautauqua?" asked the puzzled violets.

"Don't you know? Chautauqua is a beautiful place in the woods, shut in from the world by a high fence all around it, with locked gates. It is on the shore of a lovely lake. Many people come there every year, and they have meetings, and they sing beautiful songs about birds and flowers and sky and water and God and angels and dear little babies and stars. Men come there from all over this world, and stand up and talk high, grand thoughts, and the people listen and wave their handkerchiefs till it looks like an orchard full of cherry trees in blossom.

"They have lovely singers — ladies who sing alone as sweet as birds, and they have great grand choruses of song besides, by hundreds of voices. And they have instruments to play on, — organs and pianos, and violins and harps."

"How beautiful," murmured the flowers.

"Tell us more," said the brook; "tell us more, more, more, — tell, tell, tell!"

"More, more," said the wind.

"It lasts all summer, so the people who can't come at one time will come at another, though my cousin said she thought that one day all the people in the world came at once. There must have been something very grand to bring so many that day. There were not enough rooms for visitors to sleep in, and

Chautauqua is a large place, the largest I was ever in. Yes," reflectively, "I think all the world must have been there."

The little white violet looked up.

"There was one day last summer when no one came through the pasture, and no one went by on the road, and all day long we saw not one person. It must have been that day, and they were all gone to Chautauqua ," she said softly.

"I shouldn't wonder at all," said Bachelor.

Then they all looked sober and still. They were thinking. The idea that all the people in the world had come together for a day was very great to them.

At last one spoke:

"How nice it would be if all the flowers in the world could come together for a day," said the little violet.

"And all the birds," chirped a sparrow.

"And all the brooks and lakes and oceans," laughed the brook.

"And all the trees," sighed the tall elm.

"Oh! and all the winds. We could make as beautiful music as ever any organ or piano made."

"But what is it all for?" asked a bright-eyed daisy.

"To teach the people all about the things that the great God has made, and show them how to live to please Him, and how to please Him in the best way," promptly answered Bachelor.

"There is a great good man at the head of it, and I heard a lady say that God Himself sent him there to take care of Chautauqua for Him, for it is all made to praise God. They have schools, — everybody studies, but it is all about God that they learn, — about the things He made, or how to praise Him better, and all the talking, — they call it lecturing, — is to help men to praise and love God more. They have three beautiful mottoes:

" 'We study the word and works of God,' 'Let us keep our Heavenly Father in our midst,' and, 'Never be discouraged.' "

"Wonderful, wonderful, wonderful," said the old forest tree.

"It is just what we need," piped one of the birds. "We don't praise God half enough. Here we've been sitting and sulking all the afternoon because it is raining, and never one thankful chirp have we given for all the yesterdays and yesterdays when it hasn't rained. We need a Chautauqua. I declare, I'm ashamed!" And he poured forth such a glad, thankful song of praise as thrilled the old forest trees through and through and most effectually waked the napping ferns.

"Yes," said the listening daisies, when the song was done and the bird had stopped to rest his throat, "we do need a Chautauqua."

"Let's have a Chautauqua!" cried the brook.

"But how could we," said the wise-eyed violet, "when we know so little about it?"

"I will tell you all I know," said Bachelor graciously. "You see we lived just outside the gates, and people used often to come and buy my brothers and sisters. Once a young man came and bought a very large bunch of them and took them to a young lady in a white dress, and she wore them everywhere for three or four days — you know our family is a very long-lived one, and we are something like the camel, in that we can go a long time without a drink of water — well, she kept them carefully and took them everywhere she went, and they saw and heard a great many new things. One evening this young lady sat in a big place full of people, and an old lady sitting behind her said to another lady, 'Just see those pink bachelor buttons! My mother used to have some just like them growing in her garden, years and years ago, and I haven't seen any since.' The young lady heard her, turned around and gave her a whole handful of my brothers and sisters. After the meeting was out, the old lady carried them away with her, but one slipped out of her hand and fell on the walk, and some one came along in the darkness and crushed her. Quite early the next morning our neighbor, Mr. Robin, going to the market for a worm for breakfast, saw her lying in this sad state, and with great difficulty brought her home to us. She lived only a day or two longer, but long enough to tell us many of her experiences.

"After she had faded and gone, our friend Robin went every day to hear and see what was going on inside the great gates, and every night when the bells were ringing" —

"What bells?" interrupted an impolite buttercup.

"The night bells for the people to go to sleep by. They rang beautiful music on bells by the water to put the people to sleep, and in the morning to wake them, and they had bells to call them to the big place to praise God, and hear the lectures and singing."

"Beautiful, beautiful," murmured the brook.

"And every night," proceeded the bachelor, "when the bells were ringing we would wake up and Robin would tell us all about the day inside the gates. Of course I can't remember all, but I will tell you all I know."

"Perhaps I can help you a little," spoke out an old fish who had come up the stream unobserved some time before. "I lived in Lake Chautauqua myself for some years until my daughter sent for me to come and live with her in yonder lake."

They all looked at the old fish with great veneration, and thanked him kindly.

"Well, how shall we begin?" said an impatient daisy.

"I should think the first thing to be done is to make a motion that we have a Chautauqua," Bachelor said.

Then rose up a tall old fern. "I make a motion to that effect."

"I second it," chirped a sparrow.

"All in favor of the motion say 'aye,' " said Bachelor, in a deep, important voice.

And then arose such a chorus of "aye's" as never was heard before in that grove. The wind blew it, the brook gurgled it, the great forest trees waved it, all the little flowers filled the air with their perfumed voices, the far-off lake murmured its assent, the purple mountain nodded its weary old head, the sun shot triumphantly through the dark clouds, and all God's works seemed joining in the "aye, aye, aye," that echoed from hillside to wood.

"A unanimous vote, I think," said Bachelor, after the excitement had somewhat subsided.

"The next question is, When shall we have it?"

"Oh! right away, of course," nodded a buttercup. "See! the sun has come out to help us."

"But," objected white Violet, "we can't. We must invite all the flowers and birds and brooks and trees all over the world, and they will have to get ready. It will take the flowers the rest of this summer and all of next winter to get their dresses made and packed in their brown travelling seed trunks. I'm sure it would me if I were to go away from here for the summer, and it is late in the season already. We can't get word to them all in time."

"Yes," said the fish, "and there are the travelling expenses to be arranged for such a large company. We should have to secure reduced rates. They always do on Chautauqua Lake."

"Oh! as to that," said the wind, "I and the birds would do the transportation free of charge, and the brook would do all it could, I'm sure."

"Of course, of course," babbled the brook.

"That is very kind of you indeed," said Bachelor. "But I should think that the earliest possible beginning that we could hope to have would be next spring."

After much impatient arguing on the part of the buttercups and daisies, it was finally agreed that the first meeting of their Chautauqua would be held the following spring.

"It must last all summer," they said, "because some of us can come early and some late. There is the golden-rod now, it never can come till late in the fall."

"Of course, of course; certainly, certainly," chattered the brook.

"What comes next?" softly asked the wild rose.

"The next thing to do is to appoint a committee to make out the programme," remarked the fish.

"Committee! Who is that?" cried a butterfly.

"Programme! what's programme?" chirped a sparrow.

"O dear! we need a dictionary," sighed the roses.

"What's a dictionary?" asked a little upstart of a fern.

"Silence!" sternly commanded Bachelor. "Will Miss Rose kindly explain the meaning of dictionary, after which Mr. Fish will proceed to tell us about programme and committee.''

Little Rose blushed all over her pretty face, and after thinking a moment, replied, —

''A dictionary is a book that tells what all words mean.''

''Oh!'' sighed the wind, ''we must have a dictionary.''

Mr. Fish having made a dash up stream after a fly, now resumed his sedate manner and spoke:

''My friends, a programme says what we will have every day, and a committee are the ones who make it.''

''Then let's all be committee,'' said the buttercup.

''That's a very good plan,'' said Bachelor. ''Now, what shall we have? They always have a prayer meeting first at Chautauqua.''

''We can all pray,'' said the elm. ''Let us have a prayer meeting first every morning to thank the dear God for the new day, and let the rising sun be the leader.''

''That is good,'' said the flowers, and bright rays of light, the sun's little children, kissed them tenderly.

''What is next?''

''They have a large choir, and every morning after the prayer meeting they meet and practise with the great organ and piano and band.''

''We will be the singers,'' chorused the birds.

''I will tinkle, tinkle, like a piano,'' sang the brook, ''tinkle, tinkle, tinkle, —''

''I will play the band, for I have very many instruments at my command, and my friend the thunder will play the organ, while you, dear old trees, shall be my violins and harps, and every morning we will practise,'' said the wind.

''What do they have next at Chautauqua?'' asked a pert blackbird.

''Lectures,'' said the fish.

''What are lectures?''

''Talks about things.''

''What things?''

''Oh! evolution and literature and theology and philosophy and art and poetry and science, and a great many other things.''

The high-sounding words rolled out from that fish's mouth as if he actually thought he understood them.

Silence reigned for a few minutes, deep and intense, at last broken by the white violet:

''We never could have all those, for we don't know anything about them. And who could talk about such things? None of us.''

Silence again. They were all thinking earnestly.

''I don't believe it. Not one word.'' chattered a saucy squirrel. ''That's a fish story. As if *you* could get on dry land and go to lectures.''

''Oh! very well, you needn't believe it if you don't want to,'' answered the fish in a hurt tone, "but I heard a man on board the steamer read the pro-gramme, and those are the very words he read."

"If we only had a dictionary," again sighed the rose.

"Dictionary, dictionary, dic, dic, dictionary," murmured the brook, thoughtfully.

"A dictionary is absolutely necessary before we can proceed any further," said the south wind. "And as I am obliged to travel to New York this evening, I will search everywhere, and if possible bring one back with me. Anything can be had in New York. It is getting late, and I think we had better adjourn to meet again to-morrow. I hope to be able to return by two o'clock. In the meantime, let us all think deeply of what we have heard, and if any one can see a way out of our difficulty, let him tell us then."

The sunbeams kissed the flowers good-night, the forest trees waved farewell to the good wind, the brook called, "Good-night! sweet dreams till to-morrow, to-morrow, to-morrow," and all the air was soft with bird vespers.

Into the bright sunshine of the next afternoon came the winds and the eager birds to the place on the bank where the violets grew.

The daisies leaned far over the bank to listen.

The south wind came bringing two or three torn sheets of an old dic-tionary.

"It is all I could find, and I've had hard work to get this," said he. "I went in at a window where lay an open dictionary. — I had no idea that a dic-tionary was such a very large book. — It was an old one, so I had no trouble in tearing out these few leaves, as the paper was so tender. I took them out of the window and hid them in a safe place and went back for more, but just as I was turning the leaves over to find evolution, some one came up and shut the window, and I had to crawl out through the cracks. Well, I have all the 'P's' and some of the 'T's'; we can find theology and poetry.

"Philosophy, too," said wise Violet.

"My dear, that is spelled with an 'f,' " said the kind old wind patronizingly.

"O, no! I am sure you are mistaken. It is 'p-h-i-l'; look and see if I am not right."

The wind slowly turned over the leaves of his meagre dictionary, and, sure enough, there it was, — "p-h-i-l-o-s-o-p-h-y."

"Is it there? What does it say?" questioned the eager flowers.

"Philosophy, the love of, or search after, wisdom," slowly read the wind.

"Oh!" said the flowers, "is that all it is? Why, we know philosophy."

"I think the forest trees could lecture on philosophy," said the wind.

"Yes, yes, yes," they all cried. "The forest trees, for they are very old and have had longer to search for wisdom than we."

"Very well; three lectures a week on philosophy, by the old forest trees;

write it down, please," cried Bachelor.

The secretary, a scarlet-headed woodpecker, carefully carved it on the trunk of an old tree, and I think you can still find the minutes of that day written in lines of beauty all over the tree.

"Theology is the next word," announced the wind, and again turned over the leaves of their precious dictionary.

"The science of God," he read. "Science, what is science?" If we only had the "s's!"

"I know what it is," chirped a bird. "I hopped into the schoolhouse this morning, and a book was open on the desk, and no one was there, so I hopped up and took a look to see if there was anything in it to help us. The first words my eye fell on were these, — 'science is knowledge.' And I didn't wait for any more, but flew away to sit in a tree and say it over so that I wouldn't forget it. Going back a little later to see if I could get any more words, I found the schoolhouse full of dreadful boys. As I flew away again, this little piece of paper blew out of the window, and I brought it, thinking it might be helpful."

As he finished speaking, he deposited a small fragment of a definition spelling-book at the foot of the elm tree, and flew up into the branches again, for he was a bashful bird, and this was a very long speech for him to make before so many.

"Good, good, good," cried all the committee.

"To go back to theology," said the wind. "It is the science of God. Science is knowledge, therefore theology is knowledge of God. That is a very great thing. Who is able to lecture on the knowledge of God?"

Silence all. No one dared to volunteer. None felt worthy to do so great a thing.

Out spoke a shy little wren. "Last night I slept in a notch close over a church window, and the window was open and there was a meeting of the people there and the minister read out of the Bible these words: 'The heavens declare the glory of God, and the firmament sheweth his handiwork.' "

She paused a moment to gather courage, and then said, "Why couldn't the heavens teach theology?"

"Bless your heart, little wren, that is the very thing," cried the blustering north wind. And all the flowers cried, — "The heavens shall teach theology!"

The sky bowed its assent and said, "I will do my best to perform the wonderful work entrusted to me."

And the happy brook murmured, "Glory, glory, glory! the glory of God."

"Now we will see what this bit of paper has for us," said the wind as he picked up the paper at the foot of the elm.

"Ah! What have we here? Evolution! Just what we want: 'evolution, the act of unfolding or unrolling.' "

He stopped with a thoughtful look.

"Yes, I see. As the young leaves and flowers unfold. The plants must take full charge of this department, I think. I remember once turning over the leaves of a fat, dark-gray book, with gilt letters on its back. It lay on a minister's window-seat, and it looked interesting, so I read a few minutes while the minister was out and not using it, and among other things that I read was this, and it stayed with me ever since: 'A lily grows mysteriously. Shaped into beauty by secret and invisible fingers, the flower develops, we know not how. Every day the thing is done: it is God.' You see, my dear," addressing himself to a pure white lily that had only that morning unfolded its delicate petals to the sun, "you see a great many don't understand how it is done. You need to tell how God has made you able to unfold."

"Yes, we will, we can," they all cried.

"The flowers will speak on Evolution," wrote down Woodpecker.

"There are three more words spoken by our friend Fish, still unexplained, — literature, —"

"I know what literature means, Mr. Wind, it is books," announced a bright butterfly who had just arrived on the scene.

"Are you sure?" questioned the fish doubtfully.

"Yes; of course I am. I went with a big pinch-bug one day into a great room full of books, and he said, when he saw the shelves and shelves full of them, 'My! what a lot of literature!' "

The committee looked convinced, but now came the question of books, — Where should they get them? How could they lecture on books, when they knew nothing about them?

"We must just send word around to all the flowers and birds and trees and everything, to see who can lecture on books, and we must all keep our eyes and ears open," said a buttercup bud.

"We shall have to lay that on the table for the present," said the wind.

"But we haven't any table," chattered a squirrel.

"A well brought-up squirrel should know better than to interrupt. We shall have to put this aside, then, until we can learn more about it. In the meantime, let us proceed with the next word on the list, poetry."

"I know," said the brook. "A bit of paper lay upon my bank, miles and miles away from here, too high up for me to reach, but I could read it. It said, 'For poetry is the blossom and the fragrance of all human knowledge.' And I have said it over and over all the way here."

"Ah! the flowers shall give us poetry," said the good old wind.

Bachelor bowed his head and said, "We will try."

"Try, try, try," chattered the brook.

"Art is next, I believe," said Bachelor.

"Yes, art," said a squirrel.

"Art is making pictures," said the moss.

"Then the sunset must paint them, for there are no pictures made like those of the sunset," said the wind.

The sun hastened to mix his paint, and in answer to the request that he would be professor of art, painted one of the most glorious sunset scenes that mortal eye has ever looked upon. Rapidly he dashed on the color, delicate greens and blues blending with the sea-shell pink, and glowing with deep crimson and gold, till the assembled committee fairly held their breaths with delight. The crimson and gold and purple in the west were beginning to fade and mix with soft greys and tender yellows, before the committee thought of returning to their work.

"What a lot of time we have wasted," said the oldest squirrel; "to-morrow is Sunday, and of course we can't work then, and now it is time to go home."

"Not wasted, dear squirrel," said White Violet, "not wasted when we were looking at God's beautiful sunset."

Bachelor looked down at her in all her sweetness and purity, and some of the flowers say that later when he went to bid her good-night — under the shadow of a fern — he kissed her.

"To-morrow being Sunday reminds me that we have not made any arrangements for our Sunday sermons. They always have great sermons at Chautauqua, and I have often heard the passengers on the steamer scolding because the boats did not run on Sunday, for they said the great men always kept their best thoughts for sermons." This from the fish.

They all paused. "We can't any of us preach sermons, what shall we do?" questioned a fern.

"I'm sure I don't know; we might each of us go to church and listen to a sermon and preach it over again," said a thoughtful bird.

"But we couldn't remember it all, and by next summer we would have forgotten it entirely," said one more cautious.

"Well, we must go," said the wind. "Monday we will consider these subjects. To-morrow is God's day, and we must go immediately, for it is getting dark."

And so they all rested on the Sabbath day, and praised the great God, and never a wee violet, nor even a chattering chipmunk, allowed his thoughts to wander off to the great programme for the next summer, but gave their thoughts to holy things.

The busy Monday's work was all done up, and the committee gathered again, waiting for the work to go on, when there came flying in great haste, a little bluebird, and, breathless, stopped on a branch to rest a moment ere he tried to speak.

"What is the matter?" they all cried.

"Were you afraid you would be late? You ought not to risk your health; it is not good to get so out of breath," said a motherly old robin.

"Oh! I have such good news to tell you," cried the little bird as soon as he could speak. "I sat on a bough this morning, close to a window where sat an old lady, who was reading aloud to a sick man, so I stopped to listen. These are the words she read, — 'Sermons in stones, books in running brooks.' I didn't hear any more, but came right away to study that. I was so glad I had found something to help us. Two things in one."

They all looked very much amazed.

"Why, we didn't think we could do anything!" cried the stones, "and here we can do one of the best things there is to be done. Thank the dear God for that. We will preach sermons full of God and his works, for we have seen a great many ages, and their story is locked up in us."

"And the brook shall tell us of books," said the old wind. "There is good in everything, and we shall try not to feel discouraged the next time we are in a difficulty."

"Books in running brooks," said the brook. "Books, books, books. And I too can praise Him."

"This morning," said a sober-looking bird, "a small girl just under my nest in the orchard, was saying something over and over to herself, and I listened; and these were the words that she said:

The ocean looketh up to heaven as 'twere a living thing,
The homage of its waves is given in ceaseless worshipping.
They kneel upon the sloping sand, as bends the human knee,
A beautiful and tireless band, the priesthood of the sea,
They pour the glittering treasures out which in the deep have birth,
And chant their awful hymns about the watching-hills of earth.

"If the ocean is so good and grand as that he ought to do something at our Chautauqua. Couldn't he? God must love him very much, he worships him so much."

"Yes," said the elm tree. "I have heard that a great man once said, 'God, God, God walks on thy watery rim.' "

"Wonderful, glorious," murmured the flowers.

"They tell stories at Chautauqua — pretty stories about things and people; and I have heard that Ocean has a wonderful story. We might send word to ask if he will tell it," suggested Bachelor.

"I fear he cannot leave home," said the wind, "but we might try him."

So it was agreed that the woodpecker would write a beautiful letter, earnestly inviting him to take part in the grand new movement for the coming summer. The brook agreed to carry the daintily-carved missive to the lake, and the lake to the river, and the river would carry it to the sea.

Bachelor spoke next: "They have a School of Languages at Chautauqua, could we have one?"

"I have thought of that," said the fish, "but who could teach it?"

"That is the trouble," said Bachelor, slowly shaking his head.

"I know," said a little bird. "I went to church last night and heard the Bible read, and it said, 'Day unto day uttereth speech, and night unto night sheweth knowledge. There is no speech nor language where their voice is not heard.' I think the day and night could teach the School of Languages.

"The day and the night, the day and the night," said the brook.

"Yes," said the oldest tree of all, "the day and the night know all languages."

"We must have a Missionary Day and a Temperance Day," said the wise old fish.

"What is a Temperance Day?" asked a young squirrel, who was not yet very well acquainted with the questions of the day.

"My dear," said his mother, "there are some bad people in the world who make vile stuff and give it to people to drink, and it makes them sick and cross; then they do not please God, and there are some good people who are trying to keep the bad people from making it, and the others from drinking it; they are called Temperance."

"Oh!" said the squirrel, "but why do the folks drink it? I should think they'd know better."

"So should I, but they don't. Why, my dear, I must tell you of something that happened to me once. I lived in a tree at a summer resort, that year, and just under my bough was a window; a young man roomed there for a few days and every morning he would come to the window with a black bottle in his hand, and pour out some dark stuff and mix sugar and water with it, and drink it as if he thought it was very good. I watched him for several mornings, and one morning the bell rang while he was drinking, and he left the glass on the window-sill, and went to breakfast. I hopped down to see what it was, and it smelled good, so I tasted it. I liked the taste pretty well, so I drank all there was left. Then I started home, but, will you believe it? I could not walk straight, and very soon I could hardly stand up. I tried to climb up a tree, but fell off the first bough, and there I lay for a long, long time. When I awoke I had such a terrible pain in my head! All that day I suffered, and didn't get over my bad feelings for several days. I tell this as a warning to you, that you may never be tempted to touch anything to drink but water, my dear."

"You must tell that story, Mrs. Squirrel," said Bachelor. "And we will call it a story of intemperance, by one of its victims."

"I will, with all my heart, if it will do any one any good," she responded.

"Yes, we must have a Temperance Day and all make a speech on drinking cold water," said the fish.

"And dew," said the violet.

"I have always drank water, and never anything else, and I think one could scarcely find an older or a healthier tree than I am," said the elm.

"That is true," said the fish.

"Cold water, cold water, cold water," babbled the brook.

"Yes, we can all speak on Temperance Day; we will have a great platform meeting. That is what they call it at Chautauqua when a great many speak about one thing. I heard a man telling his little girl about it on the boat," said the fish.

And the woodpecker wrote it down.

"What was that other you said?" asked a sharp little chipmunk.

"Missionary Day," said the fish.

"And what is that?"

"Why, there are home missions and foreign missions," said the fish. "And they talk about them both. I think they have a day for each, or maybe two or three. Missions are doing good to some one, but I don't exactly see the difference between home and foreign missions."

"Why, that is plain to me," said Bachelor. "Home missions is when some one does something kind to you, and foreign missions is when you do something kind to some one else."

"Of course; why didn't I think of that before?" said the fish.

"One day last year I was very hungry," said a robin, "very hungry and cold. I had come on too early in the season. There came a cold snap, and the ground was frozen. I could find nothing at all to eat. I was almost frozen myself, and had begun to fear that my friends would come on to find me starved to death instead of getting ready for them as they expected. But a little girl saw me and threw some crumbs out of the window. I went and ate them, and every day as long as the cold weather lasted she threw me crumbs — such good ones too — some of them cake; and she gave me silk ravelings to make my nest of. I think that was a home mission, don't you?"

"Yes, my dear, it was," said Bachelor.

"You might tell that as one thing," said the wind.

"I will," said Birdie.

Said a daisy, "When I was very thirsty, one day, and the clouds sent down no good rain, the dear brook jumped up high here, and splashed on me so I could drink, and I think that was a home mission."

"Yes, yes," said the elm, "it was."

"I know a story I could tell," said the ferns.

"And I," said the elm; "one of many years ago, when I was but a little twig."

"I know a home mission story too," said White Violet.

"And I," said the brook. "Once I was almost all dried up and could hardly reach the lake, and a dear lovely spring burst up and helped me along until the dry season was over."

"And I, and I," chorused a thousand voices.

"But what about foreign missions?" said the fish.

"I sang a beautiful song to a sad old lady in a window, this morning," said a mocking-bird.

"That's foreign missions," said the chipmunk.

"Some naughty boys hid another boy's hat yesterday, and I found it for him and blew it to his feet," said the wind.

"I sent a bunch of buds to a sick girl, this morning," said the rose-bush with a blush.

"I think we shall have no lack of foreign missions," remarked Bachelor.

"But what can *we* do?" asked an old gray squirrel. "We can't preach, nor teach. We can run errands and carry messages, but that isn't much."

"You might be on the commissary department," said the wind.

"What's that?" they all asked.

"Things to eat. We shall need a great many, and you could all lay in a stock of nuts, enough to last all summer, for a great many."

"Why, surely!" they cried, and all that fall such a hurrying and scurrying from bough to bough there was as never was seen before. They worked very hard, storing up nuts, and the people came near not getting any at all.

It must have been about a week from the time they sent their letter to Old Ocean, that one afternoon they were assembled, waiting for the decision of a certain little committee, which had been sent over behind a stone to decide who should be the leader of the choir, that up the stream came a weary little fish.

He was unlike any fish that had ever been seen in that brook, and caused a great deal of remark among the flowers before he was within hearing distance.

He came wearily, as though he had travelled a long distance, but as he drew nearer, the old fish exclaimed, "There comes a salt-water fish! perhaps he has a message from the ocean."

Then the little company were all attention.

Nearer and nearer he came, and stopped before the old fish with a low bow, inquiring whether this was the Chautauqua Committee.

On being told that it was, he laid a bit of delicate sea-weed, a pearly shell, and a beautiful stem of coral upon the bank, and said: "I have a message from Old Ocean for you. He sends you greetings and many good wishes for the success of your plan, and regrets deeply that he cannot be with you next summer; but he is old, very old, and he has so much to do that he cannot leave even for a day or two. If he should, the world would be upside down. There would be no rain in the brooks, and lakes would dry up, and the crops and the people all would die."

"O dear! and we should die too," said the flowers.

"Yes, you would die, too," said the salt-water fish.

"He has a great many other things besides to take care of; there are the great ships to carry from shore to shore, and there is the telegraph, —"

"What is telegraph?" interrupted that saucy little squirrel who had no regard even for a stranger's presence.

"Telegraph is a big rope that people send letters to their friends on. It is under the water in the ocean, and the letters travel so fast that we have never yet been able to see them, though we have watched night and day."

"Wonderful, strange," they all murmured.

"Old Ocean says," proceeded the messenger, "that he cannot give you all of his story, as it would be too long, but that he sends some of it written on this shell, and in this coral and in this bit of sea-weed. In the shell is a drop of pure salt water that if carefully examined will tell you many more wonderful things."

They all thanked the fish kindly for coming so far to bring them these treasures, and begged him to stay and rest, but he declined, saying he had a family at home and must hasten, so he turned to go.

"Stay!" cried Bachelor. "Wouldn't you be willing to come next summer and give us a lecture on the telegraph?"

The fish laughed.

"Bless you!" said he, "I couldn't do that. I don't know enough about it myself. Ask the lightning. He is the head manager, and will give you all the lectures you want. Good-by! the sun is getting low, and I must be off." And he sped away, leaving the woodpecker writing down "telegraph" and "lightning" on one corner of his memoranda.

And now the committee returned, having decided, by unanimous vote, that the mocking-bird should be the leader of the choir, as he could sing any part, and so help along the weak ones whenever he could see the need of it.

There was a pause after the committee had been told all that had happened during their absence, broken at last by Bachelor.

"I've been thinking," said he, "that it might be as well for us to have a reply to Ingersoll."

"What is that?" they asked, for they were getting used to strange things, and did not seem so surprised at the new word.

"Ingersoll is a man that says there is no God, and he has written a great many things to prove it," said Bachelor gravely.

The other poor little flowers were too much shocked to say anything, and they all looked at one another dumbly.

"Is he blind?" asked a bird.

"He must know better," asserted a fern. "No one could possibly believe such a thing."

"I don't know whether he is blind, but I think not," said Bachelor. "They say he has made a great many other people believe as he does because he talks so beautifully.

"How dreadful!" said the flowers, in a sad voice.

"They had a man at Chautauqua who answered all he said and proved that it was untrue, but every one did not hear him. I think we ought to have a day to answer Ingersoll," again said Bachelor.

"Yes, we must," said the north wind; "and we will all prove there *is* a God. No one could have made me but God." And he blew and blew until the flowers crouched down almost afraid at his fierceness.

When all was quiet again, out hopped a dignified-looking bird. "My friends," said he, "my wife and I went to church last night, and they sang a beautiful hymn that has long been one of my favorites. I told my wife to listen hard, and this morning, with my help, she was able to sing it. I think it would help on this subject if we were to sing it for you now."

"Sing, sing, sing," said the brook.

The meek little wife at her husband's word stepped out, and together they sang this wonderful hymn:

> The spacious firmament on high,
> With all the blue ethereal sky,
> The spangled heavens, a shining frame,
> Their great original proclaim;
> The unwearied sun, from day to day,
> Does his Creator's power display,
> And publishes to every land
> The work of an Almighty hand.
>
> Soon as the evening shades prevail,
> The moon takes up the wondrous tale,
> And nightly to the listening earth
> Repeats the story of her birth:
> While all the stars that round her burn,
> And all the planets in their turn,
> Confirm the tidings as they roll,
> And spread the truth from pole to pole.
>
> What though, in solemn silence, all
> Move round the dark, terrestrial ball?
> What though no *real* voice or sound
> Amid their radiant orbs be found?
> In *reason's* ear they all rejoice,
> And utter forth a glorious voice,
> Forever singing as they shine,
> The hand that made us is divine.

When they had finished the whole congregation bowed their heads.
"Yes," they said, "every day we will show forth the greatness of God who

made us, and that bad man will see and hear and believe, and the people will not be led away from God any more.''

"We will make that our great aim, to show forth the glory of God," they all cried together.

So the little workers planned, and sent their messengers far and wide, over land and sea, and made out their programme; and the lecturers spent days and days preparing their manuscript, — for aught I know they are at it yet.

The flowers all have received their invitations to come, and some were so eager to be off that they packed their brown seed trunks and coaxed the wind to carry them immediately, that they might be early on the spot.

Next spring when the snow is gone and the trees are putting forth their leaves, and all looks tender and beautiful, you will see the birds flying back and forth, very busy, carrying travellers and messages; the squirrels will go chattering to their store-houses to see that all is right, and to air the rooms a little; the birds will build many nests, more than they need, and you will wonder why, and will never know that they are summer nests for rent, else you might like to rent one yourself.

The wind, too, will be busy, so busy that he will hardly have time to dry your clothes that hang out among the apple blossoms.

You don't know what it all means?

Wake up quite early every morning and listen. Be patient, and one morning, just as the first pink glow of the rising sun tinges the east, you will hear a watching tree call out, —

> The year's at the spring,
> And the day's at the morn;
> Morning's at seven;
> The hillside's dew pearled;
> The lark's on the wing;
> The snail's on the thorn;
> God's in his heaven —
> All's right with the world.

And then all the lily-bells will chime out the call to prayer, the great red sun will come up and lead, and the little Chautauqua will open.

You will hear the sweet notes of praise from the bird choir, and prayers will rise from the flowers like sweet incense; you will see and hear it all, but will you remember that it is all to show forth the glory of God?

THE
PARKERSTOWN
DELEGATE

1

THE PARKERSTOWN DELEGATE

The shadows are long and low on the grass, the sleepy road is muddy, the chestnuts look expectantly down from the laden tree with their eager, prickly faces, all ready to leap when the frost shall give the word, the river glides dreamily along, and the rusty-throated crickets sing and sing the whole day. A busy gray spider works hard to finish certain meshes on the railing of the upper porch. Nothing makes any difference to her any way. She builds her house in a convenient place for catching flies, and when that house fails or breaks she builds another, so on to the end, and then it is all over.

Two men come down the road in blue jeans overalls and checked blouses. One is big, with a large neck and no collar, a sunburned face lengthening into sandy whiskers, a broad, coarse, straw hat and hands in his pockets. The other is younger, with a pleasant face, a manly figure and a spade over his shoulder. They both have large, heavy boots spattered with mud, and walk much with their heels, carrying their feet after them with a sort of rhythmic curve, shaped something like a tie in music.

"Is Lois coming back soon?" asks the younger of the two men as they near the large white house on the right hand side of the road. There is much hesitation in his manner as he asks the question, but he tries to summon a matter-of-fact tone, and swings his body a little more decidedly.

The large man, however, does not notice, for he suddenly seems to be aroused to a piece of news he has forgotten to impart.

"Well, yes, now you mention it, she is." There is a pleased look in his pale blue eyes and a broad grin of satisfaction over his face as he makes this reply. He is very proud of his daughter Lois, and three months is a long time for her to have been away from home. He wishes all the neighbors to understand that it is a great thing for Lois Peters to be at home once more. "She's coming on this evening's express train, and that's what I'm hurrying home so early for."

There is a glad ring in the young man's voice which he cannot repress as he answers: "Well, I declare! I'm right glad of it. You see Harley's been taking on so of late because she's been gone so long. He says it seems as if she would never come any more."

"You don't say!" says the proud father. "Well, now, that's too bad. I'm glad she's coming. I make no doubt she'll run right over and see him the first thing. How is the little chap these days?"

"Pretty poorly. He doesn't get any better. Some days he's able to be

1

dressed and moved about, but most of the time he has to lie quite still. Mother gets discouraged about him, but the little fellow is as patient as can be. Father says he can't bear to look at him, sometimes, it seems so dreadful to think he can never be well again."

"Yes, it is pretty hard," said the rough man, rubbing his checked sleeve across his eyes; "uncommon hard for the little chap. Well, good-evening! Lois will be right glad to see you over, I have no doubt. She'll come right off to see the little chap, too," and the two men parted, the younger at his father's gate, while the older man passed on down the road toward the village.

"So Lois is coming back again. Well, I'm glad of it," said the young man to himself as he paused a moment by the gate and looked meditatively back up the road he had just come. The distant hills were purpling themselves into their nightcaps, while the sun tore the clouds into scarlet and gold ribbons to adorn them. The young man watched the process a moment as he had watched it many times before, but to-night the gold seemed more glorious than it had for many a sunset eve, and perhaps it was because it reminded him of the light on Lois's face. At least his heart felt that the sunlight of the village was coming back. He had not thought much of it in that way before, it is true; but he was glad, nevertheless, perhaps for his little brother's sake, that Lois was coming back. They had been good friends for years.

There was nothing handsome about Franklin Winters except his great, honest dark eyes, and his smile. People said his smile was like a benediction. That smile lighted up his whole face as he turned to go into the house, and made him look handsome. Although he was not a very well-educated young man, and although when he talked he did not always use the best of English, still the slow, even tone in which he spoke his words and the rare smile with which they were often accompanied, took the sharp edge from what would otherwise have grated on the refined ear, and made one feel that here was true heart culture at least, if there was not overmuch education.

It was pleasant, too, to see the tenderness with which he approached the bed of his young invalid brother, after he had removed the great straw hat which covered his well-shaped head, and stood some minutes at the kitchen sink, making a half-way toilet before the cracked looking-glass.

"Harley, I've some good news for you," he said. "Lois is coming home to-night on the evening express, and her father says he's sure she'll run right over here the first thing. Maybe she'll come in the morning."

The joy of the young invalid was quite apparent. He had very few pleasures in his monotonous life. Ever since the scarlet fever had attacked him, several years ago, his had been but a weary, painful existence.

He was not much more than thirteen years old, but his life of pain had made him old in many ways beyond his years, while the constant necessary reliance upon others had kept him quite a child too. He had the same dark, handsome eyes as his brother, but his face, though a trifle thin and pinched with the pain he had suffered, was beautiful as any girl's.

"O, Frank, I'm so glad!" he exclaimed, catching his brother's hand and squeezing it. "Now she'll have more stories to tell, and maybe some new plans for me. I'm so tired of all the old ones, and besides I've outgrown them. Three months is a long time when one has to spend it on the bed, you know, and can use the nights to live in as well as the days — that is, most of them" — and he smiled a sorry little smile.

"On the evening express did you say she was coming?" he asked again suddenly as if a new idea had struck him. "Then why couldn't you carry me into the other room for just a little while and let me watch it go by? It would be such fun to see it and then to think that there was someone I knew in the lighted-up cars. I've watched it before, you know, but I didn't ever have any one in them to feel that way about. Why, it would be 'most as good as going in a train again myself, as I did when I was such a little fellow before I was hurt, with father. I can remember real well about how the cars looked, and if I could see the express go by to-night and could think she was in it, maybe I could imagine myself in those cars whirling along beside her, coming home from the city like any boy. Say, Franklin, you will, won't you? It won't hurt me to be moved to-night, a bit, for I've had a real good day," he finished triumphantly, and then looked up to his brother's face with such pleading in his eyes as could not be resisted, albeit the brother's were so full of tears that he was forced to turn his head the other way for a moment.

"If mother says so, Harley," he managed to get out, and then strode from the room to find the mother and choke down his rising feelings.

Harley had his wish, although the troubled mother doubted the wisdom of it when she saw the fever into which her boy worked himself before the train did finally rush by. And then it was such a passing pleasure, with all his imaginings of himself on board. A few sparks, a few shrieks, a roar, a rush, a bright, quick glancing of lighted windows with dim figures in them, and then all was over, and Harley could scarcely get to sleep, so excited was he.

He was awake very early the next morning. He knew the colors of the sunrise well, and could tell you all about them, for he had watched them many times from his window, after long nights of weary hours, which it had seemed to him would never end. He watched the pink bars of the sky slowly turn to gold, and then melt away into a glory that burst over the world and filled everything, even his room, and brightened his pale face for a little. Then the world waked and went to work and things began. Harley might hope for Lois to come soon, for had she not been his friend for so long, and did she not love him dearly? She surely would come over directly after breakfast. And Lois did not disappoint him. She came while it was still early, with a great spray of chestnut burs in her hand, that the frost had opened and robbed of their nuts just to show the world what a pretty velvet lining was inside.

Lois had not exactly a beautiful face when you considered it carefully; her skin was pink, and her eyes blue, with yellow lashes, and her hands just the least mite freckled, like her father's, but the eyes were bright and sweet, and the lashes had somehow caught and tangled a sunbeam into them, and the hands were quick and graceful, nevertheless; besides Lois had hair — wonderful hair! It began by being red like her father's, but the glory of the sunlight was in it to mellow it, and the soft brown richness of her mother's had toned it down, until the red only shone through in little glints, and made it the most beautiful halo of soft, rippling light about her head; so that when you considered her hair, Lois was lovely. Harley thought her very beautiful, and I am not sure but his brother Franklin held the same opinion.

"And now, Lois," said Harley, when the greetings were over, and they had settled down to an old-time talk, "begin! What will you tell me first? Let me see. Begin with the nicest thing first. What was the nicest thing you saw in all the time you were gone?"

Lois raised her eyes a little above their level, and put on her thoughtful expression. Harley liked to see her so, and feasted his eyes upon her as she studied the ceiling, thinking how good it was to have her back with him again.

But Lois's eyes were beginning to brighten and a smile crept over her face which Harley knew was the harbinger of some good thought or story.

"I think the convention was the best of all," she said, bringing her eyes back to his face, full of pleasant memories for him to read.

"Convention! What convention?" asked Harley almost impatiently, "and how could a convention be the pleasantest thing in a visit to a big town?"

"But it was," said Lois emphatically, "the very best thing of all. I think if I had to choose between the whole of the rest of my visit and those three days of convention I wouldn't have stopped a minute to think, I would have chosen the convention — at least, that's the way I'd do, now I've been to it."

Harley looked puzzled. He could not understand why a convention should be particularly interesting to a girl, but he had unlimited faith in Lois and her taste.

"Was it politics, or a firemen's convention? And did they — why, I suppose they had a great many parades, didn't they? Was that why it was so nice?" he asked, trying to understand.

"O, no, indeed!" said Lois, laughing. "It wasn't politics nor firemen nor Farmers' Alliance nor any of those things. It's a long story, and I'll have to begin at the beginning. It was the State convention of the Y.P.S.C.E. Do you know what those letters mean?" and she stopped to watch the color deepen in Harley's cheek and his eyes shine as he tried to guess what the mystic letters could mean, but after he had made several unsuccessful attempts she went on.

"It means Young People's Society of Christian Endeavor," she said, naming each word on a finger of her hand, and nodding triumphantly as she finished. "Do you know about it?"

"No," said Harley. "It sounds stupid. I can't see how you could like it so much," and there was almost a quiver of disappointment about his mouth.

But Lois hastened to take up her story and make its scenes live again before the eager eyes of her small listener.

2

"It's a very big society," she began; "there's one all over everywhere pretty near. They even have one in Japan, they say. It's a society of the young folks all working for Christ. That's what Endeavor means, you see. It's a long story, so if you don't understand all I say you better ask questions, for I may leave out some. All the young folks get together first and say, 'We'll have a society,' and then they take the pledge and the constitution and" —

"What's the pledge and constitution?" interrupted Harley.

"I don't know much about the constitution," said Lois. "I guess it's just their laws; but the pledge I've learned by heart:

" 'Trusting in the Lord Jesus Christ for strength, I promise Him that I will strive to do whatever He would like to have me do; that I will pray to Him and read the Bible every day, and that, just so far as I know now, throughout my whole life, I will endeavor to lead a Christian life.'

"That's the first half. I didn't learn the rest. It's about being at all the meetings and helping them along, and always going to the consecration meeting once a month, unless you have an excuse you can give to God. I didn't think it was worth while to learn that part, because we haven't any society here and I don't suppose we ever shall have. They don't take to such things in this town, but I thought the first half of that pledge anybody could take and be a society by one's self, so I have written it down and signed my name to it, and I'm trying to be a Young People's Society of Christian Endeavor all by myself. Well, about once in so often — once a year, I guess it is — they have a convention. There's a great big one of all the societies in the country, in some big city — that's what they call the 'National' — but this wasn't one of those. This was a State convention. That means just the societies in that State, you know. Mrs. Brant said she invited me to come to town early in the season so that I could be there to the convention, because she thought I would enjoy it; and I did, ever so much. Well, the first meeting was in the evening, and they began to come — the delegates — along in the afternoon, from the trains that came in from all directions. Maybe you'd see a young man with a satchel, and then three girls, and then two or three youngish boys, and you'd run to the window and say, 'There come some

5

delegates! I wonder if they're the ones that'll come here to our house!' You see Mrs. Brant kept three of them, two young men, and a girl that roomed with me, and I got pretty well acquainted with her and she told me all about the society at home and" —

"But what's a delegate?" interrupted Harley again.

"Oh! they're the folks each society sends to represent them. The whole society couldn't come, of course, because it would cost too much and they couldn't all be entertained, and then some of them would have to stay at home any way, I suppose; so each society sends two or three of its members, and they call them delegates. Some of the delegates were very nice. They all wore badges just like the Grand Army men when they go to a big meeting, only these had Y.P.S.C.E. on them in big letters and the name of the town they came from, and some of them had a motto. It was ever so nice to study their badges and say to them, 'You live in Newtown, don't you? Why, I have a cousin there. Did you ever see her?' I heard from two people I used to know, that way. It was real exciting that first night before I got used to it. Mrs. Brant had raised biscuits and doughnuts and thin slices of ham and some of her nicest preserves for supper, and there was the best table-cloth and the biggest napkins, and the whole house looked so 'receptiony.' The three delegates looked as if they enjoyed it, too, when they came downstairs with their hair all combed, and their eyes shining as if they'd just got to the front hall of Heaven and expected to be shown a good way inside before the next three days were over. We had to hurry through supper, for the first bell began to ring early, and it kind of made us all uneasy to get there and begin, we'd heard so much about it and talked it over so long. I'd meant to take real solid enjoyment eating one of those doughnuts, for Mrs. Brant does make such lovely ones, but I was so in a hurry to get to meeting that I actually didn't finish mine.

"The first thing that night was a sermon, and it was a grand one. I do wish we could have such preaching here in Parkerstown. It just made me feel as if I wasn't any kind of a Christian, though I have been a member of the church for four years. Why, all those young folks are doing so much and living so differently from what I am, that I felt all sort of left out. I haven't remembered much of the sermon itself — not the words — but that's the way it made me feel, and I never shall get away from the feeling that came that night that I mustn't waste any more time living the way I'd been doing.

"When we got home, after we'd had a talk awhile in the parlor with the delegates, and they'd gone to bed, we got breakfast as near ready as we could the night before, so we could go to the meeting at six o'clock in the morning. When I heard about that meeting I thought it was a dreadfully silly idea to begin so early, and I made up my mind that whatever else I went to, I wouldn't go to that meeting. I thought I'd have enough without it, but Mrs. Brant said she wanted me to go; that they said it was one of the best meetings of the whole thing, and I felt a little curious about it after the delegates began to talk so much of it, and so we decided to go, and slip out ahead to have breakfast all ready for them when they came back. And we did. You ask about parades. They weren't exactly any parades, only when church was out they looked a little that way, everybody with badges, you know, but before those morning meetings there was just a procession of folks going. It was interesting to see them. I stood in the door and watched while the last bell was ringing, and the people came hurrying from all directions. There was a family opposite that Mrs. Brant says never go to church, and it was very funny to see them come to the door, and the man poked his head out of the upper window to see if there was a fire or anything that people were all out so early and the bells were ringing. They found out after a few hours, though, that the bell would keep on ringing all day.

"It was the most beautiful meeting that I had ever been to, then. The leader read the twenty-third psalm, about 'The Lord is my shepherd,' you know, and then we sang, 'I was a wandering sheep,' and the leader asked them all to pray, and they did, ever so many of them. I think there were twenty or thirty prayers right in a minute or two, and they didn't try to pray long and ask for everything in the world at once, but each one had some little thing he wanted for himself, or for them all, that he asked for. Then they sang, 'There were ninety and nine,' and the leader told them that as there was but half an hour for the meeting any way, that they must all be quick and short, or everybody wouldn't have a chance, and they all were.

"A girl spoke up just as soon as he got through, and said she had been thinking while he read the verses, how she had heard that it was the lambs that kept close to the shepherd that he cared for most tenderly. He found nice things for them to eat, and he took them up and carried them when they were worn out, and when there was danger they always felt safe, and she thought it was a good deal so with following Jesus: the ones that kept close to him had an easier time and loved him better than those that only followed far away. Then one of our young men delegates recited a beautiful poem, and it was so pretty I asked him to write it out for me. I can only remember a few lines of it, but you shall have it all to read when I unpack my trunk. It began like this:

> " 'I was wandering and weary
> When my Saviour came unto me;
> For the ways of sin grew dreary,
> And the world had ceased to woo me:
> And I thought I heard him say,
> As he came along his way,
> O silly souls! come near me;
> My sheep should never fear me;
> I am the shepherd true.

" 'He took me on his shoulder,
And tenderly he kissed me;
He bade my love be bolder,
And said how he had missed me;
And I'm sure I heard him say,
As he came along his way,
O silly souls! come near me;
My sheep should never fear me;
I am the shepherd true.'

"There was an old man sitting way back, and he said, right after that, that he didn't want to take up the time of the young folks as he knew he was an old man, but he had been a shepherd himself once, and he knew all about sheep. He said they wouldn't ever lie down until they had had enough to eat and were quite comfortable, and that he had been thinking that when Jesus Christ made people 'to lie down in pleasant pastures,' that it meant that he always fed them and made them comfortable and happy first. There were ever so many other pretty little things said about sheep and lambs, and some Bible verses and bits of poetry recited, and some more prayers and singing, and I really didn't think we had been in the church ten minutes, when the leader said the time had come to close.

"We all got back to the church again as soon after breakfast as we could to the business meeting. I had made up my mind by that time that those young folks could make even business interesting, if they could do so much with a half-hour prayer meeting. Besides, I intended to find out all I could about this queer society. The business was just as interesting as could be. They had a bright, quick man for president, and he made things spin; and they settled ever so many questions, and made a dozen committees to attend to things in less than no time, and then he called for the reports from societies. It was just the most amazing thing I ever did, to sit there and hear all those young boys and girls and men and women get up, one after another, and tell of what their society was doing, how many members it had, when it was formed, how it had grown, and all sorts of things about it. They kept calling for new places all the time, and I just expected they would call for Parkerstown next, and I would have to get up and say we hadn't any society here, and never had even heard of it. I was so ashamed of Parkerstown that I didn't know what to do. But they didn't call for it. That afternoon there were two speeches about doing work for Christ, and there were papers five minutes long from different people, telling the best ways of working on the different committees they have in the society, Lookout and Social and Prayer meeting and all those things. I can't remember the rest of them, but I have a constitution at home in my trunk, and that will tell you what they all mean if you want to see it. They gave some nice ideas that made me wish we had a society here, so we could do some of the things they told about.

"It was great fun in the evening when the secretary came. He is the great secretary, you know, of the 'National,' and they felt very proud to think he had promised to come to their convention, because he is so busy that he can't always go to all the conventions. He came in on the evening train, and came right down to the church without even a chance to wash his hands. We were singing when he came in, because we had been kind of waiting along for the train to come, and at the end of the verses we all waved our handkerchiefs at him as he came up to the platform. He was a splendid-looking young man, real young; you would hardly have thought him more than a boy at first, though when you looked at him closer you saw that he was a good deal older, and he didn't talk like any boy, I can tell you. He just stood up there and made everybody love him at first. He told us how glad he was to see us, and how he had come a long journey just to be with us. Then we were all so glad he had come, and began to wonder how we had gotten along with our convention so far without him and called it a good time; and we felt right away how sorry we should be when the next day was over and we should have to say good-by to him. He talked beautifully. I wish I could tell you all the stories he told us, and what wonderful things he said we could do if each one did his part. I have some of the things down in my little blank book, and when I come over next time I'll bring it, and then I can tell you more of his talk. He didn't talk very long, and then we all went home and went to sleep.

"The next morning's prayer meeting was just as good as the first one, and a little better because the secretary was there, and somehow he made us feel as if Jesus Christ was a good deal nearer to us since he came, because he seemed to love him so very much. The next day there were reports and business and talks and a question-drawer where everybody asked questions on paper and the secretary answered them, and there was a story read, a beautiful story. I'll tell you that, all by itself, another time. It's too long for now. It was a Christian Endeavor story, too; everything was Christian Endeavor. Early in the evening there was a big reception in the town hall. Everybody went and shook hands with the secretary. I was introduced to him too, and he smiled just as cordially at me as he did to the people he staid with and must have known a great deal better. Then about nine o'clock we all went in a procession to the church for the closing consecration meeting.

"Why, Harley, I never went to anything like that meeting! I can't begin to tell you anything about it. There were almost a hundred prayers in just about ten minutes. The singing was so sweet; everybody was so much in earnest; and it seemed as if Jesus was right there in the room waiting to give a blessing to everyone, to me just as much as any one else. Every body talked too, and told what the convention had done for them, and how it had helped them. I had to tell too, just a little word. I felt as if it would be ungrateful to go away from that meeting without saying how happy I felt for having been allowed to be there, and how I wanted so much to belong to that society, only we hadn't any to belong to, but I thought I would try by myself; and then some one came to me afterwards and told me he hoped I would begin a society, that I would likely find some one else to help, and that we would have a Christian Endeavor in our town before the next year's convention. Of course I didn't tell them what a hard place Parkerstown is, but I did wish with all my heart I had a society to come home to and join. I've been going to the one in Lewiston all the time I've been there, and they made me join; so I'm really a member after all.

"Well, the delegates mostly left by the midnight train, and we all went down to the station and had another reception and sort of praise-meeting there. The strangers seemed a little astonished at the queer set of young people who were singing and talking about religion. I heard one man say he never came across any like them before, but I guess it didn't do him any harm, for he threw away his cigar and went and had a long talk with the secretary. Aren't you tired now, Harley, and don't you want me to stop?"

No, Harley was not tired one bit, and he had a great many questions to ask. They were answered patiently and carefully by one who had such an intense interest in the subject that it was a pleasure to her to explain even the driest detail.

3

"If you can be a society all by yourself why couldn't I join?" asked Harley at last. "I should like to be a society. I couldn't do anything of course, but it would be nice to say I belonged to something like other boys. You said there were two kinds of members, didn't you? What are they? Tell me again. Why couldn't I be one of that other kind?"

"Yes, we have two kinds of members," answered Lois, unconsciously using the pronoun "we" in that connection for the first time, "active and associate, but the associate members are not much. They can't even vote. It is just to get hold of people and make them feel that they belong, you know. A real member ought to be an active member, I should think. You see the associate members are not Christians. An associate member is a kind of a 'half-way' thing, any way. Why couldn't you be an active one?"

"Why, what would I have to do? I don't 'act' any. I just have to lie here and 'be,' " said the boy, with a quiver about his mouth.

"Oh, don't, Harley dear!" cried Lois, with tears in her eyes. "Yes, you could be an active member. You could give yourself to Jesus and sign the active membership pledge and keep it just as well as I can, and you would find lots of little bits of work to do for Christ right here in your own room."

Harley looked thoughtful and shook his head.

"I'm afraid I couldn't be much of a Christian," he said, "for you see, sometimes when my head aches so bad I'm cross. I have to be, and then it kind of gets the hurt out a little if I talk scolding to them, and make them give me my own way. But maybe I might. What did you say was the pledge again? I'd like to have it to think about a while. It would be nice to be a member of something. If I was 'active' we could have business meetings and I could vote, couldn't I? That would be lots of fun. But it wouldn't be right to think about that part of it unless I was really willing to sign my pledge and keep it, would it?"

"No;" Lois admitted that she did not think it would. "I'll tell you what we can do, Harley," she said, "I can't remember the whole pledge, but I'll write out the part that I said off to you and you can think that over, and when I go home I will write to the place in Boston where they keep pledge-cards, and we'll each have a pledge-card to keep. It will be nice, I think, if we are going to be a society. You will like that, won't you?"

Harley showed his appreciation of it by the brightness of his eyes.

So the first half of the pledge was written out and placed under Harley's pillow for further consideration. Lois said she must go home, and Harley followed her with wistful looks, then closed his eyes to think of all she had told him, and to sleep a little while with pleasant dreams of it.

It was three or four days before Lois found time to run up to see her little friend again. He had awaited her coming with great impatience, and now he drew the rumpled slip of paper from under his cushion and said as she entered the room:

"I think I can sign it, Lois. I've thought it all over and I'll try to keep it. You see, that first sentence helped me a good deal. It says, 'Trusting in the Lord Jesus Christ for strength.' I thought I couldn't be good all the time, but if I trust in Him to help me when I can't, why then I've nothing else to do but be as good as I can and then He'll do the rest. It isn't like promising some one else, either, that wouldn't understand when I was doing my best, and when the pain was so hard that I had to cry just a little. He'll always know when I'm doing my best, and it's Him I'll have to promise and not any one else. It doesn't seem hard to do what He wants me to do, for that isn't much now, but to lie still and be patient, and be willing to give up when I can't have what I want. I think I can promise that. And then of course I can read the Bible a little while, and pray. I haven't always done it. Sometimes I would think it wasn't any use, and sometimes there was something I would want to do instead, like hearing a story or thinking about some plan I had made to amuse myself, and so I would forget to pray, but I guess I will join, Lois, if there isn't anything else in the pledge to promise."

Lois bent down and kissed the pure, white forehead and, looking into the eager earnest eyes, felt that she would have a true little Christian for her co-laborer in the Christian Endeavor Society.

"The pledge-cards have come, Harley," she said, as she took her seat by his bed. "Didn't they come quickly? I ran right over with them because I thought you'd be in a hurry to see them. They came on the noon mail."

Harley reached an eager hand for the card and read it slowly, his face growing sober as he read.

"What kind of meetings does it mean I must be 'present at?' " he asked, "and what is a 'consecration' meeting?"

Lois explained carefully about the prayer meetings and the monthly consecration meeting at which the roll was called, and each member responded to his name by telling of his progress during the past month, or by repeating a verse from the Bible.

"Could you and I have prayer meetings here in my room, do you mean, Lois? And, Lois, who would pray?"

Lois had thought of these questions a little and had made up her mind to do her duty and try to begin a Christian Endeavor Society right here, but it was nevertheless with beating heart that she answered:

"Yes, I think we might, Harley, and I suppose if there was no one else here, you and I would have to pray."

Harley considered this a moment. "Of course," said he, "you could pray. Maybe I'd get so I could too, a little, but I don't know how very well. Anyhow, I'd try if God wants me to do that."

"Then we'll be a society. Here's a constitution, and I've subscribed for the Golden Rule. That's the paper that's all about Christian Endeavor Societies, and you shall have it to read every week. I had it sent to you so you would get it as soon as it came. I thought it would interest you."

"Oh, thank you, Lois dear! How good you are to me! I shall not have any more stupid days now you've come home. The summer was so very long without you! How nice it will be to have a paper to read myself and all about our society!"

"And now when shall we have our first meeting?" asked Lois.

After much discussion it was decided to hold the meetings on Sunday afternoons at three o'clock.

"Because," said Harley, "this would be something like going to church, and I have wanted to go to church for so long. Besides, I have great trouble with Sundays. They are quite long and there hasn't been much I could do with them. Franklin reads to me a good deal, but he always takes a walk in the woods on Sundays, and I don't think he quite enjoys reading the things that mother thinks fit Sunday best; so, if you please, I'd like it on Sunday afternoon."

The paper arrived before the first Sunday meeting, and was eagerly devoured by its owner. He read to himself as long as they would allow him, and then every member of the family was pressed into service until he knew the matter of that week's issue pretty thoroughly. He had a very clear idea of what a Christian Endeavor prayer meeting should be, and he had gained much information about the various committees and their workings.

"We can't be, just us two, Lois," he announced when she came in Sunday afternoon. "I've been reading about it, and if we are a society at all, we'll have to go to work and get in some more. Besides, we need a president and secretary and ever so many committees. There's the prayer meeting committee and the lookout. I guess we don't need a social one yet, for we'll be social enough, just us two. But the lookout committee seems to be the beginning of every thing. We'll have to have a business meeting. We don't want to have that on Sunday, and we'd better have one right off Monday, and fix these things. Now begin. You'll have to lead the meeting to-day because you know how, and you must tell me what to do all along. I've been reading up about these things. Did you know there is a subject already picked out for every week? I think we'd better take that, don't you? It will be nice to think we are having the same kind of a meeting they are having everywhere else, and we can pretend there are more folks here, and pick out things for them to say and read."

Lois began her first meeting with a trembling heart. It was hard for her to do such a thing even before this little boy. But she read a few verses and then knelt down by Harley's bed and prayed: "Dear Jesus, wilt thou bless this little society of two, and help us to know how to work for thee as the other larger societies are doing? For Jesus' sake, Amen." And Harley followed without being asked, with:

"Dear Jesus, I thank thee for sending me word about this society. Please help me to be a good member and keep my pledge, and show me how I can work. Amen."

It was not a very long meeting, but it was a good one. The great army of Christian Endeavorers over the land, if they had been permitted to look in upon the two with the open Bible between them, might perhaps not have felt much inspiration from the sight; but there nevertheless was, in that small meeting, the true Christian Endeavor spirit. They had claimed the promise that "where two or three of you shall gather in my name, I will be with them," and God's Spirit was indeed there.

"I have thought of Sallie Elder," said Harley, when the solemn Christian Endeavor parting words, "The Lord watch between me and thee when we are absent one from another" had been repeated, and they had pronounced their first prayer meeting concluded. "Sallie Elder doesn't know what to do with Sunday. She told me so the other day when she was over here. I guess we could get her in. I could send a note to her all about it. I should like to write it, and Pepper could take it to her. Do you think, Lois, that it would be wicked to put Pepper on the lookout committee? If he does part of the work he ought to belong, oughtn't he? It wouldn't be wrong, would it, Lois?"

Now Pepper was a very homely little dog, who lay curled in a heap at Harley's feet during the meeting, fast asleep, and at the mention of his name he pricked up his ears, opened his bright little wistful eyes up at the two, and thumped his tail pleadingly as much as to say, "Do take me in; I'll be a very good dog."

It was finally decided that Pepper should be a sort of *ex-officio* member of the committee, and should be sent after Sallie Elder before the next prayer meeting.

Sallie accepted the invitation with delight and became an associate member immediately. Lois was glad at this addition; but when, next Sunday, Harley announced that his brother Franklin had asked for admittance to the society, or at least to the meetings, her heart beat fast, and there was consternation in her face. Admit Franklin Winters to their meetings! How could they! He was not a Christian. Indeed, he was known to have said many things which led one to think he did not much believe in the Bible. Lois had always liked him very much, but she was afraid of him. He might make fun of their meetings. But even as she thought that, her heart told her he would not do such a thing as that. Perhaps he only wished to come there to please his little brother. But who would pray if Franklin came? Surely she could not.

She had never prayed aloud before in her life until she went to Lewiston, and there only once or twice. It had been a little trial to think of having Sallie added to their number, but she had decided to bear that for the sake of the good they might be able to do, but now to have this young man come — oh! it would be dreadful. It would be an impossibility to pray, and yet what could she say to Harley? Moreover, it appeared that Franklin was waiting in the other room for admittance. Lois must answer quickly.

"Why, Harley," she said, and her voice trembled as she looked down and fumbled with some papers between the leaves of her Bible, "I am afraid your brother wouldn't enjoy it. It's just us, you know, and" —

"O, yes, he would!" broke in Harley. "I told him all about it, and he said, all of his own accord, that he wished we would let him come, and his eyes looked real 'want to' when he said it, and he asked ever so many questions about it; so he knows just what it is. He said he thought if Sallie came that he might, and that he'd like to ever so much."

Before Lois had time to reply Franklin himself appeared at the door with Sallie, and his pleasant eyes were upon Lois's face while he asked:

"You are going to let me come, too, aren't you? Harley said he thought you would be glad to have an addition. I can't do much, to be sure, but I think I might manage to conduct myself as honorably as Pepper here," and he gave the dog a pat on the head, which was highly appreciated.

4

Franklin sat down then, and there was nothing for Lois to do but submit, although she would gladly have fled the house and her newly-fledged Christian Endeavor Society and never come back any more. Harley was to lead the meeting, so she had nothing to do but await developments, but she sat with her eyes down and her whole body in a quiver. Harley asked her almost immediately to pray for the opening of the meeting. She knelt down with not a thought in her mind and scarcely a desire in her heart, except that she might be helped to get out of this trying situation, and the help came. "Thine ears shall hear a word behind thee, saying, 'This is the way, walk ye in it, … Now therefore go, and I will be with thy mouth, and teach thee what thou shalt say.' "

Surely those promises were fulfilled for her that day. She had not known what to say nor how to say anything indeed, but the young man who knelt across the room listening was amazed, and found himself wondering if it was really Lois Peters who was talking in that sweet voice, apparently to some One who stood close beside her, and in whom she seemed to have the utmost confidence. He seemed to feel that he was being prayed about too, although his name was not uttered, and for the first time in his life he believed that there was something in religion which he did not understand, a power that reached into the heart-life as nothing else could do. Harley felt the influence of that prayer too, as he took up the petition where Lois left off:

"Please, dear God, we thank thee that we have some new members to our society. Help them to get to be active members pretty soon. Let Pepper be a good member, if he is only a dog. He can run around and do the errands I could do if I were like other boys. Amen."

The little dog curled up on the bed beside his young master, opened his eyes and raised his head inquiringly at the mention of his name, but seeing Harley's eyes closed, he rested his cold nose confidingly against Harley's clasped hands and closed his own eyes until the Amen, when he gave a soft whine of satisfaction and settled down among the pillows again. Franklin's eyes were wet with tears when he raised his face from his hands, and Lois's face was grave, but little Sallie Elder sat immovable on the edge of her chair, with wide-open eyes, throughout the entire service, uncertain just what to call this strange performance to which she had been invited. It was not until Harley read slowly and carefully a story from the Bible that she began to be interested, and by and by when the reading was over and the meeting thrown

16

open for remarks, she was persuaded into repeating her one Bible verse: "Suffer little children to come unto me."

Franklin, too, had consented to read a verse if he were allowed to come, and not being very familiar with the Bible himself, Harley had selected it for him.

That was the beginning of the Parkerstown Christian Endeavor Society. It is not needful that you should know what was read or said at that meeting. There was nothing original or remarkable in it. You might think it very commonplace, but to those who were gathered there it seemed not so. They had caught the spirit of Christian Endeavor, and even Franklin felt that there was a power there, greater than any other which he knew. He promised to come again if they would let him, and even volunteered to become a temporary member of the lookout committee until some more worthy members should come in. He would that week agree to bring in at least two to the next meeting. Lois's heart began to swell with the thought of a real society right there in Parkerstown, albeit she had scarcely gotten over her panic at the rapid development of her small scheme. It was something to be thought about and prayed over, this, actually planning to speak and pray before people like Franklin Winters, every week. She was not sure she would be able to do it, though she recognized that a power higher than her own had helped her that afternoon; but would He always help? Surely He had promised, but — she must get away by herself and think it over. Happy for Lois that she had learned lately to think such things over upon her knees. The Lord presides over decisions made there, and so it was with a less fearful heart that she came to the next meeting, having herself prevailed upon three young girls to come with her.

Harley had been made president. First, because they thought it would please him, but he proved such a good president, with so many wise and original little plans for the growth of the society, that they came to feel after all that they could not have chosen more wisely. For Harley read all he could get hold of, and he knew all about the great Christian Endeavor Society; he knew all its principles and the wisest ways of working; he knew more about it than all the rest of Parkerstown put together. Moreover, he had time to think and plan and, best of all, to pray, and to grow, in this thinking and planning and praying, daily like Jesus Christ. They all saw the change in his life, even patient as it had been heretofore. There was a wondrous beauty growing in that face that spoke of an inward peace, and a sweet wisdom that had touched the child-heart and caused it to open like a flower.

It came about very gradually, the addition to the society. First, Franklin brought two boys, farm hands from a neighbor's house, and then little Sallie coaxed her older sister, and then all grew interested and the meetings became larger until it was hard to find chairs enough in the square white house by the roadside, and until Harley's little bedroom off the sitting-room became too small to contain all the members.

"Father," said Harley one evening, when he had been lying quite still for a long time with his eyes closed, so that they all began to step softly and talk in low tones, thinking him asleep, "I wish you would take me into the big south room to-morrow. I haven't been in there in two years, I guess, and I want to see it. I have a plan. Perhaps you won't like it, and if you don't I will not coax; but, father, I should like to go in there and see it."

"You shall go, my son," said the father, who could not deny Harley anything in these days. "What is your plan, my boy?"

"Well, father, if you and mother don't like it, I won't make any fuss, but it's something I think would be very nice. Do you think mother cares very much about that south room? I know it's the parlor, and there's all the best things in there, but she doesn't use it much only on Christmas days, and not much then nowadays. It seems too bad to have it using itself up in the dark when it would be so nice for our society. I shouldn't think it would hurt things very much — just once a week — would it? Or couldn't I have it for my bedroom and you move the things in here and have this for the parlor? Do you think it is a very ridiculous plan, father? Because if you do, you and mother, why, I said I wouldn't coax, but I'd like to have you think it over very hard before you say," he said pleadingly.

And so, after much calculation and some changing of household plans, with a few tears mingled by father and mother, it is true — tears of love for their afflicted little boy — the plan was carried out, and the front parlor of the Winters' household became the headquarters of the Parkerstown Christian Endeavor Society. It is true that the room had not been much used as a parlor, and that it afforded ample accommodation for the meetings of the society.

"In fact," said father Winters, "we don't need it and they do, and what Harley wants will please us better than anything else, any way."

There was much bustle of preparation after the decision was made. Franklin agreed to give as his part enough cane-seat chairs to accommodate the members. Some one sent a fine engraving of Father Endeavor Clark, Lois brought over a large copy of the United Society Pledge, neatly framed, to hang over Harley's couch, and together she and Harley planned little decorations to make the room look home-like and yet "churchified," as Harley said. A great monogram C. E., was made from evergreen and hung in the center of one wall, surrounded by the motto, "For Christ and the Church." Another wall contained the motto, "One is your Master, even Christ; and all ye are brethren." Harley made Lois describe the mottoes she had seen at the convention in Lewiston, and they made theirs as much like them as possible. When the motto, "For Christ and the Church," was put up, Harley lay thinking long about it. He didn't see how he could be working for the Church at all. But the end of his thoughts was that he wanted the new minister asked to attend the meetings. The minister was invited, and came with a glad heart. He had heard of this society with thankfulness, but had not thought it best to come until invited. Now he became one with the young people, and helped them along more than they knew. He grew to love the little president much as did every one else, and came frequently to see him, finding that in this young disciple there was much of the spirit of Jesus, and that he might sit at his feet and gather inspiration and new love and faith from conversation with this sweet, trusting child.

The work of this society was carried on according to the most approved methods. No suggestion passed by unheeded. Everything, too, was talked over carefully with the minister, to see whether in their particular society such and such measures were expedient. Every member had a pledge-card. There were cards from the National Headquarters for the different committees to use in their work, and topic cards and everything else that could be thought of; for when Harley expressed a wish for a simple little thing like that to work with, there were plenty to see that it was granted; and so it came about that there was not in all the State, a society better fitted out for work in all departments, than the one at Parkerstown.

Harley had one thing of which he was very proud. The minister brought it to him one day when he came to see him. It was a Christian Endeavor scarf-pin of solid gold; and how Harley loved that pin! He looked at it for hours at a time thinking what it meant; he held it in the rays of sunlight that lay across his bed; he wore it pinned to the breast of his dressing-gown with pleasure, and showed it to every one that came to see him.

"It seems to shine brighter than any other gold thing," he said one day. "I wonder what makes it. Is it because it is for Christ?"

The meetings were large in these days, and very solemn ones. A good many of the Parkerstown young people were beginning to find out what it is to belong to Jesus Christ, and many others were seeking him. Even the new big room was full every Sunday afternoon, and the songs that filled the air and floated out to the street often drew in outsiders who were taking a little walk or who had nothing else to do. Lois had sacrificed her organ to the cause, though it was not a sacrifice, but given gladly, and Franklin had brought it over himself, so they had good rousing singing and plenty of it, and Harley would lie on his little couch by the desk and look at the organ with admiring eyes, feeling that it lent a dignity of the church to the modest room.

But there were days, and growing more frequent now, when the little couch by the light desk was empty, and the young president of this society was unable to be moved in to the meeting, but must lie in the darkened bedroom beyond, with the door closed, and suffer. At first they thought the meetings must be adjourned when Harley was not able to be there, because the noise would trouble him, and because they felt they could not do without him, until he begged so hard that all should go on as usual that it was tried as an experiment, in hushed voices and without music. But Harley missed that at once and sent word for them to sing:

"At the cross, at the cross, where I first saw the light,
    And the burden of my heart rolled away,
It was there by faith I received my sight,
    And now I am happy all the day.''

He said the singing rested him. So, after that they went on as usual, only when the president was not there, there was a more earnest feeling manifest in all the members, and much praying done that the dear boy might be relieved from his sufferings. Some who had not cared much about the meetings heretofore seemed strangely touched by the thought that the little, patient sufferer was lying there thinking of them and praying for them.

5

It was the evening of the day after one of these sad, painful Sabbaths. Lois and his brother Franklin were sitting by Harley's bed. They had been telling him about the meeting as he had asked them. Franklin let Lois do much of the talking, he only helping her out here and there when she forgot what came next, or called upon him to know who was present. He was not yet an active member, and apparently no nearer being a Christian than when the society was first organized. He came in regularly to the meetings and did whatever he was asked to do, even to reading a verse of Harley's selection, but he never selected one himself, and always kept in the background as much as possible. People said he was doing it all for his little brother's sake, and no one dared approach him upon the subject or even urge him to do more. Very few remembered to pray for him I think, there were so many others worse than he, they thought. But Lois was praying, and so was his brother. Many a night when he could not sleep he lay and talked with God and asked him to make Franklin love him.

"I wanted to tell you something," said Harley suddenly rousing from deep silence into which they had fallen. "I have seen something, and I think you would like to know about it. I should like it if you should see such a thing to have you tell me about it. It was last Sunday when you were at meeting. The pain in my eyes was so bad that I had to close them and my head ached very badly, so that I couldn't even have the bedroom door open to hear your voices in the room, but had to close my ears, too, to bear the pain. I could just hear the sound of the song you were singing. I do not remember what it was, but it was very sweet, though it seemed far away, and it grew further away, and further, until it suddenly seemed to turn and come back again and burst into the sweetest, clearest music you ever heard. It was like, and yet it was not like, the music in our meetings. It was such as that would be if every voice was perfect, perhaps the sort of singing they have in Heaven, though I never knew before that any singing could be sweeter than what we have in our meetings; but of course Heaven has everything better.

"Well, this singing, although it was very near and loud, didn't make my head ache a bit harder, and even seemed to rest my back; at least I forgot it was aching. There was a light all around, too, and I could look up without it hurting my eyes. I didn't think how strange that was then, but just listened to the music and looked at the light. It took a shape in some clouds that were far off and yet all around — you see you were not there and so I can't quite explain it all, because there wasn't time for me to understand everything about it, and there was so much else to see. The light grew brighter and brighter and broadened out at the top as though a hundred suns were shining through one spot, and there was a long, sharp, golden crack in the clouds below, and the light changed and broadened and shaped and brightened in such a strange way until suddenly I thought of the shape of my Christian Endeavor pin, and then all at once I saw the letters at the top C. E., and the long sharp ray of light was the pin, and there it was in the clouds all gold, and growing 'golder' every minute, until I thought I couldn't look any longer; but I had to, because it was so beautiful. And then I saw that the line that made the pin was only a break in the clouds, where the light from Heaven — it must have been Heaven — shone through. Above, in the large, bright letters was a real opening into such light as you never saw before, not even when the sun sets; and then there came angels, hurrying out of the letters and down through the narrow opening and everywhere towards me, and more were beyond up there in the brightness. I watched them come out through the opening, and more and more of them seemed to come from the golden letters until all the air was full of them, and one angel came quite close to me and touched me on the shoulder where I lay — right here in my room, just think — and he said: 'Little president' — he called me 'little president' just as the secretary did when he wrote to me that nice letter after I wrote him about our new society and told him how young I was — 'Dear little president,' he said, 'you are one of us now, for we are Christian Endeavorers too, though our work is different from yours, but it is going on all the time. We are the "ministering spirits." God our Father loves your society and will bless it.' And then I felt it all so wonderful! I was just here in my bed, you know, and my head was aching so hard just a minute before, and there was the great piece of sky that I see from the window every day, and the hills at the foot of it, and there in the center of it the beautiful great gold badge, with the air full of lights and angels from it, and the most beautiful music floating all about. I was so glad and so astonished at it all that God should have taken so much trouble to send word to me, that I almost let the angel go away without saying anything but 'Thank you' to him; but just as he turned with a loving smile to fly back, I asked him if he would please see that something was done for a few people down here in our society who didn't love Jesus. Then he put his hand on my head and smiled again, and there was a look in his eyes that I'm sure meant yes, as he went back into the center of the light again. I could see him all the way, just as clearly as when he stood beside me, and when he reached the very center of the brightness the music got farther away again, and the angels all went back, and the Heaven's badge grew dim, and pretty soon was all covered up, and I only heard the music; and pretty soon the music was the hymn you were singing in the other room, 'God be with you till we meet again,' and your meeting was breaking up. But I wish you could have seen it, and don't you think it was wonderful?''

Later, after Franklin had taken Lois home, and come back to kiss the little brother good-night, Harley put his arm about his neck and drew his face close down to his own.

"Frank," he whispered, with his lips to the young man's ear, "you were one of those that I asked the angel about, and I wanted him to be very sure about you, because I love you so much."

The older brother finished the good-night greeting hastily, and drew away to hide his emotion, but there was a warmth in the quick grasp that he gave the little hand, that Harley knew meant that he understood and appreciated.

Now about this time there fell to the lot of that society a bit of good fortune and happiness such as they had not dreamed of. The society which had been expected to entertain the State convention in the spring was somewhat disabled, and wrote to say that they must withdraw their invitation, whereupon the State secretary and executive committee, having heard of the rapid growth of the Parkerstown Society, wrote to know if they would like to entertain the convention. Ah! Wouldn't they? Such honor was almost enough to take the breath away! The dear young president was so excited that they almost had to keep him away from the next Sunday's meeting. To have a real convention right there in their society, the first year, and the national secretary coming to it too, and perhaps — oh, wonderful hope! — perhaps, the dear Father Endeavor himself — for that was the hope that the State secretary held out to them.

"O, Lois!" he said, with his eyes shining very brightly, and his hands clasped tightly together with excitement, "this must have been part of what the angel meant when he came out of the letters in the sky and said God would bless our society. I can't go to much of the convention myself, of course, because our room will not be large enough, and the meetings will have to be held in the church, but you can tell me all about them as you do Sundays about the service, and we shall have some real delegates in the house to talk to, for mother said so; she said we could have four. Just think, and that perhaps they would be willing if the secretary and Father Endeavor came, that they would stop here on account of my not being able to go out to hear them. Do you think others would mind and think me very greedy? Because I should want to have a little of them you know, and then perhaps they would have just one meeting here in our room. The consecration meeting would be so grand, or a morning prayer meeting; I should so like it!"

It was decided that the convention should come, and there was much looking forward to it, and the meetings grew in interest and in spirituality.

"Oh," said Harley one afternoon at the close of the meeting, "I wish that every day was Sunday! If only our meetings could last longer. I did not want it to be out to-day at all."

But the mother looked anxiously at her boy, and was thankful in her heart that every day was not filled with excitement for him. It was getting more and more apparent to the ones who were watching him closely, that Harley was not to stay with them much longer. They had questioned whether the meetings which were so dear to him were not, after all, doing him harm, and perhaps ought to be stopped; but the wise doctor shook his head sadly, and said:

"No; if he is careful not to get too excited, it can do but little harm. The disease will have its way, do what we will. The end is not far off, I fear, but I do not think that will hasten it. The boy is getting to be such a power in this community that I do not see how we can do without him." And he went slowly from the room with bent head, while the mother covered her face with her hands, and sat down to silent grief.

Spring was coming. The convention time was near at hand, when the summons came to the little president to leave his society. He had been very ill for a whole week. On Sunday the society had met in the south room but to pray through the whole hour. Lois and Franklin were near Harley constantly. He could not bear to have them out of his sight.

It was the balmiest morning the spring had given them yet. The birds were trying some summer carols, and the breeze brought a few stray notes in at the open window. But to those in the room the notes had a sad sound, that told of some great change about to come. The whole family were gathered about Harley's bed, for he had passed through a night of suffering, and Dr. Fremont had told them he could not last much longer. He suddenly opened his eyes and looked up as Lois softly entered the room, her arms full of the splendid white lilies he loved so much.

"Lois," he said, smiling, and putting out his thin little hand to touch the flowers, "I don't think I can stay to the convention here after all. I'm sorry not to see the secretary and Father Endeavor, and all the delegates, but I think I can't stay. I saw the badge in the sky again this morning; it was brighter than before, and the angel came and spoke to me, and he said there was a convention in Heaven now, and they wanted me for a delegate from Parkerstown, and I'm to stay, Lois. The delegates to that convention all stay, and it's to get ready for the great convention when you're all coming — the angel told me so. And I don't feel so bad about not seeing Father Endeavor and the secretary now, for they will come to the great convention pretty soon. It's only a little while, and I'm to see Jesus, you know. Besides, I shall be able to do real work up there, and not have to lie on a bed, as I do here. He promised me. He asked me whom I would leave to do my work for me if I went, and I told him I didn't think it mattered about that, that I was only a little invalid boy down here, and that I had been doing pieces of other people's work. But he said no; I had a work of my own, and that I must give it to some one else to do. I thought of you, Lois, but I decided that you had enough of your own work to do, so I told him that I thought my brother Franklin would do it. You will, won't you, Franklin? You'll have to give yourself to Jesus, you know, and then you can do it, and you didn't have a work of your own. So he said it would be all right. You will, won't you, Franklin?"

The strong young man bowed his head on the pillow beside his brother and grasped the dear little hand held out so pleadingly, promising to take the commission. Harley's other worn white hand went feebly up to his breast, where was fastened the beloved gold pin, which he wore night and day. He took it off, and tried to fasten it to Franklin's coat, but was too weak to do so.

"Put it on and keep it. The angel told me I wouldn't need it up there, because he would introduce me as the delegate from Parkerstown, and they would know all about me. I think I know what makes that pin shine so now; it's the light from the letters in Heaven, that catches all the pins in the earth. You'll take good care of it, Franklin, won't you? and you'll take my place and work with Lois. She'll show you how. I wish you would find a verse to read for me at the next consecration meeting. I'm sorry not to be there, and oh! if you would say something for me at the consecration meeting of the convention I should like it, because I can't be there, you know; and if they should call my name I should like some answer to be made to it. Good-by, mother and father, I must go now, the light is coming in the sky again, and the angel will be here for me. I thought I caught a glimpse of the throne when the letters opened the last time, and maybe I shall see Jesus right away. Good-by."

And the little president of one winter passed into the "Great Convention which never breaks up," and to the "Sabbath which has no end," having accomplished more for Christ during his short winter than many of us do in a life-time.

> "Weep if we may — bend low as ye pray!
> What does it mean?
> Listen! God fashioned a house. He said:
>   'Build it with care.'
> Then softly laid the soul . . .
>   To dwell in there.
>
> "And always he watched it — guarded it so,
>   Both day and night:
> The wee soul grew as your lilies do,
>   Splendid and white.
>
> "It grew, I say, as your lilies grow,
>   Tender and tall;
> Till God smiled, 'Now the house is too low
>   For the child, and small.'
>
> "And gently he shut the shutters one night,
>   And closed the door;
> 'More room and more light to walk upright
>   On a Father's door.' "

THE CHRISTIAN LIBRARY

Classics of the Christian faith in deluxe, hardcover, gold stamped, gift editions. These beautifully crafted volumes are in matching burgundy leatherette bindings so you can purchase a complete set or pick and choose. All books are complete and unabridged and are printed in good readable print. **Only $7.95 each!**